His smile was quick and easy. "Who knows, maybe what you've got out there is a guardian angel who's new at his job and still needs to learn how to be undetectable."

She laughed, oddly comforted by the idea. "Now that would figure. A rookie guardian angel." She nodded. "Well, why not? I suppose I'd be a good case for an angel to cut his wings on, wouldn't I?"

"You'd definitely be a challenge," he said, his eyes twinkling with warm amusement. "But a delightful one."

She looked down, her face growing warm with confusion. She was surprised—and a bit disturbed—at how good his comment made her feel.

"Well," he said, stepping back, "I'd better get some rest. My boss is a regular slave driver. Believes in starting the day at the most unearthly hour."

She grinned. "Terrible the things a working man has to suffer."

"Indeed," he said. "But it's really not all that bad."

"Oh?"

He shook his head, moving closer to her again. "Nope," he said, his eyes roaming her face. "It's not bad at all." He reached one long finger to tilt her chin. "Because she's got the most amazing…" he lowered his head, his warm breath fanning her face.

*He's going to kiss me!* Her eyes widened in startled amazement, and an alarming thrill shot through her.

"Cook," he finished, pressing his lips, with feather softness, to her forehead. Then he stepped back, walked to the door, and left.

She stood frozen to the spot, a bemused smile on her face. I wonder…she thought with a sigh. *I wonder if guardian angels are tall and broad-shouldered and have smiles that can melt your insides?*

# Palisades.
# Pure Romance.

FICTION THAT FEATURES CREDIBLE CHARACTERS AND

ENTERTAINING PLOT LINES, WHILE CONTINUING TO UPHOLD

STRONG CHRISTIAN VALUES.  FROM HIGH ADVENTURE

TO TENDER STORIES OF THE HEART, EACH PALISADES

ROMANCE IS AN UNDILUTED STORY OF LOVE,

FROM BEGINNING TO END!

A PALISADES CONTEMPORARY ROMANCE

# REUNION

## KAREN BALL

PALISADES

This is a work of fiction. The characters, incidents, and dialogues are products of the author's imagination and are not to be construed as real. Any resemblance to actual events or persons, living or dead, is entirely coincidental.

REUNION
published by Palisades
*a part of the Questar publishing family*

© 1996 by Karen M. Ball
International Standard Book Number: 0-88070-951-0

Cover illustration by George Angelini
Cover designed by David Carlson and
Mona Weir-Daly
Edited by Judith Markham

Printed in the United States of America

For information:
QUESTAR PUBLISHERS, INC.
POST OFFICE BOX 1720
SISTERS, OREGON 97759

96 97 98 99 00 01 02 03 — 10 9 8 7 6 5 4 3 2 1

*To Mom and Dad—*
*You taught me to love and respect the beautiful world*
*God gave us—and you endured me owning nearly every kind*
*of four-legged creature (and a few feathered ones)*
*known to man! I love you.*

❧

*To Angie, Frani, Gil, and Johnnie—*
*You've been telling me for years to get out there and write.*
*So this is all your fault!*
*I'm grateful to each of you for your encouragement, guidance,*
*and instruction—but most of all for your friendship.*

*Speak up for those who cannot speak for themselves…*
*speak up and judge fairly.*

PROVERBS 31:8–9, NIV

# Prologue

November, 1994

"Okay, you guys, this is where we put on the blindfolds."

A chorus of moans and groans met his announcement, and Josh Sorensen grinned. He looked over the nine boys standing in the clearing. Though varying in age from twelve to eighteen, they were all dressed in flannel shirts, jeans, and hiking boots, ready to take on the wilds of a Wyoming mountain.

Josh took a deep breath of the clean, cold mountain air he loved. His only regret was that this was the last day of his annual week-long camping trip with the youth group.

"Do we have to be blindfolded?" whined Eric, one of the younger boys, scanning the rough terrain and woods around them. Eric's family had moved to Wyoming less than a year ago, and the boy was still getting used to the rugged wilderness that surrounded their new home.

"Course you do!" Josh grinned at this quick response from Mike—one of the juniors—who added emphasis by tapping the bill of Eric's baseball cap. "That's what makes this so much fun."

"But—" Eric said.

"Don't worry, kiddo." Mike slung his arm around the smaller boy's slender shoulders. "I'll be there to make sure you survive."

Noting the uncertain look on the boy's face, Josh decided it was time to step in. "You'll be okay, Eric," he assured him,

11

handing him one of the strips of cloth they used for blindfolds. "You might even have fun."

Josh was grateful that he had two seniors and a junior to help him oversee the trust hike this year. The younger boys were a good group, but they could be a handful sometimes.

As he scanned the eager faces before him, Josh felt a surge of pride. These boys were ready to face the challenges waiting for them in high school and beyond. All were strong, physically and spiritually, and Josh was pleased that he'd had something to do with that.

"Who are you gonna go with, Brad?" Eric asked the tallest of the seniors, and Josh's sense of satisfaction dimmed a bit. Well, almost all of them.

Tall and athletic, Brad Momadey was the kind of young man who drew attention. There was something about him: the way he stood and walked; the look in his brooding, dark eyes; the remote yet kind way he treated others. Everything about the boy spoke confidence and dignity and gave an impression of underlying strength and intelligence. He was a natural leader, for the most part perceptive and considerate. Though Brad always held himself apart, Josh had never seen him treat the other youth group members with condescension or disdain. From all Josh had seen, Brad treated even the youngest or geekiest kid with respect.

*Too bad he can't extend that to Jim and me,* Josh thought glumly. All he or Jim Wilson, the youth pastor, had to do was say "white" and Brad would respond with a resounding "black." Nothing the men did or said seemed good enough for Brad, and despite their most determined efforts to befriend him, the boy had made it abundantly clear he wanted nothing to do with either of them. Or with their God.

Taylor, Josh's wife, had helped him understand the situation a little better.

"Brad's Native American heritage goes deep," she told him. She was a part Ojibwa herself. "He knows the importance of honoring his elders"—she grinned at his incredulous look—"his *tribal* elders. He's loyal to those who are in his world"—her cheeky grin peeked out again—and indifferent to those who aren't."

Watching Brad now as he leaned against the tall trunk of an evergreen, his arms crossed over his chest, that slightly mocking light in his dark eyes, Josh knew Taylor had been right on target. Bradson Momadey respected and loved his parents and did his best to honor them—which was the main reason he came to the youth group at all.

Clearly, though, he had no use for Josh. Or Jim. But Jim was the lucky one today. He'd stayed back at the camp to start cleaning up. Josh laughed inwardly; this was the first time cleaning up had ever seemed like the better duty.

Brad's only response to Eric's question was a casual shrug. Josh sighed and turned his attention to his eager charges.

"Okay, guys, line up and let's count off."

When the boys were paired up, he asked, "Everyone have a blindfold?"

"Yeah!" they yelled with gusto, waving the pieces of white cotton in the air.

"Okay, here's how it works," he told them. "One of you gets blindfolded, and the other leads him for ten minutes. The one who's leading stands or walks behind his partner, telling him where to step, what direction to go, and making sure he stays out of trouble."

"Yeah," one twelve-year-old remarked to his partner with an elbow to the ribs. "No walkin' me into trees—"

"Or off cliffs!" another boy added gleefully.

"Or into the river!"

"Or a bee hive!"

"Or—"

"Or anything!" Josh commanded. "The whole point is to be a good guide, to prove trustworthy. After ten minutes, switch places and head back to the clearing. We'll rendezvous here in twenty minutes, so you older guys keep an eye on your watches. And one final caution: Make sure your team sticks to the path. Don't let your partner wander off it. It's been unusually warm lately, and the higher temps have caused some thawing. There are a lot of places that look safe, but aren't. Any questions?" When none were forthcoming, Josh nodded. "Okay, seniors and juniors, pick a team to follow."

Each of the older boys moved to stand next to one of the pairs—except Brad. He didn't budge. He just stood there, leaning against the tree with casual disinterest.

"We get Brad!"

This pronouncement came from Billy, a sturdy sixth-grader, who grabbed his partner, the hesitant Eric, and hauled him over to stand next to the senior.

*Now there's an interesting team,* Josh thought. *Eric, who's scared of his shadow out here, and Billy, who's not scared of anything.* He smiled inwardly, recalling Billy's youth group nickname: Destructo. Josh's delight grew. Those two would drive Brad crazy. If that wasn't poetic justice, he didn't know what was.

"All set?" Josh said. "Go to it!"

The group exploded into activity. Each of the teams was off and running—even Eric and Billy, except they didn't exactly explode into action. Rather, they launched into a heated debate over who would wear the blindfold first. From his nearby leaning post, Brad watched the two push the cotton cloth back and forth between them.

Of course, Josh hadn't expected Brad to intervene. Not really. In his three years in the youth group, Brad had never participated willingly. His only contribution to group discussions was to snort in disbelief from time to time. As for activities, he only joined in grudgingly when one of his friends asked him to do so. Even then he made a point of ignoring Jim's or Josh's directions or requests.

Brad wasn't blatantly defiant or disobedient. He didn't refuse to cooperate or argue in front of the others. He would simply listen as Jim or Josh talked, wait until everyone else was involved in his or her activity, then go his own way. Quietly. And alone.

Several times Jim had come close to asking Brad to leave the youth group, but Josh always talked him out of it.

"The kid needs someplace to belong. Someplace where he'll hear truth, even if he doesn't seem to respond." Reluctantly, Jim had agreed. But with graduation around the corner, Brad's time with the group was coming to an end, and he and Jim weren't any closer to the boy than the first night he'd come to youth group.

*What's it going to take to reach this kid, Lord?* Josh asked for the hundredth time.

With a sigh, he walked over to Brad. "Well," he said quietly, "looks like you've got quite a job here with these two."

Brad didn't budge. His dark gaze raked Josh with disdain.

*There's got to be a way to get through to him, Lord!* Josh thought. The memory of the morning they'd left for this trip ran through his mind. He'd held Taylor close and kissed her good-bye.

"Pray for me," he said softly. "I have a feeling something incredible is going to happen on this trip. Something Brad won't be able to resist."

"Something other than your boyish charms and disarming sincerity?" she'd teased.

The image of her laughing eyes and sweet face lifted his sagging spirits. Even after nearly eight years he could scarcely believe God had blessed him with such a wife. Their parting that morning had been bittersweet. She'd seemed uncertain, worried. So he'd held her close, kissed her, and promised her, "I'll miss you. I'll see you soon."

He smiled. Taylor's love and belief in him always made Josh feel he could do anything, overcome any obstacle. Even the solid steel walls Brad seemed to have erected around his heart.

*Somehow, Father…somehow we're going to do it. We're going to open this guy's eyes to the incredible love you have for him.*

"You know it would only take a word from you and they'd stop fighting."

Josh watched the mocking light deepen in Brad's eyes.

"Hey, they're not my responsibility." The challenge was clear: You want them to stop fighting, you talk to them.

Josh shook his head. "Actually, I'm afraid they are." He met and held Brad's defiant gaze.

"I don't have to do this," Brad said in a low voice. "Or I could start off with them and then just walk away. You wouldn't even know it until they didn't show up at rendezvous time."

"True enough." Josh was amazed at how everything had to be a contest of wills with this kid. "So go ahead. Whatever happens to these two is up to you. But I just want you to know I trust you."

With that Josh turned and headed for the path into the woods. As he reached the edge of the clearing, he tossed one last comment over his shoulder. "By the way, Mike and I have a bet on how long it takes."

"For what?" Brad asked with a snort.

"For those two to drive you totally crazy." He turned and grinned at Brad. "I give them two minutes. Tops."

Brad watched Josh disappear down the path, then looked away impatiently. *What a jerk. "I just want you to know I trust you." Yeah, right! Like that matters. He probably thought that would make me feel guilty or challenged or something stupid like that,* Brad thought. *Well, no way. I'm not going to—*

A loud wail interrupted his thoughts, and he looked to see Billy sitting on top of Eric, trying to tie the blindfold on the smaller kid's head. With a disgusted sigh Brad stepped forward, grabbed Billy by the back of the shirt, and lifted him off his victim.

"Hey!" Destructo complained, and Brad let him go. The boy flopped on the ground in a pile next to his partner.

Both boys looked up at him angrily, but Brad held up an imperious hand.

"Just knock it off!" he barked. They fell silent at once. Eric's lip started to tremble.

Oh, no…not tears!

"Here." Brad quickly stepped toward Eric and extended a hand. Eric took it and Brad pulled him up. "You go first, buddy. I'll make sure Billy leads you right. And since you've spent at least five minutes fighting, you'll only have five minutes to be blindfolded instead of ten. And that's no sweat. You'll be done in no time."

Eric took the blindfold, then looked up at Brad doubtfully. "You'll watch him? Close?" He shot a glare at Billy. "Make sure he doesn't send me off a cliff?"

"Oh, right!" Billy shot back. "Like you could walk that far!"

Brad silenced the older boy with a look and put his hand on Eric's shoulder. "I'll watch him."

Eric nodded and put the blindfold over his eyes. Brad tied it at the back of his head.

"Okay, Destructo. Move it out."

Five minutes later, Brad was bored out of his mind. Billy had done a pretty decent job of leading Eric once he got started. Now it was Billy's turn. Brad watched as Eric whipped off the blindfold with a triumphant grin and tossed it to Billy.

"Tell you what," Brad whispered to Eric as Billy tied the blindfold in place. "You go ahead and lead Billy down the path. Do as good a job for him as he did for you. I'll head back to the clearing and let Josh know everything's okay."

Eric frowned. "I thought you were supposed to stay with us."

"Just until you got the hang of things. Besides, you know the way back, right?"

Eric nodded slowly. "Right."

"So no sweat." Brad thumped Eric on the back. "See you there."


Josh stood in the clearing, watching the teams straggle in and checking off names to be sure everyone was back. The boys were whooping and hollering, laughing as they took off their blindfolds and shaking hands. Everyone was talking at once about what they'd done.

Then he spotted Brad, once again leaning against his tree. Alone.

"Mike, have you seen Eric or Billy?" he asked, fighting the sudden apprehension that was tugging at his gut.

The blue-eyed senior cast a quick glance over the group, then shrugged. "No, come to think of it, I haven't." He frowned. "I thought Brad was with them."

"Yeah," Josh said. "So did I." With a sigh he walked over to Brad.

"Where are the boys?" Josh tried to remain calm. Surely Brad hadn't left them alone in the woods.

Brad looked at him, his expression bored. "They're coming."

"What do you mean, 'they're coming'? Why aren't you with them?" Though quiet, Josh's voice held an ominous quality.

Brad stiffened visibly. "Hey," he shot back. "I told you they weren't my responsibility!"

"And I told you they were."

Before Brad could respond, Eric burst into the clearing, his eyes wide, his face pale.

"Josh!" he screamed. "Josh, you gotta come! Quick!"

Josh pushed past the other boys who had swarmed around Eric. "What's happened? Where's Billy?"

Eric was breathing heavily, as though he'd run for all he was worth to get back as fast as he could. "He-he's in trouble. He's on a ledge. I-I think he's gonna fall! I told him I'd come get you." He grabbed Josh's sleeve and pulled. "You gotta come! Now!"

"Mike, you and Brad stay here with the other boys."

"Brad's gone," Mike answered. Josh shot a glance at the tree; Brad was nowhere in sight. He shook his head. "Okay, you and Aaron stay here. I'll send Eric back if I need more help." He didn't wait for a response. "Let's go, Eric." He broke into a run.


Brad raced down the path, his eyes narrowed, searching. Five minutes away from the clearing, he spotted two sets of tracks in the snow leading into the woods, away from the path.

"Stupid!" he muttered angrily. "Stupid, stupid kids!"

He followed the tracks, jumping brush and dodging low-hanging branches as he ran. Suddenly he burst out of the woods and slammed to a halt. What he saw made his blood run cold.

He stood at the edge of a steep drop-off. Below was an icy slope, and at the bottom were huge, scattered boulders. To his left was a narrow ledge that followed the mountainside. From what Brad could tell, the ledge, which was barely two feet wide, was primarily made of ice. And there, fifteen feet out on the ledge, was Billy, face pressed to the rocky mountainside, tears running down his red cheeks.

"Oh, man..." Brad breathed. "What have I done?"


Standing just behind Brad, Josh heard his horrified whisper.

"Good question." His voice was low and angry. Brad spun around to face him. He'd been so focused on Billy, he hadn't heard Josh and Eric come up.

Josh stepped past Brad without giving him a chance to respond. "Billy." He kept his voice calm. "Billy, you hear me?"

The boy didn't answer. He just stood, shaking, plastering himself against the frozen mountain.

"I told him not to go there." Eric's voice was choked with tears. "But he said he could do it. He was just going to go out and come right back. But when he started to turn around, he got scared..." His words trailed off.

Josh looked below the ledge, noting the ice and the boulders.

*Now that would be a nasty fall,* he thought. And a deadly one.

"I'm gonna get him." Brad started to move toward the ledge, but Josh's hand shot out to grasp his sleeve.

"No!"

"It's my fault he's there!" Brad snarled. "I'm going after him."

Josh held him fast. "Listen to me," he ordered, his words clipped and fierce. "I can't let you go out there, so forget it." When Brad moved to shake his hand off, Josh gripped him more firmly. His blue eyes locked with Brad's dark, angry gaze.

"You want to help?" Josh said, his voice low. "Then stay here. Watch Eric and make sure he doesn't do anything stupid. And stay close to the edge."

Brad's eyes narrowed. "Close to the edge?"

Josh looked at Billy, studied the ledge he was perched on. "I'll do what I can to bring him back safely." His gaze swiveled back to Brad's. "But if I can't, if that ledge goes, I'll throw Billy your way. He's small. If we can get close enough, I should be able to get him to you. But I need you there to catch him."

Brad's eyes held his for a moment, then he gave a curt nod. "I'll be there."

Josh's grip on the boy's arms slackened, and he nodded. "Okay. Good." He let go and moved toward the ledge.

"What about you?" Brad's question was hoarse, almost desperate.

Josh glanced at him quickly. "I'll be okay."

"Yeah? You Superman or something?" Brad asked with a meaningful glance toward the boulders below.

If the situation hadn't been so critical, Josh would have laughed. He just shook his head. "No. Not hardly. But I've got God with me. No matter what happens to me, I'll be with him. I know where I'm spending eternity." He stepped onto the ledge. "That's another reason I'm going out here and not you."

"Because you don't think I'm going to heaven?" Brad's voice was incredulous. "You're going out there because you don't think I'm going to heaven?"

"Not entirely." Josh smiled wryly as he moved cautiously along the narrow shelf. *Lord, I don't believe this! Now he wants to talk about you?* He paused, and drew a deep breath. There was barely enough room for him. He had to plaster his back against the mountainside, his arms spread out, his hands flat against the rough, cold stone. *Help me, Lord. Don't let that little boy fall. Please.*

"Not entirely?" Brad echoed.

Keeping his eyes on the ledge beneath his feet, Josh inched his way toward the spot where Billy stood in terrified silence. "I'm doing this," he responded, "because Billy needs help. And I won't let you do it because I don't know where you stand with God. I'm not willing to risk losing you for eternity."

He tossed a quick glance back at Brad. The boy was standing in silence, his dark eyes mirroring the tortured dullness of disbelief.

A jolt of understanding shot through Josh. *He wants to believe in you, Father! But it's as though he's afraid of something.* Another step closer. "Brad, God cares about you. Whatever you think, whatever you've been told, the only truth is that. God cares about you."

Brad flinched and looked down. "Okay," he said at last, so quietly that Josh wasn't sure for a moment if he'd really spoken. "Okay, I hear you." He looked up again, his expression one of entreaty. "But I've had enough of this little lesson, you know? So get Billy and get back here."

"Believe me, that's exactly what I intend to do." Now Josh was only a few feet away. He could see the way Billy was trembling, the way his fingers were trying to dig into the dirt and rock of the mountainside.

"Billy, I'm right here," Josh said as he reached the boy. He brought his hand down and rested it gently on the slim, trembling shoulder. "We're going to be okay, son."

The boy cautiously turned his face to look at Josh. Tears had left streaks across his dirt-smudged cheeks, and his eyes were red and swollen—and filled with fear.

"One step at a time, buddy," Josh said. "Just hold onto my hand and inch your feet along." He smiled. "We'll be back on solid ground in no time, okay?"

The boy gave a quick nod. "O-okay," he managed in a quavering voice.

"That's the spirit," Josh encouraged as he took the boy's small hand. Though the day was unseasonably warm, Billy's hand was like ice. Josh smiled, doing his best to appear unconcerned. "Ready?"

Billy kept his eyes fixed on Josh. "I-I guess so."

Josh started to take a step toward safety, but he felt Billy stiffen.

"I'm scared, Josh!"

Josh nodded. "I know. Me, too. But we're going to do this together, okay? You and me and God."

Billy swallowed, then nodded. Together, they started back toward solid ground.

Brad raked a hand through his hair, and from the corner of his eye Josh noted that it was shaking slightly. Brad turned to Eric, who still stood a few feet away from him, watching him with wide eyes.

"C'mere, kid. It's okay." Relieved, Eric moved into the circle of Brad's muscular arm, leaning against him.

Josh stepped sideways again, testing the ledge gingerly before he put his weight down. Billy followed his lead, sliding his feet to the side slowly and carefully.

*It's as though Brad is out on a ledge, too, Father,* Josh thought. *Perched on the edge of some huge black hole, feeling helpless and forgotten.*

Josh tried again. "God loves you, Brad, but he won't force you to accept his love. You can turn your back on him. Or you can let him in. If you do, he'll take care of you. He'll make things bearable. He gives you the strength, the wisdom, the peace you need." He looked up again with a quick grin. "Take it from someone who lives life on the edge: He's the only one who can."

Brad stared at Josh, his expression one of doubt—though Josh wondered if the boy was doubting his words or his sanity.

*You've got to admit it's a little crazy, Father, carrying on a conversation about you while I'm out here, inching my way along! But it's the first time the kid has listened!*

"I hear what you're saying," Brad said at last. "You really believe God's the only answer." A slight smile tipped Brad's tight lips. "So prove it and get off the ledge."

"Okay," Josh said amiably. *Okay, Lord,* his heart echoed. *He not only listened, he heard me! It's a start.* He continued inching along the ledge, elation sweeping through him. "What do you say, Billy? You ready to get back on solid ground?"

"Yes!" the boy responded vigorously.

Relieved laughter bubbled from Josh's throat. They were only three feet away. They were going to make it.

"I'll tell you one thing, guys," he said with a grin. "This fresh air is getting to me. I'm so hungry I could—"

Josh froze. Every ounce of awareness raced to focus on his

foot, on the spot where he'd just stepped. It shifted, sank—and a chill of terrible understanding touched Josh's spine.

"Josh?" Billy's voice was small, terrified.

Josh's eyes flew to meet Brad's disbelieving gaze.

"No!"

Brad's horrified denial washed over Josh, and Josh surged into action. He jerked Billy into his arms, sliding his hands under the boys armpits and lifting him quickly as he threw his back against the mountainside. The ledge shuddered ominously and Josh threw Billy forward as hard as he could.

Billy screamed as he went airborne, his arms and legs windmilling. He landed with a thud in Brad's outstretched arms, and the two of them fell backward in a tangled heap. In the next second, Brad sprang to his feet, scrambling back to the edge, reaching for Josh.

He was too late.

The ledge seemed to dissolve beneath Josh's feet, and in one blazing flash, Josh knew with awful clarity what was coming. An odd mixture of anticipation and regret flooded him.

He was going home.

He was going to break his promise to Taylor.

*Jesus!* The prayer bolted from Josh's mind as everything seemed to go into slow motion. *Don't let Brad go! Don't lose him!*

For a second Josh seemed suspended in midair, almost as though he were hovering, and then he fell.

"Noooo!" Brad's scream pierced the air, following Josh as he plummeted toward the boulders.

*Father, take care of Taylor.* It was Josh's last thought before everything went black.

# One

✒

*May, 1995*

Taylor Sorensen couldn't remember a spring this hot in years. She shifted her weight in the saddle, pulled off her hat, and fanned herself as she squinted against the merciless sun to study the hills in front of her.

What a rotten day.

*How appropriate,* she thought dismally. She shoved her hat back in place, her movements abrupt and angry. *The hottest May in decades and I'm out here. You'd better appreciate this, Josh.*

Pushing her sunglasses back up her nose, she took up the reins and urged Topaz, her ten-year-old buckskin, forward. The two of them had been together since Topaz was a yearling, and the trust they had in each other was implicit. Taylor knew if any horse could make it to Reunion in this blistering heat, it was Topaz. And he'd do it without a complaint.

Why couldn't men be more like horses?

Slowly, choosing his steps with both caution and confidence, the gelding climbed the rocky rise. Taylor breathed a small sigh of relief when they reached the top. Now there was only the descent left. Tricky, but nothing they hadn't done hundreds of times.

*Never for this reason, though.* The thought came unbidden, unwelcome. As did the tears. And then, as though some inner conspiracy had been set in motion, images flooded her mind.

She saw, as clearly as though she were there again, the last time she and Josh had come to the small, hidden valley.

He'd stood at the bottom of the steep path waiting for her, the picture of rugged masculinity. His electric blue eyes laughed up at her; his gaze was warm and aware.

"I told you I'd win." His deep voice, filled with teasing humor—and not a little macho pride—wrapped around her, and she felt again the thrill of knowing he was hers.

"Only because I took mercy on you and slowed Topaz to a crawl," she shot back.

His grin only broadened as he came forward and reached up to catch her as she slid from the saddle. She rested her hands on his solid shoulders, looked into his laughing face, and gladly lowered herself into his embrace....

A sudden jerk pulled her from her memories and her eyes widened in alarm. Topaz whinnied once—a piercing sound—and then Taylor was airborne.

She landed with a thud on the rocky ground, her momentum causing her to roll a few feet until she came to a halt in a breathless pile at the edge of the grass. She lay still, panting, wondering if anything was broken. She moved gingerly, one limb at a time. When she was sure her arms and legs were only bruised, she slowly pushed herself into a sitting position, testing her back and shoulders. Everything seemed to be in working order. She'd be sore, no doubt about that, but at least she was in one piece. With a sigh of relief, she leaned back on her elbows and drew in a calming breath, then glanced at Topaz. The buckskin was regarding her with a decidedly sheepish expression.

"Got a little careless those last few steps, did we?" she asked him, and he tossed his head, then stepped forward to lower his nose and nudge her.

With a moan she sat up, then stood. She brushed herself off, straightened her shoulders, and looked around. The beauty of this valley never failed to stir her. Unless they stumbled on it as she had, no one would ever imagine it was here, nestled in the rocky outcropping. She'd found it when she was a teen, riding aimlessly, exploring her parents' Wyoming ranch. She didn't know what had drawn her attention to the rock formation. It didn't look any different from dozens of others on the ranch: steep inclines covered with scrubby brush and loose rocks that led to narrow plateaus. If you'd seen one, you'd seen them all. But she'd climbed it all the same. And when she and her pony reached the top, she was stunned at what she saw.

The majesty and ruggedness of northwestern Wyoming had always awed her. Her parents' ranch, Galloway Glen, was just east of the Grand Tetons and just south of Yellowstone, and its location was so remote that it was almost wilderness. Here, Taylor had seen nature in all its splendor—and all its power— for as long as she could remember. But discovering the hidden lushness of the valley had been like tripping over a two-pound nugget of solid gold: unexpected and wonderful.

At the top of the rise, instead of the expected plateau there was a narrow ledge. From there Taylor looked down into a pic- turesque valley. It wasn't large—no more than 150 feet long and about 80 feet wide—but every inch was a feast for the senses. The steep path leading to the valley floor ended at a carpet of emerald grass that was dotted with masses of wildflowers. Lupine, phlox, and wild iris danced in the breeze, as though beckoning her, inviting her to come down into the beauty. From her vantage point, she saw that small stands of lodgepole pine and other conifers bordered a clear, deep, spring-fed pool.

The descent into the valley was steep, but her sure-footed pony had managed without any mishaps. Taylor had slid from the saddle and spent the rest of the afternoon getting acquainted with what would become her own private haven. Over the years she had enjoyed every aspect of the pool, from using it to quench her thirst after a long ride to letting it cool her skin with a refreshing swim.

Then, on her second or third visit, while exploring, she'd discovered a treasure within a treasure: a cave, located on the far side of the pool. The entrance had been concealed by brush and trees, which Taylor's unending curiosity had prompted her to push aside. Heart pounding with excitement, she'd scrambled onto the lip of the ledge at the cave entrance, then stepped inside to explore with a youthful disregard for safety.

She'd inspected the main chamber carefully and had been thrilled when she saw a narrow corridor branching off to the right. She squeezed along it, going as far back as the light would allow. When she could no longer see, she turned around and raced back to the entrance, jumped into the pool, and went to pull a flashlight from her saddlebag. Back in the cave, she'd discovered that the narrow corridor turned and opened up into another small chamber—a perfect hiding place.

She hadn't told anyone about the valley; it was hers and hers alone.

Until Josh.

They had met in college, in November during her senior year. Taylor could still remember the first time she'd seen him—tall, broad-shouldered, sandy blond hair bleached from days spent in the sun, blue eyes aglow with humor and passion. The first time their gazes met she'd known something monumental had happened. Apparently he'd felt the same, for within six months they were married.

She could recall that day with vivid clarity. They'd come to Galloway Glen during spring break, when the colors of spring were exploding everywhere. She remembered the emotions that flooded her as she placed her hand in Josh's and vowed to love, honor, and cherish him. It was the happiest day of her life.

May 6. Eight years ago today.

And with those vows, Taylor's life had suddenly taken on a dimension she'd never imagined was possible. Without even trying, Josh had managed to pull her out of her reclusive shell and help her see how incredible life could be when you opened yourself to someone. He brought her love and laughter and the certainty that life was good.

Or at least it used to be.

All that had changed six months ago on the youth group camping trip.

Taylor had known these trips were the highlight of Josh's

year. He loved the kids, loved the adventure, loved sharing his faith. As with everything else in his life, he gave of himself 110 percent. That was one thing about Josh: He lived life to the hilt. He took every experience by the horns and rode it into the ground. It was what made him so exciting, so passionate. It was what made him a favorite with the teens in the youth group.

In Taylor's opinion, it was also what got him killed.

She remembered the last words he'd spoken to her on the morning he left for the trip. "Pray for me."

She'd done that.

"I'll see you soon."

She'd believed him. She'd had no reason not to. No solid explanation for the gnawing apprehension that seemed to hover on the edge of her awareness for the next several days. Numerous times she stared at the phone, willing it to ring, willing Josh to be on the other end, laughing and telling her of the group's exploits. If it had been possible, she would have called them herself. But this was a wilderness trip, and the camp was miles from a phone.

The call never came. But a knock at the door did. Taylor peered out the peephole, and when she saw Jim Wilson standing there with her parents and her brother, Ryan, her heart seemed to freeze in her chest. She rested her head against the door for a moment as the niggling apprehension became a wave of dread.

"God…" she whispered, "please." Then she drew a breath and pulled the door open.

She didn't remember much of what Jim told her. She'd known immediately from his pale, strained expression that the news wasn't good, but from the moment he'd said Josh was dead, she'd stopped listening. It wasn't until days later that she'd been able to take in the facts and had learned of Brad Momadey's part in her husband's accident.

Rage washed over her now, as it had when she'd first understood what had happened. Brad hadn't been to church since the accident, but Taylor couldn't find any regret in her heart. She was glad he was gone. She couldn't stand the thought of seeing him. If it hadn't been for his carelessness, none of this would have happened.

*He should have been the one to go out on that ledge, Lord,* she thought, as she had many times since that day. *He should have been the one to die.*

At the funeral, Taylor's grandmother had taken her aside. Taylor had been grateful that her grandmother had come. Her home was nestled in a remote section of Idaho's Sawtooth National Forest, several hours away, and her health had not been good enough for much travel. But it would take more than a long trip to keep her grandmother away when someone she loved was hurting.

Taylor had been so lost in her grief she hadn't even noticed that the old woman had dressed in her ceremonial Ojibwa garments, her way of showing honor to "the one who has left us." The daughter of an Ojibwa woman and an Irish sheepherder, Taylor's grandmother had a great respect for her Native American heritage. She had done all she could to pass that respect on to her own daughter and to her grandchildren.

Taylor had followed her grandmother wordlessly as she led her to the garden. She wanted to refuse, to leave the empty phrases and uncomfortable condolences and hide herself at home. But she'd learned at an early age that her elders were to be honored and the wisdom of their words respected. Often at their family gatherings everyone remained silent until the elders had spoken, for it was reasoned that those who were wise must speak first.

"I see the grief that washes over you," her grandmother said, as Taylor sat on one of the wooden benches. She didn't reply. Instead, she glanced around the garden where she had played so often as a child.

*Was life ever that simple, Lord?*

"It is sad when those we love leave us, little one," her grandmother went on. "But there will be many times in life when we face loss. The challenge is to remember that the beauty of each life remains forever in our hearts. That is what you must remember, Taylor Moira. The beauty your Joshua brought you.

And you must thank Gitchi Manito for sharing this man with you."

*Gitchi Manito.* The Great Spirit. God. Taylor had drawn a deep breath, fighting against the fear and anger that threatened to overwhelm her. If one more person told her God was in control, she would scream.

She knew it was true. Believed it with her whole heart. And yet belief didn't keep her heart from breaking or from crying out that if God were so in control, why would he allow someone so alive, so vibrant and loving, to die? Why would he take away the only person outside of her family who had ever made Taylor feel as though she belonged?

The pain of her memories cut at her heart, and Taylor turned abruptly, her eyes scanning the sun-kissed valley.

*Stop it,* she ordered her swimming mind. *Stop thinking. Stop remembering.*

She went to Topaz's side, lifted the flap on the saddlebag, and reached in. Her hand closed around the cool ceramic container she'd slipped into the bag earlier that morning. The container holding Josh's ashes.

Clearly her gray matter was ignoring her, for as she turned back to the pool, her mind burned with the memory of the first time she and Josh had come here together.

Their honeymoon.

Delight had filled his eyes when he'd looked down into the valley, a delight that only increased as he discovered the wonders waiting for him in this small piece of paradise. It hadn't taken long for him to fall as hopelessly in love with her special place as she was.

"Will you do something for me?" he'd said one dusky evening as they sat beside the campfire. She was cradled against him, her back to his chest, feeling warm and safe. Loved. Protected. Cherished.

"Maybe," she said, shifting to look at him. "What?"

"If I die—"

"Oh, Josh!" she'd exclaimed and turned away. But he'd held her fast, smiling at her.

"It could happen, Taylor. Life isn't certain, not for any of us. Only eternity can be counted on."

At the memory, Taylor frowned. Had he known even then how short their time would be?

She recalled wanting no part in the conversation. This definitely was not honeymoon talk. She'd leaned back against him, refusing to look at him. He'd laughed, and teased, and asked her to humor him. She'd muttered something uncomplimentary under her breath.

But when she turned to look at him, the somber look in his eyes brought an end to her resistance.

"All right. Tell me."

"If anything happens to me, will you bring my ashes here and scatter them on the water?"

Quick tears had pricked at her eyes, and she'd nodded, then nestled against him. He rested his chin on the top of her head.

"I like the idea that, in a way, I'd be a part of this place, this beauty. Besides, that way we'll always be together, Taylor. This will be our forever reunion place."

At the time it had been a nice sentiment. Now it was reality. Undeniable, dreadful reality.

She'd resisted fulfilling that request, afraid that doing so would mean finally letting go of Josh. But when their anniversary had approached, she'd realized it was time. Time to do as Josh had asked.

Now, calling up every ounce of determination, she moved through the small stand of conifers that surrounded the water, oblivious for once to their beauty and grace. She stopped at the edge of the pool.

"Well, Josh." Her voice was deep and dusty. "Here we are. At Reunion. I wonder if you knew when you named this place how appropriate that name would be." Tears begged for release, but she pushed them away. "This was supposed to be our retreat, our spot of restoration. Nothing was going to be allowed here that would keep us apart." A humorless laugh escaped her, and she was almost startled by the sound. Shivering, she closed her eyes. The valley had always seemed to hold a remarkable peace, and she stood for a few moments, willing herself to feel it now.

But it wasn't there. All she felt was…empty. Hollow.

She brushed at her eyes with the back of her hand. *What good does it do to let someone in, Lord? I trusted Josh, gave him my heart, and he risked it all…*Pain shot through her, and she hugged the ceramic container tightly. *He risked it, and I lost. How is that right, Father? How do I live without him?*

Silence answered her, and she felt a wretchedness of mind and spirit that she'd never known before. It was as though icy fingers seeped into every pore and left something deep within her—some part that had been vital and living—brittle, fragile, ready to shatter.

"Get a grip, Taylor!" she hissed impatiently, willing herself to ignore the deep, stubborn pain in her chest.

There was silence all around her, as though even the birds and wind had stilled with regret. Then, almost in a dreamlike slow-motion, she removed the lid, lifted the container, and turned it upside down. The ashes spilled out with a slight *whoosh,* and Taylor smiled through her tears. Even in death Josh was in a hurry to get where he was going.

She sank to the ground, setting the container beside her and pulling her knees to her chest. Resting her forehead on her knees, she surrendered at last to the grief she'd been wrestling for the last six months.


It was growing dark by the time Taylor lifted her head, her eyes sore from weeping and her cheeks still wet with tears. Her head ached and her throat felt tight and raw. She'd always heard that crying was healthy, cathartic, the beginning of healing—so why didn't she feel better? Maybe some pain went so deep that even tears couldn't touch it.

Listlessly she stared across the pool, her gaze resting, unseeing, on the cave…and then she froze.

She was being watched.

There, at the edge of the rock face, on the rise just above

the cave entrance, sat a wolf.

*So this is what it's like to go crazy,* Taylor thought, stunned. There weren't any wolves in Wyoming. Hadn't been for sixty years. There was no possible way she could be seeing one now.

She squeezed her eyes shut, then opened them again.

The wolf was still there, his head held high, his ears perked, his amber gaze fixed on her. Apparently he didn't know he was an impossibility.

Taylor leaned forward, and the animal crouched slightly, as though ready to flee. She stilled, and after a moment he seemed to relax. His haunting, penetrating eyes were brilliantly intelligent, startlingly compelling.

He was more slender than Taylor had thought a wolf would be, but his demeanor was positively aristocratic; he gave the impression of a sovereign surveying his domain—and one of his subjects. His coat—a study of light grays, browns, and flecks of black—was so thick and luxurious that Taylor's fingers itched to touch him, to bury themselves in what promised to be remarkable softness. The look on his gray face, though watchful, was disarmingly sweet, and she had the distinct impression he found her fascinating.

A quick and disturbing thought coursed though her, bringing alarm on its heels. Did wolves attack people? Was this majestic beast looking at her with such interest not out of curiosity but because she was a threat? Or an enemy?

Or, worse yet, an item on his dinner menu?

Her eyes widened at the thought, and she swallowed with difficulty. Frozen in place, loathe to move and precipitate any response, she could only continue the furtive exchange of glances. Then, for a brief, incredible moment, her eyes met the wolf's golden gaze. The contact lasted only a second, but before his eyes flicked away, something clicked in her mind.

She was in no danger.

Her apprehension melted as the assurance resonated within her, filling her with a peaceful certainty that she had nothing to fear. In fact, she had the oddest feeling that the wolf was watching her out of concern. And a kind of protectiveness.

They sat in silence for a few moments, regarding each other without ever repeating the eye contact. Taylor was mesmerized. The creature was a barely controlled store of power coiled in a slender frame; he was everything that was wild and graceful and beautiful.

And then, as suddenly as he had appeared, the wolf was gone. It was as though he'd simply melted into thin air.

Taylor blinked twice, then frowned.

*Okay, God,* she prayed, a tumble of confused thoughts and feelings assailing her. *What are you doing now?*

CHAPTER

*One Year Later*

Connor Alexander strolled down the carpeted hallways of the home office of Wildlife Awareness Coalition, unaware of the ripple of interest that followed in his wake. Had he stopped and glanced behind him, he would have seen a dozen women, standing on tiptoe, watching over their office dividers as he walked by. More than one had an appreciative glimmer in her eyes, and several were rummaging in their desks for mirrors and makeup.

Their dreamy-eyed fascination was due in part to Connor's classic good looks, broad shoulders, and lean, muscular build. But those assets, as attractive as they might be, weren't the greatest source of women's response to him. What seemed to draw the most attention were his eyes. Many a woman had found herself speechless when fixed with that penetrating blue gaze—a gaze made even more captivating by its curious blend of sincerity, respect, and audacity.

More often than not, Connor would listen to others silently, content to take in what they had to say. When asked, however, he didn't hesitate to express his thoughts, beliefs, and values. He spoke what he believed, even when the words were difficult to hear. He did his best to be kind, but kindness did not always remove the sting of tough truths. Especially when those truths had to do with his feelings toward the women who so often pursued him.

Connor enjoyed women, even enjoyed dating occasionally. But he did not have time in his well-ordered life for a relationship. He was "married" to his career. That was his focus. So he made it a rule not to play with anyone's emotions. He kept his distance. It was much safer that way. For the women. For him.

Thus it was that he walked along in determined ignorance, blissfully unaware of the havoc he was wreaking in several women's hearts. Instead, his attention was focused on the fact that today, as on most days, WAC—or "Wacky," as some of the politicians in D.C. liked to call their organization—was buzzing with activity.

Connor smiled, listening to the lively discussions emanating from the offices he passed. He'd spent some of his most enjoyable—and infuriating—days caught up in similar meetings. Brainstorming, venting, screaming, cheering.

He was going to miss this place.

The clean white walls were adorned with strikingly beautiful prints of bears, eagles, dolphins, wolves—every sort of endangered or threatened species. One wall was dedicated to plaques and certificates, most of them commending WAC for its work in educating the public regarding wildlife management issues. That was what had first drawn Connor to WAC: their profound dedication to raising the public's awareness and deepening their understanding of wildlife issues. The organization had enjoyed remarkable success through programs that were both educational and entertaining. "Information, Not Persuasion" was the motto by which they lived. And it was this ideology that had drawn Connor to the organization sixteen years ago when he emerged from college with a degree in wildlife biology and a head full of idealistic goals and passions.

He paused to study a print of an eagle, admiring the beauty of one of God's most magnificent creations, remembering with wry humor the young man he'd been—enthusiastic, fervent, eager to take on a world that seemed all too ready to destroy nature in the name of progress. Ask him to live in the wilds, to stand against any foe, to sacrifice comfort, society, and human relationships—he would have done it all. All that mattered was protecting God's wonderful wild creatures who, despite claws, fangs, or seemingly gargantuan strength, could not protect themselves from mankind and its constant efforts to "subdue the earth."

He turned to continue down the hallway. That young man had been so sure he could change the world. Instead, he'd run head-on into reality, learning some hard facts about the politics of wildlife management. He'd discovered that many of the true battlegrounds for effective wildlife management weren't in the wilderness, but right here in Washington, D.C., in people's offices. And contrary to his idealistic beliefs, human relationships were one of the most vital factors in the battle. With God's help and guidance, he'd learned to deal with all kinds of people—politicians, ranchers, educators, government officials—even others involved in wildlife management, many of whom had their own agendas and prejudices. Talk about being refined by fire!

Fortunately, Connor was blessed with a quick mind, a teachable heart, and a spirit committed to following God's principles. It hadn't taken him long to discover that his most effective tools were tact, respect, and honesty.

"Well, it's about time you showed up."

The comment met him as he rounded the corner, and Connor glanced down to see Irene Smith looking up at him from her desk, her expression one of tolerant affection. Her salt-and-pepper hair framed her face softly, and her brown eyes glowed with an amiable courtesy. All in all, she had the appearance of a sweet grandmother—but Connor knew WAC's executive secretary could be an iron-willed tyrant when she had to be.

He smiled at her fondly and perched on the edge of her desk. "I suppose he's waiting patiently?" he asked, folding his arms across his chest and angling a look at the office door beside her desk. "President" was etched in the decorative frosted glass of the door.

"Oh, of course. And penguins can fly."

He laughed.

"Well, what are you waiting for?" she demanded, giving him a push off her desk. "Go forth and conquer."

He was still smiling as he opened the door and entered the cluttered office. His amused gaze roamed the room. One thing he could always count on: Harry Crowley, the founder of and visionary behind WAC, would never change. "Harried Harry" he was called by those who knew him well, but always with a smile and a wink. His office bore mute testimony to the appropriateness of the nickname. Shelves lined both walls, doing their valiant best to hold the multitude of volumes Harry had collected over the years. But the large oak desk and the equally large conference table gave clear evidence that the shelves were outnumbered, for both were buried beneath piles of books and papers.

"So nice of you to honor me with your presence, Mr. Wonderful."

The dry remark came from behind a particularly large pile of papers, and Connor grinned. "I just hated to interrupt you, Harry, knowing how busy you always are."

"Hmpf!" the man snorted, standing and coming to clamp a large hand on Connor's shoulder.

Big and bearlike, Crowley presented an imposing figure. His height was well-balanced by his breadth—where he found such stylish, tailored suits to fit his bulk, Connor would never know—and his eyes snapped with intelligence and awareness. Harry had been in the Capitol city for a lot of years. He knew everyone, and his keen wit, ready laugh, and enviable knack of understanding and being able to relate to opposing sides of any debate had earned him the respect of many—an amazing accomplishment in a city filled with potential enemies and proven adversaries. Connor's boss wasn't timid about taking a stand, but he did so in such a way that people seldom felt disregarded or discounted.

*No, not my boss,* Connor corrected himself. *My ex-boss. Almost.*

"Sit! Sit!" Harry swept books from one of the leather chairs in front of his desk, then eased himself onto the edge of his desk and regarded Connor with sparkling eyes. "So! How's the world-famous wildlife photographer?"

Connor arched an eyebrow. "Now, Harry, we both know you didn't call me in here to talk about my change in professions. A change, I might add, that you considered…let's see, how did you put it? 'Ludicrous and lunacy,' wasn't it?"

An impenitent grin crossed the big man's face. "Nice alliteration, don't you think? Kind of fits with 'morosely moronic' or 'downright doltish' or—my personal favorite—'clearly and concisely crazy and cockeyed.'"

"So," Connor said, laughter in his deep voice, "why have you called me here, O great guru of the gazelles?"

"You're learning." There was an appreciative twinkle in Harry's eyes. "And that's exactly why I think you should stay with us."

Connor shook his head. "Harry, we've talked all this over. You've done too good a job of teaching me. I think you're right on the money when you say the most effective way to get people fired up about supporting wildlife management is to educate them, to let them see for themselves what the issues are and why. 'Information, Not Persuasion,' remember? I just happen to think I can accomplish more through the lens of a camera than by participating in yet another debate with yet another opponent in some bureaucrat's office."

Harry gave a deep sigh of disappointment. "So you intend to go through with this, eh? Just travel around the country, looking for unexplored wilderness and wildlife in all its glory and taking pictures."

Connor grinned. "Yup. Pretty much. Take pictures, write articles, maybe even put together a showing or exhibit. After all, if my work is good enough to hang in the hallowed walls of WAC—"

"I only bought those prints to placate what I thought was a phase you were going through. You're one of my best field reps. I never figured you'd jump ship on me!"

"Hmmm," Connor replied. "Of course not. That's why you asked me to supply you with prints of my work to sell at your fund-raisers—"

"Pure marketing acumen. Wealthy people love to spend money on artsy stuff like your photos."

"—which led to some of my photos being published in a nationally known wildlife magazine—"

"Hey, can I help it if they thought you were some kind of creative genius?"

"—and an offer from one of your pals, who just happens to own a D.C. art gallery, to hold a showing of my work next spring," Connor finished, his eyes twinkling with humor.

Harry crossed his arms over his broad chest. "Well, now that you mention it," he said, his eyes wide, as though just realizing some great truth, "I guess your success is entirely my doing. I just hope you're appropriately grateful!" he huffed with mock haughtiness.

Connor's eyes grew serious. "You know I am, Harry." All jesting gone, his voice was low and sincere. "You've helped give my dream life and breath, and I'm more grateful than I can say."

"Good!" Crowley boomed, moving to sit in his large, sturdy leather desk chair. "Then you won't mind doing me a little favor."

Connor paused, eyeing his almost ex-boss suspiciously. "A favor?"

"Nothing big. By the way, have you decided where you're going first on this photo expedition of yours?"

"Not yet."

"Terrific! Then it shouldn't be a problem to start in Wyoming."

Connor leaned back in his chair. "Okay, Harry, out with it. What's in Wyoming?"

"Nothing, as far as I'm concerned." He pulled some papers from a folder and handed them to Connor. "However," he continued as Connor scanned the sheets, "there are those who don't agree with me."

Connor looked up from what he'd been reading, his eyes

thoughtful. "Wolves in Wyoming. Do you think this is for real?"

Harry shrugged. "Normally I wouldn't give reports like these a second thought. But with the wolves that were released in Yellowstone last January, who knows? It's improbable, but…"

Connor nodded. "Not impossible. A wolf could have made its way further south."

"Right into the backyard of a whole passel of ranchers, none of whom would send the Welcome Wagon out to greet him."

"More likely the meat wagon." Connor's face was grim.

Harry inclined his head in agreement. "So, circumstances being what they are, I figured it would be a good idea to take a look. A purely unofficial look, mind you. One where no one knows who you are or why you're there. Don't want to get the locals any more worked up than they already are, now do we? And who better to send on such a delicate project than my most experienced field rep?" He smiled, thoroughly pleased with himself.

Connor was already shaking his head. He hated doing "unofficial" investigations. There was too much deceit, too much concealing of facts. It went against everything he believed in.

"No way, Harry. You know how I feel about this kind of thing."

"I certainly do. I'm well aware of your stand on honoring God and truth and all that stuff. That's why you're going to be completely aboveboard with these folks."

Connor looked at him, unconvinced.

"You're going to tell them you're a roving photographer, out to shoot some great pix, who has just discovered the wonders of Wyoming."

"Harry…"

"It's the truth, isn't it?" Harry's eyes dared him to deny it.

"Well, sure, but it isn't the whole truth—"

"So what? You're not lying to anyone. After all, isn't it the Good Book that says something about being shrewd as snakes and innocent as doves? Well, you're just going in there as quietly as possible, thereby avoiding upsetting people unnecessarily.

And if anyone happens to ask you if you're there to check out the wolf rumors, you can honestly tell them you are." His eyes gleamed as he played his trump. "I mean, what wildlife photographer wouldn't jump at the chance to get shots of the first wolves to come to Wyoming in sixty years?"

Connor sat there, his arms crossed, a frown creasing his forehead. The thought was attractive. Extremely. He couldn't deny that. And he wouldn't actually have to lie to anyone. So why did he feel so uneasy?

"I don't know…"

"Great!" Harry was grinning from ear to ear. "I knew you wouldn't let me down. After all, Wyoming has a lot of unexplored wilderness. Heck, it's the least populated state in the union! It's nothing but unexplored wilderness. And what better time to go than in the spring, when all the pretty flowers are blooming." He pulled a face. "Just be sure to credit me for leading you to what are sure to be award-winning photos, okay?"

"And if the wolves really are there?"

"Then we notify Wyoming Fish and Game or our friends at U.S. Fish and Wildlife, and we send one of our teams to the area to start a host of public education and awareness programs," Harry replied. "If there's even one wolf out there, we'll do our best to put people's fears to rest, and hopefully keep our furry friend from ending up as a rug on someone's floor."

"Or buried beneath the daisies in someone's backyard," Connor added grimly.

"So, it's settled then. Here are your tickets." Harry slapped an envelope down on the desk in front of Connor. "You leave tomorrow at 7:00 A.M. Sharp."

Connor looked from the tickets to Harry's expectant face, then shook his head with a resigned chuckle.

Harry beamed. "There's a rental car waiting for you at the airport. A Jeep Wrangler from Rent-A-Wreck, I think." He grinned. "Wouldn't take anything less than a four-wheeler into that area! See Irene about your expense check—" he broke off, a slightly pained expression crossing his face, "and try to keep costs down, Con. Your last trip almost broke us. That money

42

tree we planted in the backyard still hasn't bloomed."

"I don't know why not," Connor quipped as he took the ticket and started for the door. "There's enough horse manure flying around this office to keep a dozen trees in bloom."

# Three

*April, 1996*

"Taylor Moira, you're an amazing and courageous woman!"

Taylor cocked an eyebrow and looked over her shoulder at her brother, Ryan. He sat at the kitchen table, his booted feet resting on her clean tablecloth, his chair balanced on the back two legs. Dressed as he was in Wrangler jeans and a denim shirt, Taylor knew most would consider him the epitome of a brave and heroic cowboy of the Old West. More rugged than handsome, Ryan still gained his share of feminine attention. Taylor had seen more than one woman do a double take when her brother walked past, but he seldom noticed. For the last fourteen years, the only woman he'd had eyes for was Lisa, his wife.

"Clearly a lead-in of some sort, Taylor," Lisa remarked from her seat next to Ryan. "I'd avoid it if I were you."

Taylor laughed. "You're probably right, but I can't resist." She turned to her brother. "So I'm amazing and courageous, am I?"

He waggled his eyebrows at her and grinned. "Either that or you're plumb daft."

"She's not daft!" This quick defense came from Ryan's eleven-year-old son, Mark.

Taylor smiled at him. "Of course I'm not, sweetie. And I'm glad you're smarter than your daddy and can see that."

Ryan snorted, then yelped when someone delivered a sharp rap to the back of his head. He turned wrathfully, then stopped in mid-rant when he spotted his mother standing behind him. At her slightly reproachful expression, he turned sheepishly to take a drink of his coffee.

"Really, Ryan," Donelle Camus chided as she moved to the stove to pour hot water into a mug. "I should think you'd try to be a better example for your sons. Instead, you sit in your chair like a monkey, put your filthy boots on the table, and talk to your sister in tones that could hardly be considered respectful. Sasha is exhibiting better manners than you are."

At the sound of her name, the black-and-white Siberian husky, who was curled up in the corner of the kitchen, lifted her head and fixed her intense blue gaze on Taylor's mother.

"Never mind, Sash," Taylor said. "Mom doesn't have any treats for you."

The Siberian's velvety, pointed ears perked, and her gaze switched to Taylor expectantly, her tail giving one hopeful thump.

"Oh dear, you used the 't' word," her mother said, laughing. Taylor grinned and knelt to scratch the dog's broad head.

It was always fun to have her family visit—which happened often, since her parents also lived on Galloway Glen, about a half-mile away in a log home of their own, and Ryan and Lisa lived just a few miles down the road. Some people might not like having their family so close, but Taylor loved it.

"Now, Ryan, where were we," his mother said thoughtfully. Then she smiled. "Oh, yes. Your manners…" Her gaze rested pointedly on his feet. "Or should I say lack of them?"

At fifty-seven, Donelle Camus was one of those women who always seemed at ease. Her dark curly hair was cut in a flattering short cap, and the occasional fleck of silver only added a touch of sophistication. Her green eyes sparkled with humor and sagacity, and her manner was warm and welcoming to anyone she encountered. Little escaped her notice, though she seldom offered advice where it wasn't requested. She was the emotional anchor of her tight-knit family and the very picture of elegance, vitality, and patience. All factors that made her especially effective when dealing with her spirited, fun-loving children.

"You're absolutely right, Mother mine," Ryan said as she drew out a chair and sat down. He removed his offending feet from the table and set his chair in place, then gave Taylor an intent look. "Now let me see…" he continued, his face creased in concentration, "there must be *something* respectful I can say about you."

Taylor glared at him, tempted to throw the dish sponge right between his twinkling eyes.

"Come on, Dad!" Mikey, Mark's twin brother, urged. "How 'bout saying she's pretty?"

"Okay, guys, time for another topic of—" Lisa started, but they went on before she could finish.

"Yeah!" Mark said enthusiastically. "Her hair's pretty, too. Same color as Chestnut, and all shiny, just like his coat after we treat it for a show."

Ryan considered his sons, then shrugged. "Okay, I can go for that. Taylor, you're as pretty as a greased-up show horse."

Temptation won out. The sponge hurtled through the air and connected with a satisfying, squishy *thud* squarely in the center of Ryan's broad, muscular chest.

"Taylor!" her mother scolded, but this time she had little effect. The twins exploded into laughter as their father vaulted out of his chair and went after his sister, who fended him off with another sopping sponge.

Seeing her offspring were out of control, Donelle settled back in her chair and sipped her tea.

"Better not hurt her, Dad, or Sasha will take your leg off!" Mikey chortled, but the dog was far too accustomed to such events. She was lying, unconcerned, with her head on her paws.

"Well, I thought sure we were in the midst of World War III," a deep voice remarked from the doorway, "but I see Mother has her wee cuppa, so all must be right with the world."

Taylor, who was locked in her brother's bear hug and suspended a good foot off the floor, grinned at her father. "All's right except that Ryan is being his typical juvenile self."

"Right," her brother retorted, "and you're an angel. That's why my shirt is soaking wet and smells like dirty dishes."

"Exactly," Taylor agreed. Her father chuckled as he stepped into the kitchen.

"You can't say you didn't ask for it," Lisa remarked dryly.

"Ryan, be a good lad and put your sister down, please"— Holden Camus took the seat next to his wife—"so she can tend to her duties as hostess."

"And do it gently, dear," Taylor's mother cautioned, seeing the gleam in her son's eyes at his father's request.

With a disappointed sigh, Ryan lowered his sister to the floor. She tossed him a triumphant smirk and went to hug her father. His blue eyes were bright with merriment and his rugged face creased into an affectionate smile.

Tall, broad-shouldered, and muscular even at sixty-one, Holden Camus looked more like a lumberjack than a minister. But his gentle eyes were a clear window to a heart that was totally dedicated to serving the Lord. While he was a loving husband and father, he was also a man uniquely designed to shepherd God's people. His devotion to God, his quick sense of humor, and his caring heart eventually won over even the most reticent or cantankerous parishioner and had endeared him to his congregation and the community.

"Thanks, Daddy. You know how hard it is to control the brute. Not even Lisa's wonderful influence has made him fit for civilized company."

Ryan ignored Taylor, choosing instead to walk back to his seat and lift his coffee cup, holding the handle daintily between his forefinger and thumb, keeping his pinkie out.

"Oh, yuck! Dad!" Mark and Mikey protested together. "You look like a sissy!"

"Not at all, my dear lads," he replied in affected tones. "I'm simply being snivilized."

"Ry, old boy, read my lips." Taylor blew a less-than-ladylike raspberry.

"Uh-oh, Dad, sounds like a grudge to me!" Ryan said, his expression full of mock horror.

"Why don't you just sit there and—" Taylor began, but Ryan held up a hand, cutting her off.

"Father, if you please. Your wayward child is in desperate need of words of truth and wisdom."

Taylor looked at her father, outraged. "Dad! Don't you dare…"

Her father merely smiled serenely, his brilliant blue eyes brimming with laughter, then tilted his head and tapped his chin with a long forefinger, as though thinking deeply. "Ah, I have it. 'Therefore, as God's chosen people, holy and loved—'"

"'*Dearly* loved,'" his wife broke in gently, and he looked at her, a slight frown creasing his brow.

"'Dearly'? Are you sure?"

"Oh, for heaven's sake!" Taylor blurted, startling Sasha from her nap. The husky jumped up, cast her mistress one disgusted look, and padded from the room to find some peace and quiet.

"Taylor, please," her mother said. "Your father is talking. You should know better than to interrupt." She turned back to her husband. "I'm sure. 'Dearly loved.'"

He nodded in good-humored assent. "'Holy and *dearly* loved,'" he went on, "'clothe yourselves with compassion, kindness—'"

"'Humility, gentleness, and patience,'" Ryan chimed in, looking inordinately pleased with himself.

Taylor merely huffed.

"'Bear with each other,'" her father's voice raised in mock sternness, "'and forgive whatever grievances you have against one another—'"

"'Forgive as the Lord forgave you—'" Taylor's mother joined in.

"'And over all these virtues—'" Lisa's voice joined the chorus, too.

Then the twins chimed in, their faces glowing with excitement that they actually knew one of their grandfather's many quotations from the Bible.

"'Put on love, which binds them all together in perfect unity—'"

Taylor's father cut them off, holding up one hand, and everyone paused, their eyes coming to rest on Taylor.

"No way," she said, standing with her arms crossed.

No one moved. All eyes remained fixed on her.

She shrugged nonchalantly. "I'm not doing it."

Clearly it was a battle of wills.

"Dad…"

Clearly, she was going to lose.

"Oh, all right!" she blurted, throwing her hands up in surrender.

Her father's eyes crinkled with affectionate amusement and he raised his hands, poising them in the air like a maestro before an orchestra. With a slight nod he lowered his hands in a swooping downbeat, and the kitchen rang with their collective voices.

"'Let the peace of Christ rule in your hearts, since as members of one body you were called to peace!'"

"Colossians," her father said, then nodded to Mark.

"Chapter three!" he said with a triumphant jump, his fist punching the air. Then he pointed at his twin.

"Verse…twelve?" Mikey said slowly, relief washing over his face at his father's smile. He nudged his grandmother gently.

"Through verse fifteen," she finished.

Taylor shook her head. "Has anyone ever told you people that weird runs in this family? Because it does. It definitely does."

Her father let out a deep, rich chuckle, and Taylor leaned over to give him a hug. "You're a beast, Dad. I can see now where Ryan gets it from." She grinned at him. "Now, how 'bout a wee cuppa?"

Like the rest of her family, Taylor used the phrase without thinking. Her mother had picked it up as a little girl from her Irish grandfather, and it had become a "Camusism" for anything hot to drink. In her mother's case, "wee cuppa" generally meant Mint Medley tea with a generous dollop of honey.

"Coffee will do me fine," her father replied, leaning back

and sliding his arm along the back of his wife's chair. "And you can tell me what started the ruckus this morning."

"Dad said Aunt Taylor looked like a horse," Mikey replied around a mouthful of Cheerios.

At his father's raised eyebrows, Ryan grinned. "I said she was as pretty as a show horse, to be exact. But that's not really what started the whole thing. It was Taylor taking exception to my calling her daft, which I still think she is."

"And why, exactly, is that?" Taylor asked in saccharine tones as she poured her father's coffee.

Ryan regarded her with humor mixed with compassion. "Because you're determined to push ahead with the repairs and preparations for the upcoming retreat season."

Taylor gave a nonchalant shrug, setting the cup of hot liquid in front of her father. "It's only April, Ry. There's plenty of time to get things done before July. I don't want to delay the opening this year."

"Why?"

His quiet question stopped her cold. She could give him a million reasons, but she knew he'd see through them all. No matter what she said, Ryan would know she wanted to push ahead because she needed to. She couldn't stand being immersed in grief and letting life pass her by any longer. She met his understanding gaze.

He leaned forward to touch her arm. "Sis, I know how much these retreats mean to you. And normally I'd be behind you a hundred and ten percent, you know that."

Taylor nodded. It was true. Ryan was one of her staunchest supporters. He always had been. For as long as she could remember, he'd been there to cheer her on, offer encouragement, or just listen.

"But to push ahead with your plans, when you know you'll have to handle a lot of the preparations yourself…" his words trailed off, and he shrugged. "I'm just not sure it's wise."

Taylor started to reply, but her father spoke up first. "Ryan may be right, Taylor. Don't you think you should give yourself more than a few months to get things done? There's a lot to accomplish, hon, and not enough people to do it."

Taylor looked at her father thoughtfully, then shook her head. "I don't know, Dad." She was a bit surprised at how tired she sounded. "I just know I don't want to put the retreats off again."

Silence fell over the room as she went to perch on the counter and sip her cocoa. She was touched that her family was so concerned about her, yet determined to stick to her plans. If there was one thing Taylor Sorensen was not, it was a quitter. Her perseverance and tenacity were what had carried her through her second year of college after she had realized that she just wasn't cut out for pastoral counseling, her chosen major. It was too draining, too depressing, too hard for her to distance herself from the pain others felt. Through this process, however, she'd discovered another way to accomplish what she'd always felt God had created her to do: give families in ministry a place to be refreshed and nurtured.

With a growing sense of excitement she'd gone to her advisor and developed a specialized major that combined counseling, business, and camp management. When she met Josh and realized they were falling in love—which happened within forty-eight hours of their first encounter—she shared her dream with him. He caught the vision that had captivated her heart, and together they worked and planned and prepared to take on the task they believed God had given them.

Their first step, when they came home together during spring break of their senior year, was to talk with Ryan, and Taylor was thrilled to find her brother a ready advocate.

"Talk with Mom and Dad," he told them. "Let them know Lisa and I are behind you. We may even want to take part, but we need some time to pray about it."

Elated, Taylor and Josh sat down with her parents.

"You've always said Galloway Glen belongs to Ryan and me, that we have an even share in it. I've talked my ideas over with him, and he's all for it."

"What exactly is it that you want to do, Taylor?" her father had asked.

"I want to open a retreat center at Galloway Glen for ministers and missionaries and their families."

Taylor smiled now, remembering the surprise on her parents' faces. But it hadn't taken long for them to catch her vision and Josh's enthusiasm as together they explained what they wanted to do and how they would go about it.

Eight years ago, after they had graduated from college, they came back to Galloway Glen, ready to put their dreams into action. Within three years, Taylor had seen her dream come true. They'd built small, cozy cabins just east of the ranch house, and converted the old bunkhouse into a caretaker's cabin for Luke Narbona. The Navajo was like an uncle to Taylor and Ryan.

Luke had been a part of Galloway Glen for as long as Taylor could remember. He'd come to the ranch as a young man to work for her grandfather and had never left. When her father married her mother, Luke had helped open the way for him to be accepted in his new congregation. When Ryan and Taylor came along, Luke appointed himself their guard and playmate.

Taylor had been Luke's shadow since she started walking. And, as though recognizing the girl's lonely spirit, Luke took her under his wing. He regaled her with tales of his Navajo ancestors, taught her the Songs of Talking to God, and listened as she shared her thoughts and dreams.

When Luke heard about their plans for Galloway Glen, he had been full of creative ideas for transforming the ranch into a retreat center, for making things work more smoothly and efficiently. He'd even helped out with the public relations and advertising, commandeering several local young people to help send out mailings and put up flyers.

Josh and Taylor began talking with the leaders of churches in neighboring communities, and most listened with interest. But their eyes really lit up when Taylor told them the retreats would be free of charge. Contributions were welcome, of course, especially from the congregations, but not required.

The "no charge" idea had been Josh's. He'd felt they could carry the center for the first few years with their savings and let

God use the church to bring in the rest. The risk had paid off. Congregations had been generous in their donations; one denomination even gave an annual contribution for the center's operating expenses. Though they seldom had an excess, there was always enough money to keep the center running and cared for.

The first season brought three ministry families to the ranch; the second, seven came. When a family sent in a reservation, Taylor and Josh would pray together, and then send brief questionnaires for each family member to fill out. The two of them did their best to discern the needs of each family, then used a mixture of guided discussions, Bible study, organized play sessions, and free time to meet those needs.

So far, the retreats had been a success. Numbers had grown steadily, and now Taylor had families scheduled for a year in advance. Because of Josh's death, however, she'd had to cancel last year's retreats. She had still felt emotionally raw, unable to go ahead with their dream without Josh.

Now…now she was ready to start again. It was time to get on with life.

Which was why she was so hesitant to delay the much-needed work or the start of the coming retreat season, just because her work crew was deserting her.

Ryan came over and slipped his arm around her shoulders. "I'm not trying to be the voice of doom here, Sis, but facts are facts. When we're all here, we can divide the work into reasonable amounts. But with this wilderness expedition Dad and the boys and I are going on, and Lisa heading out to visit her folks for a while, you're pretty much on your own."

Ryan was one of the top guides for Wilderness Outfitters, an operation that took people on expeditions into the wilds of Wyoming. Ryan's love for and knowledge of the out-of-doors and his easygoing manner had made him a favorite of the firm's clients. Because of that, the company let him take his family for a trip once a year. This year he was taking the twins and his father on a rafting expedition.

"You and Dad will be back in three weeks," Taylor reminded

him. "And I've handled at least a week or more of the preparation on my own in previous years."

"No, not on your own," Ryan corrected her quietly. "Josh was here. He was able to take on a lot of the physical work and leave the administration to you and Mom. But that's changed now."

A wave of pain washed over Taylor, and she fell silent. It was hard to believe it had been a year and a half since Josh's death. It frustrated her that every time she thought she was finally getting used to her loss, the reality would once again sucker punch her and leave her feeling empty and cold. Well, this time it wasn't going to get to her. She had spent the last eighteen months doing her best to get along on her own, and she wasn't going to let this setback make her feel hopeless again.

"I'm sorry, Sis," Ryan said, seeing the way his words had affected her. "I just want you to take a realistic look at the situation. As much as you'd like to think you can, you can't do it all yourself."

"It's okay, Ry." She willed her voice to be steady. "You're right. Josh took up a lot of the slack. But I've still got Luke. He can help some, even if he isn't as young as he used to be." She surveyed her family's worried faces, then smiled resignedly. "Besides, I already realized things were going to be a bit much this year. So I took the proverbial bull by the horns—"

"There's a bull here?" Mark looked up with interest.

"Not a real bull, dummy. A figurative one," Mikey replied with a superior air.

Taylor just grinned and went on. "—and put an ad in the paper for a temporary handyman and ranch hand."

At the stunned silence in the room, her grin broadened.

It didn't happen often, but the Camus clan was speechless—and the fact that she was the one who'd rendered them so brought Taylor a surge of gleeful triumph.

For once in her life, she'd actually had the last word!

CHAPTER

# Four

❧

D on't look so shocked, everyone," Taylor finally said into the
silence. "I can show common sense from time to time."

"It's just so novel," her brother replied smoothly. "At
least give us time to get used to the idea."

"Har de har," she said, pulling a face at him.

Her mother sipped her tea before offering her encouragement. "That's a good idea, Taylor."

Uncertainty creased Taylor's brow. "I thought so, too, at first.
But I haven't had any calls, and the ad's been out for a week. I
thought I'd at least get some high schoolers responding, but no
one's called." She shrugged. "Unfortunately, the odds of anyone
from out of town even seeing the ad aren't exactly high."

Ryan leaned back in his chair. "You don't think someone
would come to the booming metropolis of Wilson looking for a
temporary job as a handyman and ranch helper, eh? Not even if
they'd have the prettiest boss in the area?"

"I hardly think that would be a draw," Taylor replied with a
laugh. "Besides, when you consider that the last time a stranger
came to town for any length of time the news made the front
page of the local rag, it doesn't exactly bode well for my poor
little ad."

Ryan's grin broadened. "Hey, there are strange men walking
through our town all the time! I mean, they don't get much

stranger than some of the tourists who come here!"

She laughed and took a sip of hot chocolate. "Oh, now *there's* an idea. Say, mister, I know you came to Wyoming to ride horses, soak in the hot springs, and follow your wife around to every shop in the county, but wouldn't you rather come on over and dig some post holes? Or muck out a few stalls?"

"I'd rather muck stalls any day than go shopping," Mark piped up, disgust ripe in his young voice.

"That's my boy!" Ryan said with a deep laugh.

Lisa shook her head, looking at the others with a shrug. "I do my best with them, but you can see what I'm up against," she said with a grin.

Taylor laughed. "It's okay, Lisa. Ryan was hopeless long before you came on the scene. But I doubt I'll have any tourists lining up to answer the ad. At any rate, I'll know this afternoon if I've had any luck. I'm going to check out the post office box when Duncan and I go into town today."

Her mother looked up with interest. "You're going in with Duncan MacEwen again, hmmm?"

Taylor shrugged. "Just to pick up supplies and return some books to the library, Mom. It's no big deal."

"I'm glad you're getting out more, Sis," Ryan said approvingly.

"Duncan is a friend." The words came out between clenched teeth. "Nothing more."

"Hey, I think it's great you're spending time with Mr. Scottish Hunk," Ryan replied, and Taylor's eyes narrowed with suspicion.

"What are you up to?" she demanded.

Ryan laughed and shook his head. "Nothing. Honest." His eyes were open and frank. "I'm just glad to see you getting away from the ranch for a while."

"Well, it's not like that's so terribly unusual," she huffed.

"Actually, hon, it is," her father said. Taylor turned to look at him in surprise. His eyes held a tender concern as he said, "You've kind of hidden yourself away here for the last year, Taylor."

"I love Galloway Glen." What was the problem with spending time in her own home, for heaven's sake?

"We know you do, dear, and we're glad." Her mother's voice was kind but firm. "But you need to be around people."

"I go to church!" she defended. "There are all kinds of people there."

"Sorry, Taylor, but Mom and Dad are right," Lisa said. "No one ever gets a chance to talk with you. You come in as the first hymn starts and leave as Dad is finishing up the benediction." The understanding expression in her eyes softened the words. A little.

Taylor stared at her cooling chocolate, her lips pressing together tightly. It had been easy to socialize when Josh was with her. His vibrant personality and warm heart drew people to him like bees to honey, and Taylor had benefited from that appeal. But without Josh, she felt herself falling back into old patterns. As a child she'd often struggled with feelings of not fitting in, of being somewhat different, even odd. Since Josh's death, those feelings had come back in force, compounded by the fact that she was now a widow. A young widow. If she'd felt odd as a child, she felt downright freakish now.

"I suppose they're talking about me," she said, somewhat bitterly.

Her father's eyes chided her. "Sweetheart, I'm not concerned about what people are saying. I'm concerned about you, about how much time you spend alone."

"Which is why we're pleased Duncan is coming over," her mother added.

"Though why a good-looking fella like him would want to be around a prickly pear like you is beyond me!" Ryan put in.

"I like Duncan!" Mark piped up, forestalling his aunt's heated response to his father. "I like his accent and some of the funny words he uses—"

"Yeah, like 'canna' and 'ken' and stuff!" Mike agreed. "He's Scottish, you know," he said to his mother.

"Yes, dear." She nodded. "I know. He's charming."

"Yeah, but that's okay. I mean, he's not a sissy or anything. He can fight real good. I saw him once with Dancy Blocker—"

"Okay, sport, that's enough." Ryan tried to put a halt to the story, but Mark could be stubborn when he wanted to make a point.

"I *did*, Dad. Dancy said something about Aunt Taylor, and Duncan told him to hold his tongue or he'd be eating it—"

"Marcus Riley!" Ryan barked, and his son's eyes widened and his mouth clamped shut.

"Sorry, Mom," Ryan said with a sigh.

She nodded and smiled. "It's all right, dear. I'm well acquainted with men and their set-tos, especially when they have to do with young women." She glanced at her husband, and Taylor was surprised to see a dull blush creep across her father's face.

"Yes, well," he said quickly, "I'm sure Duncan was only doing what he thought was right,"

"Right, Grandpa," Mark said, casting his father a cautious glance. When Ryan nodded he went on. "Duncan's always doing something nice for people. He even lets me drive his Blazer sometimes. Or steer it, anyway," he amended at the quick frown that crossed his father's face.

"Yeah, Duncan's cool," Mikey chimed in, reaching for another piece of toast. Then he paused, his hand in mid-reach, and looked at Taylor with a grin. "Hey! I know! You should just marry Duncan! He's big an' strong and he could do all your work for you!"

"What a good idea, Son." Ryan was clearly starting to enjoy the conversation. "Or, better yet, we could have a contest. You know, invite all the able-bodied, eligible men in the area to compete against each other and see who can do the most work the fastest. The prize will be our very own Taylor as a sweet little bride!"

"Ryan..." Lisa warned, but she was too late.

"Sure!" Mikey said, taking it all seriously. "I'll bet ol' Mr. Wanamuc would come. He's always watching Aunt Taylor when she comes in his store—"

"Yeah!" Mark's eyes shone with excitement. "And Eddie Running Elk said Aunt Taylor was real pretty, even if she did keep to herself like a wounded cougar hiding out in the woods. He'd come too, I bet!"

"Oh, I'm sure he would," Ryan said, laughing so hard now there were tears in his eyes.

"You guys are a laugh a minute," Taylor remarked dryly.

"But I still think Duncan would be the best one," Mikey stated, as though that settled it.

"I've always thought so, though I'd like to know what I'm the best one for."

The group at the table turned as one to stare at the man standing in the doorway.

"Duncan!" Taylor said, mortified. "I didn't hear you pull up—"

"A bit hard to with all the racket you Camuses are makin' in here," he said playfully, coming to tousle Mark's hair and tweak Mikey's nose.

As the twins jumped from their chairs to wrestle with Duncan, Taylor took the opportunity to regain her composure. She hoped he hadn't noticed her discomfort, but that hope was dashed when he turned to give her a decidedly amused look.

"Now, what's all this about?"

Her embarrassment almost turned to blind panic when Ryan pulled out a chair and remarked, "Duncan, old boy, have a seat and I'll tell you all about it! The twins here just made the most fascinating suggestion—"

Taylor bolted from her perch on the counter, uncaring if she dumped the remnants of her chocolate on the floor. She all but tossed the mug into the sink, snagged her jacket and hat from the peg by the kitchen door, and grabbed the pile of library books from the counter—all the while nudging Duncan toward the door.

"Sorry." She paused only long enough to lean down and give her mother and father quick good-bye pecks. "Gotta go! Loads to do! See you later."

"You will let us know about any response to the ad, dear?" her mother asked, and Taylor paused to smile at her. "Sure, Mom. And try not to worry, okay? God will work things out.

Isn't that what you two are always telling me?"

"Hmmm," was all her mother said, and Taylor felt her speculative gaze follow her all the way out the door.

# Five

~

As Duncan MacEwen's Blazer bounced over the rough road-way leading to the highway, Taylor eased back against the seat and drew a calming breath.

She loved her family. She really did. But some days she would gladly trade them in, part and parcel, for a pack of basenjis. Not so much because she liked the dogs, although she thought they were delightful, but because that particular breed had the marvelous distinction of having no vocal chords.

The very thought of her family being mute brought a smile to her face.

"Ah, a smile. So am I safe in assuming you're not plannin' to sit there in wounded silence the whole ride to Wilson?" Duncan asked lightly.

She glanced over at him apologetically. "Sorry, Duncan. They just get to be a bit much sometimes, you know?"

"Aye, I know. My family's the same way, though I must admit they're even more vocal than yours. Scots are notorious for their volume and verbosity when they're tryin' to prove a point."

"Well then, my family must have some Scot in them some-where."

"Either that or it's the Irish tryin' to make more of itself than it really is." He winked. She laughed, and he reached out to capture her hand in a brief clasp. "For all of their Irish heritage, though, I have to admit your nephews show a rare insight and intelligence."

She met his warm gaze and leaned back with a groan. "You heard it all, didn't you?"

"Aye. But it's nothin' new, now is it? I've been tellin' you for some time now that we do well together, darlin'. You know it's true."

"Yes, I know…"

"So why don't you marry me, Taylor?" Duncan smiled broadly, and his dark eyes sparkled with humor and affection. She turned her head and studied him thoughtfully.

Duncan MacEwen had moved into the area about five years ago. Born and raised in Scotland, he had come to help his uncle work his ranch, the Bar T, which was only a few miles from Galloway Glen. When he'd shown up at church on his first Sunday, Josh had been among the first to welcome him. Before long, the two men realized they shared many interests, and a solid friendship was born.

From their first meeting, Taylor had considered the darkly handsome Duncan absolutely charming. He had a way of winning people over without really trying, and he'd always treated Taylor with kindness and a winsome courtliness. And he'd never missed an opportunity to tell Josh just how lucky he was.

"You've got yourself a remarkable woman, Sorensen. I hope you realize that," he'd tell Josh with that cocky grin. "Of course, if I'd been here first, you'd never have had a chance."

"Taylor knew we belonged together the first time we saw one another," Josh would reply with an even cockier grin. "Which goes to show she's not only remarkable, but possessed of great insight and wisdom."

Duncan had become a close friend to Taylor as well as Josh, and soon they were a merry threesome, attending church together, going to movies, and having dinner at each other's homes. Josh and Taylor watched with interest—and considerable amusement—as Duncan dated a steady succession of women. They never knew who would be accompanying him to their get-togethers, but they didn't mind. It kept things interesting.

During the months after Josh died, Duncan's friendship and support became an emotional anchor for Taylor. He was always there to help out, to talk or listen, to nudge her from her depression or to pray with her.

Remembering those dark days and the blessing Duncan had been, Taylor reached out to touch his face gently. He angled a look at her, and the expression in his eyes sent a thrill racing along her nerves.

Though Duncan MacEwen might be a "man of the nineties," he sometimes seemed more like a dashing lord of the Scottish Highlands—an image strengthened by the thick, shoulder-length black hair that he often wore tied back in a ponytail. While such a style might have looked odd or out of place on many men, it only increased Duncan's roguish appeal. An appeal that was especially difficult to resist when he looked at her in a way that said he was aware of her, drawn to her, and waiting.

*Stare into those eyes long enough,* she thought, *and a woman might never come out again. Or want to, for that matter.*

The direction of her thoughts jolted her, and she felt her cheeks blush with a wave of guilt. She leaned away slightly, and Duncan smiled gently at her withdrawal.

"It's not unfaithful to Josh, you know. Being attracted to me."

Taylor was amazed that such a quietly spoken comment could cut her so deeply. She turned to stare out the window, trying to blink away sudden tears. She was successful, too. Almost. But an errant tear made its defiant way down her cheek, despite her most determined efforts.

"I know it's hard for you, Taylor. But Josh wouldn't want you to stop living, too. He loved you—and life—too much to want that. I may sound like I'm teasing, but you know I'm serious when I ask you to marry me."

She nodded, chewing her lower lip slightly, then turned to

meet Duncan's understanding gaze. "I know. And I wish I could say yes. You've been so good to me, so kind and patient and abiding—"

"For the love of MacDougal, Taylor, you make me sound like the faithful family dog!"

She laughed, shaking her head. "You know that's not what I mean."

"Aye, but just once I'd like to hear you talk about my massive shoulders, or rippling muscles, or granite jaw—"

"Or your compelling brown eyes or rakish grin or your really cool Blazer—" she cut in, a grin overtaking her features.

"Or *something* that lets me know you've noticed me as a man and not just a friend."

She crossed her arms and leaned back against the door, giving him a serious appraisal. "Well, I'm not all that impressed with the Blazer. I mean, Luke has one too, you know. And it's blue, not green. I mean, isn't green kind of a sissy color?"

"Taylor," he growled.

"Okay, okay. Now that you mention it, I suppose you are somewhat manly in appearance."

"Oh, aye! *Somewhat* is it?" he yelped. Without warning he pulled the vehicle to the side of the road and threw it into park.

"Duncan!" Taylor exclaimed as nervous laughter bubbled up inside her. "What are ya doin', mon? Have ya gone pure daft?" Her exaggerated Scottish accent only fired the determination in his eyes, and he leaned toward her. With one lithe movement he stretched his arm across the back of the seat, slipped it around her shoulders, then pulled her close. He smiled down at her, his dark eyes full of mischief.

"*Somewhat* manly, is it now? Well, my fine lass, we'll see aboot that…"

His gaze held her captive as he lowered his head, and an involuntary sigh escaped her before his lips eased over hers. Warmth filled her, and she nestled against him, content.

When Duncan finally lifted his head and looked down at her, his eyes were slightly dazed. "Well…" His voice was even huskier than usual. Taylor stared up at him in silence. "Well…"

he said again, then shook his head and set her away from him.

Taylor scooted to her side of the seat, wondering who had tilted the truck on its side. It took a few deep, steadying breaths, but the world finally righted itself again.

When a deep chuckle came from the other side of the cab, she risked a glance at Duncan.

"I thought to teach you a bit of a lesson." Duncan's eyes glowed with laughter. "But I'm thinkin' maybe I'm the one who learned something."

"Oh?" It wasn't exactly the scintillating response she wanted to make, but it was all her foggy brain could muster at the moment.

"Aye." He reached forward to start the Blazer again and ease it onto the road. "When I told Josh you were a remarkable woman, I didn't know the beginning of it, Taylor Moira. You're nothing to trifle with, and that's for certain."

"Oh, come on now—"

"No, it's gospel truth!" he insisted. "You're the kind of woman who infects a man, lass."

"Thanks a lot!"

He laughed, shaking his head. "Indeed, you are. And I doubt there's a cure for it, either. So you'd better agree to marry me soon, else I'll suffer untold miseries and ailments and die a horrible death from a shattered heart."

"And what a romantic proposal *that* is," she shot back.

"Face it, lass. We're meant to be together, you and I. Besides, you won't find a more lovin' man, and you know it."

"Or humble!"

His grin was purely impenitent. "In truth, yer beauty makes me forget myself, darlin'." The brogue thickened until Taylor was sure she could cut it into chunks. "I canna ken livin' without ya, and the mere threat of it sets my mind to whirlin'. So you'd best say yes. You wouldna want me to drive meself off the mountains, now would ya?"

"Och, the way ya do talk, Duncan MacEwen of the clan MacEwen. And how the clan must miss such a golden tongue."

"Indeed, I'm sure they must," he replied, his warm, rich

laughter filling the Blazer. "And though I hate to say it, we've reached our destination."

She looked up in surprise and saw that they were indeed entering Wilson.

The small town, inhabited by roughly 500 people, was a study in rugged beauty. As a restless teen, Taylor had given Wilson the disdainful title of "the town that never was." But four years attending college in overpopulated L.A. had given her a new appreciation for Wilson's small-town warmth and familiarity. Now she cherished the fact that traffic jams were unheard of in Wilson. And she enjoyed the uniqueness of the town's landmarks—the post office, Hungry Jack's General Store, and Nora's Fish Creek Inn—a far cry from L.A.'s happening, frenetic hot spots.

Of course, if Hungry Jack's didn't carry what she needed, all Taylor had to do was head six miles further east, to Jackson. With a population of nearly 7,500, Jackson was the area's center of commerce. It had definite old-time appeal with its town square, shopping center, and an abundance of Western-fronted shops custom-designed to send any tourist into paroxysms of delight.

"Supplies or library first?" Duncan inquired.

Taylor patted the books beside her. "Library. Definitely."

"I love a woman who knows what she wants and goes after it." His eyes twinkled at her decisive response. "Almost as much as I love one who's ready when she says she will be," he added as they pulled up in front of the building.

"And you know it goes without saying, dear Duncan," she quipped as she gathered the books, opened the door, and stepped from the vehicle, "that the only thing that matters to me is making your sweet Scottish heart happy."

"That's as it should be, lass," he shot back.

"I'll be done in twenty minutes. Thirty, tops."

"I'll wait as long as it takes," he replied, a spark of some unfathomable emotion in his dark eyes. And as she turned to enter the building, she had the strong impression that he was talking about a good deal more than her visit to the library.

# Six

W ell, I was wondering when we'd see you in here again."
Taylor smiled at the librarian as she approached the desk. "It has been a while, hasn't it, Linda?"

"Mmmm, longer than usual." The woman's blue eyes wandered to the doorway behind Taylor. "Is Duncan with you?"

Suppressing a grin at the woman's hopeful expression, Taylor shook her head and laid her stack of books on the desk. "No, he decided to make a quick stop at the hardware store while I'm here."

Linda's mouth puckered in disappointment, and then her eyes came back to rest on Taylor.

"Congratulations, Taylor." A smile lifted Linda's lips. "You returned these just under the wire. No late charges this time."

Taylor grinned. "I'm turning over a new leaf. The last batch almost broke the bank."

Linda laughed and turned to her computer. "A new book on wolves just came in." Wilson might be remote, but the Wilson Memorial Library, named after one of the town's oldest families, had the latest in library technology. Donations from the Wilsons had ensured that. File cards had given way to microfiche and computers; everything, from the reference desk to interlibrary loans, was connected to the computer super highway.

As Taylor watched Linda key in the title with swift, efficient fingers, she sighed. Personally, she missed the card files. There had been something satisfying in thumbing through the drawers of cards and finding just the right book, or in discovering some unknown treasure by pulling open a drawer, closing your eyes, and flipping to a card at random. Computers might be faster, but they weren't nearly as much fun.

Linda peered at the screen, then jotted the information down on a slip of paper and handed it to Taylor. "Since you've read almost every book we have on wolves, I thought you'd be interested in this one. It's got some wonderfully creative essays and great photographs."

Taylor glanced at the paper, then smiled. "Thanks."

"By the way," Linda said, "have you heard the latest rumors—that we've actually got wolves around here?"

Taylor, about to turn toward the shelves, stopped cold, her heart pounding in her chest. "Oh?" She hoped she sounded far calmer than she felt.

Linda laughed lightly. "Oh, don't worry! I'm sure there's nothing to it. Just like there's been nothing to all the other rumors we've heard over the years about killer wolves invading the area and decimating the elk and cattle populations." She shook her head. "I swear, if wolves did half of what people accused them of, they'd have to be able to fly, leap tall buildings with a single bound, and disappear at will."

Taylor smiled weakly. "So who reported a sighting?"

"Oh, no one. But Mylon Hogan said he heard howling a few nights ago. And you know how the ranchers are about wolves. Someone thinks he hears one and they all head for their guns."

*Oh no! Lord, please, don't let this happen.*

"Did Mylon send a report to the officials?" Taylor dreaded the answer. If the government agencies found out about her wolves, they'd be pounding on her door.

Linda snorted. "Think about what you're saying, Taylor."

Taylor frowned. Then realization dawned—and her sense of dread doubled.

When she saw the light of understanding in Taylor's eyes,

Linda nodded. "Right. You know how the saying goes: 'Shoot, shovel, and shut up.' I doubt any of the ranchers would even consider reporting a sighting. They don't want the government coming in to catch and move the wolves."

"You think that's what they'd do? Capture them and move them someplace else?"

"I would certainly hope so. But they'd have to do it fast if they wanted to find the wolves before somebody killed them."

Taylor nodded soberly. What Linda said was true. The ranchers were much more inclined to "take care of things" themselves, rather than let the government agencies and their restrictions in the door. She'd heard the arguments all her life: The government had no right to tell people what they could and couldn't kill on their own land. Especially when what they wanted to kill was something hated and feared, something that many men would willingly risk fines—and even possible imprisonment—to kill.

Like wolves.


Taylor stood on the curb outside the library, wishing she'd told Duncan five minutes rather than thirty. Her conversation with Linda had left her with a heavy heart, and all she wanted to do was go home. She hadn't even taken time to look for the book Linda had suggested.

Shoving her hands in her jacket pockets, she glanced around, hoping Duncan was parked nearby, waiting. A young man was coming up the sidewalk, apparently heading for the library. His head was down, his chin all but buried in his chest, and his thick, shaggy hair fell over his face like a black curtain, blocking his features. Taylor narrowed her eyes. She wasn't sure why, but there was something disturbingly familiar about his walk, the straight way he held himself, the overall impression of grace and contained strength.

As though sensing her scrutiny, the young man looked up and their eyes met. A shock of recognition jolted through her, followed quickly by a wave of pure loathing.

Brad Momadey.

She wanted to turn and run. Or to scream and rage at him. She did neither. She simply stood there, stiff with emotion, holding his stunned gaze.

Somewhere, in a corner of her mind, it registered that his dark eyes were haunted, his face gaunt and strained. His coppery skin was unnaturally pale, as though all the color had been siphoned away. He wore the anguished expression of someone consumed by a burning, unrelenting pain. She knew, because it was the same expression she had seen many times over the last year in her mirror.

Faint stirrings of sympathy brushed at her heart, and she furiously pushed them away. She would not feel sorry for him. She would not! She was *glad* he was suffering! It was only right after what he'd done.

*"Forgive whatever grievances you have against one another."*

Her father's voice echoed in the black stillness of her mind.

*No!* Her rejection was fierce, determined.

*Forgive as the Lord forgave you.*

Her heart twisted with pain, and she turned away sharply.

*How do I forgive him, Lord? It's his fault Josh is dead. His fault my heart is dead!*

The cold, bitter thoughts ran through her, and she closed her eyes, sickened by the realizations washing over her.

*Duncan deserves an answer, Father, but how do I give him one? I have nothing to give him! No love. No trust. Just an empty, dead heart….*

She wrapped her arms around herself, fighting the emotions that threatened to envelop her.

*That boy killed my heart, Father.*

She felt a gentle touch on her arm and jerked away, turning, ready to fight.

"Whoa!" Duncan's eyes were wide and startled. "It's only me, Taylor."

Her breath came out in a rush, and she put out a shaking hand. He took it in his own and drew her against him, cradling her, sharing his warmth with her suddenly chilled body.

"I'm sorry." The words were hushed and ragged. "I—it just was a shock to see him—Brad, I mean."

Duncan nodded. "I see him." The sadness in his voice disturbed her. "The boy looks like he's in a bad way." She stiffened, and his hold tightened. "I'm sorry, lass. I'm sorry it still hurts so much."

"Take me home, Duncan." Her voice was flat. "Please… just take me home."

He didn't question, didn't remind her they hadn't gotten supplies yet. He simply led her to the Blazer, opened the door, and helped her get in. As he came around to the driver's side, she cast a quick glance out the window.

Brad was still there, his face ashen…and as the truck pulled away, she was hit with the terrible realization that the boy's face was streaked with tears.

Duncan drove in silence. The only contact he attempted was to reach out and clasp Taylor's chilled fingers in his large, warm hand. She leaned her head back against the seat and struggled to hold back the tears. Her empty book bag sat on the floor by her feet.

"Did you find what you wanted at the library?" Duncan ventured after several miles. She started, the memory of her discussion with Linda flooding back.

"No," she answered. "I—I left after a few minutes."

He glanced at her curiously. "Why?"

Instead of answering, she turned to look at him and asked a question of her own. "Duncan, do you hate wolves?"

He glanced at her, as though a bit concerned about her sanity, and she didn't blame him. The question sounded odd even to her own ears—abrupt and out of left field.

She shook her head impatiently. "I'm sorry. I know that sounded weird." She explained. "Linda told me some of the ranchers in the area are getting worked up over some rumors about wolves."

"'Worked up' meaning they're getting their guns ready?"

She nodded stiffly. "Shoot, shovel, and shut up. It's still a way of life for a lot of people. Especially ranchers." She looked at him, her eyes pleading with him to understand. "I couldn't help wondering if you felt that way, too."

"Would it bother you if I did?"

A sharp pang shot through her, and she nodded, biting her lip.

He sighed. "Taylor, to be honest, I don't know how I feel. I've heard tales about wolves since I was a boy. Tales that make them out to be monsters. My grandda used to tell me bedtime stories"—he grinned wryly—"though I seldom slept afterward. Grandda knew how to spin a truly terrible tale."

"About wolves? But why?"

He shrugged, his expression troubled. "My grandparents, and their parents and grandparents...they saw wolves differently than Americans do now." He glanced at her, a faint smile on his lips. "Most Americans, anyway. In Europe, wolves were considered monsters, killers. I think a lot of the hatred stemmed from the dark days when Europe was devastated by the Black Plague. Grandda painted a vivid, horrifying picture of wolves, roaming to and fro, seeking something to tear apart. He made it so real, I could almost see it."

"Did the wolves actually attack anyone?"

"I don't know. But he told me how, when people were dying in droves across Europe, the wolves pulled corpses from shallow graves and devoured them." He angled a look at her. "Believe me, lass, you hear those stories often enough and the last thing you feel for the creatures is compassion. Fear, definitely. Anger, even hatred. But surely not a sense that these are the fine, noble beasts the environmentalists want us to believe they are."

"But stories like your grandfather told are more fairy tale than truth. Myths and legends. Like stories about werewolves."

"Och! Don't even get me started on those!" he exclaimed, laughing.

"Wolves aren't at all like the stories make them out to be, Duncan. They really are fine and noble. And they don't attack people."

He smiled. "Here now, are you telling me Red Riding Hood was a liar?"

She laughed weakly. "I'm telling you a lot of people are. Real people…though I'm not sure why."

"What makes you say so?"

She tilted her head thoughtfully. "Did you ever hear about the time, several years ago, when people here got all upset about that wolf attack in British Colombia?"

He nodded. "Aye, New Chetwynd, wasn't it? Two hunters shot and killed a wolf that came after them."

"That's just it, Duncan." She turned in the seat so she could face him. "The wolf *didn't* come after them."

He frowned. "But the paper said—"

"I know what the paper said. It was wrong. I read a book that gave an account of the official report the hunters made. The wolf was just following them. They admitted it never made any movement toward them, never demonstrated any aggression, but they got frightened—"

"Understandably so," he remarked.

"Getting frightened, maybe. But shooting the wolf wasn't understandable. They had the decency to take the dead wolf to the authorities, but they weren't charged with anything. Then the local news magazine picked up the story and splashed 'Wolf Attack in New Chetwynd!' across the front page." She crossed her arms over her chest, disgust evident in her fine features. "Everything I've read says there's never been a verified account of a healthy wolf attacking any person in North America."

He looked at her disbelievingly. "Never?"

She shook her head firmly. "The only wolves that have attacked people were rabid, and even those instances are ridiculously rare. So all those tales about the 'big bad wolf'? They spring from imagination and superstition. That's what these guys are basing their fear on. Not the facts."

He inclined his head. "Maybe you're right. I've never been around the beasts myself. They were gone from the area long before my family came here. So I can't say one way or the other

73

what they're really like. But I do know this"—his eyes darkened—"we're a small band here, and we depend on each other to survive and endure. Ranchers like my uncle make their living on their livestock, and they aren't greatly inclined to risk their families' welfare just to placate some wolf-lovin' environmentalist. Or the government, for that matter. And I'll wager that anyone who chooses a pack of beasts over their friends and neighbors is making a regretful decision. If someone is actually hiding the existence of those creatures, they'd best keep it a well-guarded secret. My guess is they'd become as much a target as the wolves."

The words struck Taylor hard. She knew he was right. If her neighbors found out about the wolves, they'd kill them. And hate her. If government officials found out about them, they might take them away. Relocate them. To someplace safer.

Someplace other than Galloway Glen.

She sat back and stared out the window with unseeing eyes. A fierce determination swelled up and filled her. No one was going to hurt her wolves. And no one was going to take them away from her. The wolves were hers! They came to her, they were on her land, and she'd fight anyone, friend or foe—even Duncan, she realized in amazement—who dared to set foot anywhere near them! True, she'd seen the large male only that one time, at Reunion, but she'd heard him and the others several times in the past year, howling, joining their voices in a mournful, discordant, incredibly beautiful chorus. She'd been thrilled to discover the beautiful beast who had watched her was not alone. And she was fairly certain they were establishing territory on Galloway Glen. She'd hoped against hope that no one else had seen or heard them, that they were as much her secret as Reunion was.

Now she knew that wasn't the case. And she was terrified of what that meant. For her. And for the majestic creatures who had finally, against all odds, defied the dangers and hatred and returned to the area after being completely annihilated over sixty years ago.

"Why does this trouble you so, Taylor?" Duncan's deep

voice broke into her thoughts, and she looked at him, startled. It was on the tip of her tongue to tell him, to ask him for his help, for his counsel...but something held her back.

She believed he would listen, would promise to help her.

*But people can't always keep their promises, can they, Lord?*

No, this was her battle. She would handle it on her own. She wouldn't ask for help, not from her family, not from Duncan, not from anyone. There was too much at stake to trust anyone but herself to handle things: her relationships with her neighbors, the wolves' lives...

*Your hopes,* a voice whispered from deep within. *Your heart.*

Keeping her face devoid of emotion, she shrugged. "I don't know, it just didn't seem fair, somehow. But I suppose it doesn't really matter one way or the other, since there's nothing to back up the rumors. I mean, who's really gullible enough to believe there are wolves in Wyoming?" She laughed and settled back in her seat, hoping Duncan was buying her disinterest.

But his dark, probing eyes reflected doubt—and a vague glimmer of hurt disappointment. She swallowed with difficulty, wishing he would talk about something else.

Instead, he reached for her hand again, closing his strong fingers around it. "Someday, Taylor, I hope you'll realize you can trust me."

"Duncan—"

He stopped her with a shake of his head. "It's all right, lass. I understand. You're just not sure of me yet." He smiled into her troubled eyes and a gently teasing tone filled his next words. "But don't fret. I'm not giving up. I'll just have to work harder at showing you I'm not just the handsomest man you know, but the finest as well."

# $\mathscr{S}even$

Linda Williamson loved books—almost as much as she loved men. So when she heard the front door of the library open and glanced up to see a tall, ruggedly handsome stranger walk in, she was definitely in her element.

She put on her most dazzling smile as the man approached. "Welcome to the Wilson library, sir. May I help direct you to something of interest?"

The man glanced at her and nodded briefly. "I'm interested in anything you have on wolves."

Undaunted by his lack of response to her friendly overture, Linda turned up the dazzle a notch. "Well, you're in luck! One of our patrons just returned several of our best books on wolves. And we just received a new book on the subject. It's a beautiful combination of writings and photographs."

His eyes lit with interest, and she reached for the books Taylor had returned and set them on the desk in front of him.

"I was just about to shelve these, so you couldn't have timed your arrival any better." Her eyes met his with a flutter. *Electric blue,* she decided. *Like a summer sky when a thunderstorm is brewing.* "I'd be more than happy to show you where the new book is located."

He tilted his head to one side and regarded her curiously. "Is the book hard to find?"

"Well, no…of-of course not," she stammered, taken aback as much by the effect of his deep, sensual voice as by the question. "You look well equipped—I mean, well, I'm sure you know what to do—where to go—for what you want."

His eyebrows arched slightly.

"For the *book* you want!" she amended quickly, feeling increasingly flustered under his startlingly blue gaze. She stuck her hand out abruptly, handing him the slip of paper on which she had written the book title and location for Taylor.

He took the paper, glanced at it, smiled slightly, and then moved toward the shelves.

*Oh, my,* she thought, watching him walk away. *Oh, my!*


Connor Alexander leaned back in the hard wooden library chair and laced his fingers behind his head. He stretched his shoulders back, trying to work out the kinks in his weary muscles.

The flight from Washington, D.C., had been delayed a few hours, and they'd experienced considerable turbulence all the way. By the time he finally arrived in Jackson, he was bone weary. Fortunately, the Jeep Wrangler he'd rented was ready and the drive to Wilson had been uneventful.

His first stop, the general store, had been profitable. He'd noticed a small group gathered as he entered the building. Four or five men stood watching two old-timers play checkers, and Connor's interest had been immediately peaked by their raised voices and heated exchange. He was willing to bet they weren't discussing checkers.

He eased his way to the shelves closest to the group. Doing his best to look engrossed in selecting just the right bag of chips, he focused on the men's words.

"They come on *my* land," a heavyset man declared, "and they'll get a gut full of poison!"

"Or lead," another chimed in.

"I say we follow Brody Camus's lead," a dark-haired man commented. "We kill off as many of the vermin as we can."

"Now there was a hunter!" Mr. Heavyset agreed with relish. "My dad saw old Brody come in once with more than a hundred wolf pelts."

"Did more to rid this area of wolves than ten men combined, so I hear," Dark Hair chortled.

"I *want* those wolves to come on my land." This comment came from one of the checkers players, an older gentleman whose baseball cap was pushed back to reveal a craggy, weathered face. Clearly he had spent a good portion of his life outdoors.

His bald statement was met with confusion and exclamations of censure from all.

"Sure," he responded, a grin splashed across his face. "I been wantin' a new rug in my den!"

At that, a chorus of approval sounded around the laughing man, and Connor shook his head slightly. He grabbed a bag of chips and headed for the cashier.

The talkative young clerk also proved to be a source of information.

"I heard those men talking about wolves," Connor said casually, nodding toward the group of men at the back of the store. "Thought they were extinct around here."

"They musta come over the mountains from Idaho," the clerk, a gum-chewing, fresh-faced teenager, volunteered, explaining that the locals suspected the animals were somewhere to the north of town, on one of the ranches near Phelps Lake. Connor noted the way the kid's eyes gleamed with excitement. "I'd sure hate to have 'em show up on my ranch. I hear tell a pack of them killers can take down a bull!"

"So they say," Connor had said, paying for his purchase.

His next stop had been the library, where he'd scanned copies of the town's weekly paper for the past few months—not a big task considering how small the paper was. The paper gave him a glimpse of local events and topics of interest. If the Help Wanted ads were any indication, things weren't exactly hopping economically. Seasonal help at the resorts seemed to be the big opportunity. Either that, or working as a ranch hand.

Sighing, Connor set the paper aside and looked over the books the librarian had given him.

He glanced at the desk, where the librarian seemed engrossed in her work. After that first *intriguing* encounter with Mrs. Williamson, as her nameplate identified her, the woman had treated him with a professional, slightly distant attitude. But he knew it would take little more than a friendly word, an interested smile, and she would once again be the welcoming charmer he'd encountered when he first came through the door.

He shook his head slightly as he looked down at the table again. A fan of library cards was spread out in front of him. They were the check-out cards from the wolf books, and each one had the same name on it: Taylor Sorensen.

He bit his lip thoughtfully. Why did that name sound familiar? He stood abruptly, heading for the newspaper archives once more. He selected last week's paper and returned to his table.

He hadn't seen the name in any of the articles, of that he was fairly certain. So that meant it had to be something from the classifieds.

A satisfied smile crept over his face as he spread the newspaper out in front of him, reading over the ad in the Help Wanted section:

Temporary, full-time handyman/ranch hand needed.
Work will last 1-2 months. Mechanical and riding skills
a must. Housing provided. Good pay. References
required. Contact Taylor Sorensen, Galloway Glen.


His smile deepened. Perfect. Absolutely perfect.

With a grin he stuffed the cards back into the books, swept them and the newspaper up, and headed for the desk.


Linda looked up uneasily at the sound of firm footsteps approaching. He was coming to talk again. Stiffening her shoulders, she watched him stroll up to the desk, looking completely at ease.

The least he could do was have the decency to show some awareness of the way he was affecting her! From his bland expression, she might as well have been a cold piece of toast. Without jelly. Or butter.

"Did you find what you were looking for?" she asked as he set the books on the desk.

He nodded. "I think so."

"Is there something else you needed?" The second the words were out, Linda could have kicked herself. Why was she being so accommodating? The man was entirely too sure of himself as it was! She should have turned her back on him.

"If you could direct me to Taylor Sorensen's ranch, that would be a help."

"Galloway Glen?" She regarded him with slight surprise. He seemed almost smug, as though quite pleased with himself, and Linda had to fight the urge to dump her coffee over his head. Still, the quicker she answered, the quicker he'd be gone.

"I'll draw you a map." She pulled a notepad toward her. "It's north of town. Just follow the signs for Teton Village and Phelps Lake." She sketched a quick map and handed it to him. "Are you…a friend of Taylor's?"

He shook his head. "No, never met him. I'm going to see him about a job."

"Him? Oh, but—" She broke off as the last part of his comment hit her. "A—a job? You're going to…stay in the area?" Aware her voice was becoming high and slightly shrill, she clamped her mouth shut, staring at the desk as though fascinated by its wood veneer.

"For a while, anyway."

She clenched her teeth at the hint of laughter in his deep voice. Looking up, she met his gaze squarely. "Well. Isn't that nice. I hope it works out. So, here's your map." She knew the words had come out rapid-fire, but she just didn't care. She shoved the map at him.

"Thanks for your help." He took the paper and turned to head for the door.

"Wait!"

He halted abruptly, turning back to her, his eyebrows raised in inquiry. She smiled sweetly. "Just thought I'd offer you some friendly advice. Watch out for Taylor's dog."

A wary look entered his eyes. "His dog."

Keeping her expression friendly, compassionate, Linda shook her head. "*Her* dog. Taylor's a woman. And Sasha—that's the dog—is a bit…unpredictable. Especially where men are concerned."

"And how does Mr. Sorensen feel about that?" Connor asked.

"Josh Sorensen was killed a year ago last fall. Taylor's a widow."

The man frowned. "Then she lives on the ranch alone?"

"No, not at all. Her parents live on the ranch, and her brother and his family are close by, too. Her father, Reverend Camus, is the minister here in town."

"Camus?" he repeated, his frown deepening. "Any relation to a Brody Camus?"

Linda nodded. "Brody Camus was Taylor's grandfather. And his father established Galloway Glen."

From the look on the man's face, this information was less than palatable.

"Anyway," Linda pushed on, "watch out for Taylor's dog. One minute she'll seem just fine, the next she'll be snapping and snarling and going for your throat."

The man blinked. "And she lets this animal run loose?"

Linda shrugged, all wide-eyed innocence and concern. "You know how some people are about their animals. But I wouldn't say anything if I were you. To Taylor, that is. About the dog. She's kind of sensitive."

He frowned, hesitated, then nodded. "Thanks for the warning."

"My pleasure," Linda said. As the door closed behind him, a smug smile tipped her full lips. She picked up the books he'd been looking at and set them on the reshelve cart. "Entirely my pleasure, I'm sure."

# Eight

❧

Several hours after she returned from town, Taylor stood staring out the tall, elegant windows of her living room. She never grew tired of the view, of her home and the wilderness surrounding it. Many people would go crazy in such a remote location, but she thrived on the challenge. As had Josh.

She pictured his face—and felt a pang of startled sorrow that it wasn't as clear and immediate in her mind as it had been. She could scarcely believe his image was already beginning to fade.

If only the pain would fade as well.

With an impatient sigh, she turned and walked to the kitchen. Actually, the living room, dining room, and kitchen were one large room, a spacious floor plan with furniture arrangements defining each area. That was one of the things Taylor loved about her home: the light, airy feel of the open rooms.

When she pulled the fridge door open and took out the milk jug, Sasha rose from her place on the rug and came over, watching her with interest, her tail wagging with enthusiasm.

Taylor smiled at the dog. "Hey, you greedy beast. You ate your breakfast already, remember?" Sasha tilted her head to the side, her eyes fixed on the milk jug, and Taylor laughed, patting the dog's head. "Duncan's right. You're a walking garbage disposal."

At the mention of the Scotsman, Taylor frowned slightly. As she poured her glass of milk, she thought about the conversation she and Duncan had had on their return from Wilson. *Why didn't I tell him about the wolves?* she asked herself, but no answers came.

She moved back to the living room and sank into her favorite overstuffed chair. Leaning back, she took a deep breath, soaking in the sense of peace she so often felt in this room. She loved the openness of the living room, the way it was so often washed in sunlight, thanks to the tall windows on the southern wall and the skylights in the high, vaulted ceiling. The sheen of the log walls and the wood floor created a richness and warmth; the simple design of the alderwood chairs and couch with their black, oversized cushions offered homeyness and comfort. Decorative pillows scattered across the furniture added a touch of color and playfulness. From the lighting to the plants to the glorious view, it was a room designed to uplift sagging spirits.

Taylor plopped her feet on the ottoman and leaned back, staring at the high ceiling. Would the walls around her heart ever come down again? She'd lowered them for Josh, allowed him to come in and draw her out of the inner fortress she'd built as a child. Nurtured by his love, encouraged by his openness, her long-buried desire to find acceptance and friendship had finally pushed through her defenses and blossomed. Until she'd met Josh, she'd always been a loner, except for her family and her animals.

She glanced at the portrait on the mantel of the river rock fireplace. Her family's faces smiled down at her. Her family. They'd always made her feel accepted, as though she belonged. They gave her security, an anchor. Only with them did she feel safe. With them, and at Reunion—her retreat, her refuge.

It didn't matter a bit that she was always by herself. In fact, she preferred it that way. As a child, Taylor had never felt she really fit in with her schoolmates. She was…different. During her teens, she'd thought the girls in her class were scatter-brained, self-involved, and far too focused on their looks and boys. As for the boys, she'd never met one she couldn't out-wrestle, outrun, or outthink.

Put simply, she saw little point in spending time with people with whom she had little or nothing in common.

"I have more interesting conversations with my dog," she told her mother once when she inquired why Taylor didn't spend time with any of the girls in her class. Her mother had raised an eyebrow and cast a glance at the husky lying in the middle of the room.

"Have you ever really talked with any of these girls?" she asked when her gaze came back to rest on her scowling daughter.

"Why bother?" Taylor snorted. "All I have to do is watch and listen. They stare at themselves in the bathroom mirrors every chance they get, they moan about how ugly they are, and they sigh all over themselves if Bobby Ravenhill even *looks* their way."

Her mother had listened patiently, but her expression clearly told Taylor that she wasn't fooled. She knew how hard it was for her daughter to overcome her self-consciousness and reach out. She also was aware of how cutting teenage girls could be, particularly about anyone who didn't think and act the way they did.

Still, whatever Taylor had lacked in social skills she more than made up for in inquisitiveness and out-and-out daring. Not with people—they were too intimidating. But Taylor was always *trying* things. The proverbial bookworm, she read every-thing she could get her hands on. But just reading wasn't enough. She had to *do* something with what she'd read.

Once, in the sixth grade, she watched a TV special on sky-diving. Fascinated, she promptly checked out every book the school library had on the subject. Then she'd fashioned a hand-kerchief parachute for one of her dolls and launched it from her bedroom window. Her delight when the contraption worked convinced her she could do even better. Soon she was perched on the edge of the hayloft, a homemade parachute—a sheet and some clothesline—tied to her back. She barely missed landing on her father as he came in to feed the horses. Fortunately, she didn't miss the hay pile. The stunned look on her dad's face as she sat there, half-buried in hay, sheet and clothesline draped over her head, was a memory that still made her smile.

Then there was the time she slipped though the fence surrounding the field where their nearest neighbors kept their bull. She'd wanted to see how long it would take the nearsighted beast to spot her and react.

Ryan, who had timed the experiment with the new stopwatch he'd gotten for his birthday, said she should go out for track. When he showed her her time for getting from the middle of the field to the fence, she couldn't argue.

"Course, we don't know if you'd run as fast without a bull on your heels," he commented as they mounted their horses and headed for home. She couldn't argue with that, either.

It hadn't taken long for the stories of her exploits to spread. She became a celebrity of sorts, a curiosity—someone the other kids tolerated, even defended at times, because she was intriguing. She knew and did things—amazing, crazy things—that girls didn't generally know or do. She might not be the life of the party, but she sure kept the party *interesting*.

Not that she cared what her classmates thought of her. She wasn't around them enough for their opinions to matter. Most of her time had been spent on her pony, roaming the ranch, exploring. Then, once she discovered her hidden valley, she had all but lived there. Sometimes she read, sometimes she explored, sometimes she just sat and soaked in the peace and isolation.

Until Josh.

And now, with him gone, isolation was something that had grown more and more attractive to her. She recognized that fact as clearly as her parents and brother did. This morning was the first time they'd said anything, but she'd known they were worried about her, about her lack of interest in being around anyone outside of her family and her home.

*Well, they'd better get used to it,* she thought half-rebelliously. *I don't need anyone more than I have here. My family. My animals.* Her gaze moved in the direction of Reunion. *What I have here is enough.*

A loud knock on the door pulled her from her thoughts, and she hopped up as the front door opened.

Luke Narbona came in, smiling at her, his dark brown eyes filled with warmth. "You returned, but you didn't call me to help you unload the supplies, *Yazhi.*"

The Navajo endearment warmed her. *Yazhi.* Little One. She smiled and went to toss her arm around her friend's broad shoulders. Few people would have guessed Luke was old enough to be retired. He had the straight carriage and fit build of a far younger man. His copper skin glowed with health, and his aquiline features were smooth and free of wrinkles. Only a few streaks of gray in his long black hair, worn in a braid, betrayed him. He was a man who thrived on activity—especially activity that improved Galloway Glen or the retreat center. Taylor's home had become as much a passion for Luke as it was for her.

"That's because I didn't get any supplies, Luke." He looked at her sharply, and she forestalled the questions she saw in his eyes by leading him from the house. "But I'm sure we can find something to keep you busy."

"What happened in town, Taylor?" The question was quiet but firm. "Why'd you leave before you got supplies?"

She considered telling him about Brad, but the thought of reliving the experience was too overwhelming. Instead, she told him about the ranchers and their reaction to the rumor of wolves.

"The wolves are gone from this area," he said. "These men are foolish, like worried old women, to think they could return."

"That's what I said," Taylor agreed with a smile. "There haven't been wolves in this part of Wyoming for more than sixty years. I don't know why anyone would believe they'd suddenly come back."

Luke nodded, then glanced around him. They were in the horse barn. He shot Taylor a pointed look. "Hmpf!" he grunted. "Why do I think I know where this is leading?"

She grinned. "That's what I've always liked best about you, my friend." She handed him a shovel. "Your remarkably keen sense of the obvious."

The moon was high and bright in the sky later that night as Taylor sat and rocked on her front porch. She snuggled more deeply into the soft quilted comforter her grandmother had made her, then reached a hand out to rest it on Sasha's broad head.

The husky turned, and a twinkle of moonlight caught her ice-blue eyes as she glanced at her mistress. Taylor smiled at the dog fondly.

Sasha was Taylor's second Siberian husky. Her parents had given her a pup, Vanya—a name meaning "gift from God"—when she was ten, and she and the husky had loved each other completely and unconditionally. When Taylor came home from college, new husband in tow, Vanya fixed him with a dubious stare, then moved to sit between the two of them, her unblinking gaze fastened on Josh as though warning him that Taylor was hers and not to be trifled with. Fortunately Josh loved dogs, and it had only taken him a few weeks—and an entire box of dog biscuits—to win the Siberian over.

When Vanya died at the ripe old age of fifteen, Taylor had been devastated. Josh put up with her moping for a week, then told her to get her coat and get in the car, they were going for a drive. They ended up at the home of a local husky breeder, who just happened to have a litter of pups. It was there Taylor found Sasha.

Actually, it was more accurate to say Sasha found her.

Taylor had gone to sit on the back stairs, where she was petting a five-month-old male, when she felt something warm and moist nudge the back of her neck. She turned to find Sasha behind her. The dog looked at her for a moment with the most amazing pair of white-blue eyes, then laid her chin on Taylor's shoulder and licked her neck with the tip of her pink tongue. Taylor was lost. Just under a year old, Sasha had been returned to the breeder by a woman who had developed severe allergies to the dog's thick, double coat.

When the breeder saw Sasha's action, he smiled broadly. "Well, the dog's made her choice. I guess the final decision is up to you."

Taylor took her home that very day. And though one dog could never replace another, Sasha quickly became an integral part of the Sorensens' lives. In no time at all it became clear that Sasha was not only thoroughly devoted to Taylor, but also perfectly suited to her chosen mistress in personality and temperament. She enjoyed nothing more than trotting along beside Topaz, roaming the ranch with Taylor. Like most huskies, she was as independent and stubborn as she was loyal and loving.

"It's like the two of you were cut from the same cloth," Josh said, grinning.

"Well, then, you should count yourself the most fortunate of men to have us both," she shot back.

The memory of that exchange brought a watery smile to Taylor's face as she reached out to rub Sasha's velvet-soft ears.

"You miss him, too, don't you girl?" she asked. Sasha merely turned her head to stare into the night.

Taylor sighed deeply.

"Sometimes," she whispered, "I still expect to see him, you know? I walk into a room, or come back from a ride, and wonder why he isn't there." Her voice choked, and she brushed an impatient hand at her eyes.

*God, I know Grandmother was right, Josh was a gift from you. But I can't stop wondering why he had to leave. I mean, what did it accomplish? It almost seems as though his death was meaningless. Wasted.*

The sharp image of Brad Momadey's face floated through her mind, and she pushed it away.

*I need Josh, Father. I need his wisdom, his insights. He would know what to do about the wolves. He would know—*

Her prayer was cut short by the sound of movement in the nearby woods. Taylor stilled, staring into the darkness. Sasha stood slowly, her ears twitching, a low growl rumbling in her chest.

Heart pounding, Taylor stood, too, possibilities running through her mind. A bear? Maybe, though it wouldn't have been so quiet. Raccoon? Could be, though it had sounded larger. Actually it could be any number of nocturnal animals…

*It could also be human.* The unwelcome thought nudged its way into her mind, and she stiffened. If that was so, it was an intruder. Neighbors or friends would have identified themselves right away.

Her eyes swept the woods, trying to discern any activity in the moonlight.

Sasha growled again and tensed beside her, ready to bound into the trees. Taylor quickly place a hand on the dog's head. "Stand!" she commanded softly, and the dog obeyed, standing motionless—her eyes fixed on the woods.

"Who's out there?" Taylor asked loudly, putting as much confidence in the question as she could. Never let 'em see you sweat. She'd learned that early on.

Silence was her only response—until Sasha suddenly turned her head sharply. Startled, Taylor jumped.

So much for appearing cool and confident!

"What is it, girl?" she asked, but the dog didn't even look at her. Something had caught her full attention, and she tilted her head, angling her ears as though listening more carefully to whatever night sound was drawing her.

Taylor strained her ears…and heard the faint rise and fall of a wolf howl.

Relief swept through her, and she looked down at the Siberian. Sasha was lifting her chin, as though tempted to join in the distant song. Taylor smiled.

"I understand, Sash. I've been tempted, too." She cast another look toward the dark woods, but all was silent. If something, or someone, had been there, it seemed to be gone now.

She lowered herself to sit next to Sasha, draping her arm

around the dog and resting her head against the animal's soft, fur-covered neck. Together they sat there, listening to—and oddly soothed by—the eerie, resonant song that rose and drifted on the wind.

# Nine

❦

The sound came to him in the night, and at first he thought it was just another nightmare. But it continued even after he awoke, and a shudder gripped him.

He threw the covers off and moved to the window, looking out on the moonlit landscape. He concentrated, listening intently. Had he really heard the howling?

Yes, there it was again, distant and haunting. Wearily he leaned his forehead against the cool glass of the window, his long black hair falling like a curtain to hide his face as he fought the sadness welling up within him.

So the rumors were true. He'd granted himself the luxury of not believing, of dismissing what he felt were the tales of old women masquerading as hunters. He knew how quick men were to label any howl wolf howls, even if they knew within themselves that it was really just dogs in the area venting their canine angst. It always sounded so much better to say, "Hey! I heard a wolf howling last night," than "Tommy Black Elk's old hound dogs were at it again."

But this…there was no mistaking this haunting, sonorous song rising in the night. The ever-changing pitches, the discordant symphony that lifted and danced on the wind, as though wooing its listeners to join in. His dark eyes narrowed. This was not Tommy Black Elk's hounds. This was a wild song, full of excitement and an almost seductive entreaty. It was hard not to be drawn.

As Taylor apparently had been drawn.

His heart lurched painfully. She'd lied to him—told him she didn't think there were any wolves in the area. But clearly those howls were coming from her ranch.

The fact that she'd sided with them against him was galling. Didn't she understand what these animals were? It wasn't even so much that they were killers. Many animals could be accused of that fault. No. The greatest danger lay in what they could cost Taylor. If she sided with them, she would be siding against her neighbors. She would become a target. He couldn't let that happen.

He turned from the window and went back to his bed. Morning would be soon enough to begin. He needed to get some rest, to find some sense of restoration and oblivion before he took up the battle.

His eyes glittered with a fierce resolve as he pictured his adversary: the amber eyes, the falsely sweet expression, the sharp, jagged teeth. And then, superimposed on the image of the beast, came the reflection of a beautiful smiling face framed by long dark hair, of emerald green eyes brimming with laughter and sincerity.

He sighed and turned over, punching his pillow into submission. For now, he needed sleep. Tomorrow he would plan and prepare.

He would have to be cautious. He couldn't let Taylor know what he was doing. He didn't want to alienate her, to destroy what they were building. He'd have to be as clever and skilled as his opponent if he were to succeed.

Yes, tomorrow he would begin to plan. And by next week he would be ready to begin the killing.

On that determined note, he closed his eyes.

Connor turned his Wrangler off the highway and drove under a tall arch made of logs. At the top of the arch was a large sign with the name "Galloway Glen" carved into it. The librarian's map had been clear and exact, a pleasant surprise. He'd half expected her to lead him to the edge of a cliff somewhere.

He drove slowly down the long, winding gravel drive, admiring the scenery. Fields of wildflowers bordered the drive. Just beyond the field to the west was a thick forest of evergreens, and beyond that the Tetons loomed in all their craggy majesty. Galloway Glen was a wilderness paradise.

*Perfect location for a pack of wolves,* he thought, and a pang of regret shot through him. Too bad such a place was owned by wolf-haters.

*You don't know that for certain.*

The caution breezed into his mind, and he found himself arguing aloud. "I know, Lord, but if her grandfather was all those men say he was…"

*People change.*

Connor couldn't argue with that. Still, it seemed wiser to follow Harry's instructions, as much as they galled him. He would have preferred to knock on Taylor Sorensen's door and tell her who he was and what he wanted. But until he was sure she wouldn't run him off her land—and then follow in her grandfather's footsteps—he'd just have to play this Harry's way. Fortunately, he had the perfect plan to accomplish his task.

Provided Taylor Sorensen still needed a handyman.

Within a mile or so he saw the ranch buildings. As he drew nearer, he passed a herd of horses grazing lazily in a fenced-in field. The driveway opened into a parking area, and he pulled into a spot in front of a large barn. As he stepped from the Jeep, he looked around appreciatively.

The buildings were well-cared-for log structures. To the east of the barn were several small cabins, complete with porches and rocking chairs. In front of him, opposite the barn, was a beautiful, ranch-style, two-story log home made of lodgepole pine. The wraparound porch, with its rocking chairs and large pots of flowers, gave the house a welcoming appearance.

Heavy double doors and a large, circle-head window graced the front entrance, which jutted out slightly from the rest of the house. From what Connor could see, the entryway had to have a vaulted ceiling. On either side of the entrance were windows as tall as the front doors, and these were flanked by double windows topped with fanlights. The overall effect was one of rustic elegance.

In fact, everything about Galloway Glen seemed to proclaim beauty, clarity, and balance. It was a far cry from D.C., that was for certain.

Drawing a deep breath of the crisp, clean air into his lungs, he went up the steps to the front doors. It was time to go to work.


Taylor was sitting at the kitchen table with her mother, just finishing a second cup of coffee, when the doorbell rang.

"Who can that be?" she said with a slight frown.

"I suppose you could always answer it and find out," her mother recommended mildly.

"I suppose so," Taylor agreed with a grin. It wasn't Luke—he would have pounded on the door, then come in. And

Duncan always came to the kitchen door.

The only people who rang the front doorbell were people who didn't know her.

She walked across the living room and peered through the peephole in the massive pine door. Her eyes widened slightly. Standing on her front porch was the proverbial tall, dark, and handsome stranger. Well, okay, he wasn't dark. But he was tall. And definitely handsome.

"Wow!" she said under her breath, then jumped when a hand came to rest on her shoulder.

"'Wow'?" Her mother stood on tiptoe to look out the peephole, then turned to look at her daughter. "Wow indeed."

Taylor grinned and went for a second look.

What was a man like this doing in the middle of nowhere—particularly in the middle of *her* nowhere? Before a suitable answer came to her, he rang the bell again.

"Do you intend to stand there and gawk all day, dear, or are you going to invite the poor man inside?" her mother said softly.

"I wonder what he wants?" Taylor murmured, matching her mother's quiet tone.

"I'm sure I don't know, dear," her mother replied, turning back to the kitchen. "But you certainly won't find out if you don't let him in." The last three words were spoken in a raised voice, and Taylor swiveled quickly to shoot her mother a warning look.

Her eyes drifted back to the peephole—and she found herself eye-to-eye with the man. The full impact of his intense, magnified blue gaze hit Taylor as solidly as a splash of cold water and she stepped back quickly, unaware that Sasha had padded over soundlessly to stand behind her. Her heel came down on one of the husky's paws, and Sasha yipped in pain, scrambling out of the way. Taylor gave a yelp of her own as she lost her balance and landed in a heap on the floor.

"Ohhhhhh," she groaned, rolling on her back and staring up at the ceiling. "I knew I should have stayed in bed."

"You certainly would have gotten into less trouble," her mother agreed amiably.

With a resigned sigh she pushed to her feet. *Please, God, let him be gone.*

She peered out the peephole again.

He was standing there, completely at ease, his arms crossed, his eyes fixed on the peephole, as though he knew she was there. A slight smile tilted his lips, making him even more attractive—a fact that Taylor found particularly irritating.

*Well, nothing to do now but admit defeat.* She reached down to turn the handle and, with what she hoped was complete calm, pull the door open.

"Yes?" she asked innocently.

"Mrs. Sorensen?" His voice was deep and resonant, and she had the oddest feeling that it was reaching out to envelop her.

Tall and broad-shouldered, he had thick golden brown hair that just brushed the collar of his leather jacket. The man looked as though he'd just stepped from the pages of an Eddie Bauer catalog, for heaven's sake. A straight, Roman nose gave way to his finely chiseled mouth and a strong, squarish jaw. The set of his cleft chin suggested a definite stubborn streak. The only thing that saved him from being too perfect was a small scar that ran from his right brow to his cheekbone, yet even that seemed to add to the man's rugged appeal.

All in all, he gave the impression of confidence, power, and strength. Taylor could easily picture him barking out orders and expecting...no, *demanding* immediate obedience.

*For Pete's sake, Taylor, get a grip!* she chastised herself.

"Yes, I'm Mrs. Sorensen."

"Ma'am, I'm Connor Alexander. I'm here about your ad."

She stared at him blankly. "My...ad?"

His dark, expressive brows lifted a fraction higher. "For a handyman." He spoke slowly, cautiously, as though she were either hearing or understanding impaired.

"Oh! Yes. Of course," Taylor responded, trying to sound businesslike. *This* man was a handyman? "Won't you come in, please?"

He stepped inside. "I realize I should have called you first, but if the job is still available, I wanted to get things moving as quickly as possible—" He broke off abruptly, his eyes focused on Sasha, who was sitting near Taylor, watching him.

Taylor looked at him inquiringly. "Is something wrong?"

He looked at her, seemed about to say something, then snapped his mouth shut and shook his head. "No, nothing."

"Well, why don't you come on in." She moved aside, motioning toward the living room. "As it happens, the job is still open."

He moved into the room, keeping a wary eye on Sasha, then stopped with a slight start when her mother came into the room. Taylor saw his eyes widen slightly with admiration and she smiled. Her mother's beauty and elegance seldom went unnoticed.

"Mr. Alexander." She extended a slim, graceful hand. "I'm Donelle Camus, Taylor's mother. I couldn't help overhearing that you're here for the job. I assume you brought references?"

"Of course." Taylor gave him two points for not being the least bit flustered at her mother's blunt question.

"Well, that's fine then. Please, have a seat." Her mother turned a gracious smile her way, and Taylor noted with alarm the mischievous twinkle that suddenly sparkled in her mother's eyes. "I'm certain my daughter has several questions she'd like to ask you—"

At the teasing tone of her mother's voice, Taylor gave her a warning glance.

"About your qualifications," Donelle continued, "experience, marital status—"

Taylor grasped her mother firmly by the elbow and propelled her toward the front door, which still stood open.

"Actually," Taylor tossed over her shoulder, "Mother was just leaving."

"Was I really? Well, I hadn't noticed." There was a hint of laughter in her mother's voice. When they reached the door she stopped abruptly, and Taylor barely avoided running her over.

Taylor stepped back, her arms crossed, and received one of her mother's haughtiest looks. "For heaven's sake, dear, if you want me to leave, all you need to do is ask."

Taylor felt her cheeks flush as her mother glanced at the man, who was now watching them with clear amusement.

"It was a pleasure to meet you, Mr. Alexander. I hope we'll see more of you." With that, her mother turned and made a regal exit.

Shaking her head ruefully, Taylor came back into the living room, Sasha padding along beside her. She glanced at her visitor, noting the watchful way his eyes trailed the husky as they approached. Taylor paused, frowning. "Are you uncomfortable with dogs, Mr. Alexander?"

"Not as a rule," he muttered.

Taylor dropped into one of the large, overstuffed chairs. The man sat at one end of the couch, his gaze still glued to Sasha as she circled the floor next to Taylor's feet, then plopped down with a contented sigh.

*This is getting ridiculous!* Taylor thought with a twinge of irritation.

"Mr. Alexander, I assure you there's no need to be uneasy around Sasha."

He lifted his eyes, and her irritation increased when she saw the doubt reflected in that blue glance.

"Now, look!" she said in a huff. Sasha started at the sharp tone of her voice, coming to her feet and moving between Taylor and the man, a low growl sounding deep in her chest.

In a flash the man was on his feet, tensed and ready for action. Taylor stared at him, dumbfounded.

"Sit!" she commanded. Sasha obeyed; the man did not.

"Okay, I know you don't like to talk about this," he began, "but if you can't control your animal, I hardly think you should let it roam loose when there are strangers visiting. You seem to know dogs, so you should be aware how intimidating some of the larger breeds can be."

"If I can't control—" she echoed, incredulous, and then she was on her feet as well. "Look, you! My dog is as well-behaved as they come—"

"You call attacking people well-behaved?" he broke in.

Taylor stared at him in amazement. Had she let a nut case

98

into her house? "She hardly attacked you!"

"No, but—"

"For that matter, she's never attacked anyone! She simply wouldn't—not unless I was in danger!"

Clearly that surprised him, and he turned a quick, assessing gaze on the husky. His eyes narrowed suddenly, as though he'd just figured out some perplexing riddle, and he shook his head ruefully.

"Mrs. Sorensen—" he began, but Taylor wasn't listening.

"I don't know where you get off implying Sasha isn't safe—"

"Mrs. Sorensen, I—"

"—when you've never even *met* her before—"

"Please, there's been a mistake—"

"But if she *were* to attack someone, Mr. Alexander, I could certainly understand why she would attack *you!*"

Taylor felt a nudge against her leg and looked down to find Sasha sitting there, staring at her with a worried expression. She laid her hand on the dog's head, trying to calm down—and almost jumped out of her skin when a large, tanned hand covered hers where it rested between Sasha's soft ears. She turned and found herself almost nose-to-nose with her irritating visitor.

"Mrs. Sorensen, I'd like to apologize."

The quietly spoken words struck her as utterly sincere, but before she could formulate a response, the man knelt in front of Sasha and scratched her velvety chin. "And I apologize to you, too, girl. I judged you unfairly."

Sasha leaned forward to bestow a quick lick on Connor Alexander's nose. Her tail thumped approvingly, and she gazed into his eyes with adoration. Taylor sat down, thoroughly disgusted.

What in the world had just happened?

The man's eyes met hers, and he smiled slightly. "I realize I've hardly made a great first impression, Mrs. Sorensen, but I promise you I had a reason for my...odd behavior."

Taylor raised her eyebrows. *This ought to be good.*

But instead of explaining, he rose and moved back to the

couch, picked up an envelope he had laid on the cushion, and handed it to her. "My references," he said in response to her questioning look.

"Ah." She lifted the flap and drew out several neatly typed sheets of paper. Scanning them, she found that, according to several previous employers and professional contacts, Connor Alexander was a veritable paragon of virtues.

"So I take it you didn't insult any of their dogs?" she asked at last.

A quick smile creased his face. "No, I was much more well-behaved with them."

"Hmmm." She started to relax a bit. "I see you've had experience on a ranch."

"Raised on one," he replied.

"And you worked as a handyman when you were in college."

The smile was back. "Obviously a few years ago." His voice was laced with repressed laughter. "But I remember what I learned."

She nodded. "Well, it seems you're qualified, but…"

"But?" he prodded.

She looked at him in silence, then decided to be blunt. "Why do you want the job, Mr. Alexander?"

"Why does a man want any job?"

"Yes, but this is something more suited to a high school or college student. It hardly seems the kind of job that would attract someone of your—"

"Advanced years?" he inserted, smiling again.

"Experience," she amended, refusing to let him distract her—no matter how charmingly he smiled at her. "I confess I'm a bit confused. And I would appreciate some clarification."

That said, she fixed him with a steady look and waited.


Connor held Taylor's gaze, controlling his features to remain as impassive as possible. He settled back in the cushions of the couch and regarded her thoughtfully.

It was clear she expected an answer, but he was loathe to lie. So he gave her as much of the truth as he could.

"You're right on one point. This job does seem well suited to a student. But it also happens to be perfectly suited to my needs at the moment."

Her delicate eyebrows arched, but she remained silent.

*You're a tough one, aren't you?* he asked her inwardly, noting the glint of steel in her moss-green eyes.

"I'm a freelance photographer," he went on. "Or I'm trying to be. I've had some success doing shoots in wilderness areas, but I'm still learning, still new to the profession. So I decided to take a few months and travel around, checking out different regions, looking for places that are unique and ruggedly beautiful, but relatively undiscovered. Wyoming seemed an ideal place to start."

It was all true. The fact that it wasn't the entire truth hardly bothered him at all. What small pangs of discomfort he felt, he pushed aside. There was too much at stake to be squeamish.

"But if you're a photographer, why do you want a job as a handyman?"

Connor looked at the woman sitting in front of him and felt the stirrings of admiration. She was sharp. He could almost see the wheels turning as her mind worked to bring the facts in line with reason.

"Because I don't make money until I sell my photos"—he smiled wryly—"and I prefer eating to starving. This job was particularly attractive because you provide housing as well. Another expense I don't have to deal with."

Still all true. The lower he kept his expenses, the better.

"If I hire you, I expect to keep you busy. When do you plan to take your photos?"

"Whenever I can. My equipment is fairly easy to take along. And I assume I'll get a break or two during the day."

"Of course."

"And time for meals."

"Well, yes—"

"So there will be opportunities. Believe me, Mrs. Sorensen,

if you hire me I'll give you a decent day's work. And I'll do my best to stay out of your way when I'm not working. You won't even know I'm around."

"Hmmm," was her less-than-convinced response, and her green eyes studied him intently. Despite her closed expression, he sensed something...a certain caution, a vulnerability. It was almost as though she were afraid of him. Or of herself.

She glanced away, looking at her dog and reaching out to scratch the husky's neck. He took the opportunity to study her profile, taking in the oval-shaped face, high cheekbones, and well-defined brows. Her dark brown hair was thick and long and glimmered with red-gold highlights. She wore it parted in the middle, and it flowed in a graceful wave to well below her shoulders.

Dressed in a Henley shirt, jeans, and brown leather boots, she was the picture of simple beauty. Given the opportunity, he knew how he would photograph her: standing in the woods, trees decked in autumn colors all around her, the wind lifting her hair, those amazing green eyes shining with pleasure and excitement.

She turned to look at him again, and their eyes collided unexpectedly. A startling awareness shot through him, and his heart thudded once, then settled back to its natural rhythm. He let out a slow breath. He'd never realized just watching a woman could be such a disturbing experience.

"Okay."

He blinked at the short comment. "Okay?" he echoed, relieved to hear his voice was steady, calm. Not a bit like his erratic pulse.

She nodded. "Okay. You're hired." Before he could respond, she stood and motioned toward the door. "I assume you have your things with you?"

He stood as well. "Out in the car."

"Good. I'll show you to your cabin." She glanced at her watch, then smiled at him. "While you're settling in, I should have plenty of time to check your references."

He nodded. He wouldn't have expected any less.

"Assuming everything's on the up-and-up, I'll give you a tour of the ranch, and we'll go over meal times and other information. Then we can get started on the work tomorrow, first thing in the morning." Her smile deepened. "There's a fence on the back forty that's been waiting for you for quite some time now."

"And if my references don't check out?" he asked, following her to the front door and out onto the porch.

She glanced at him over her shoulder, a surprisingly impish gleam in her eyes. "Then I'll just send Sasha out to get rid of you," she replied. "Which could mean anything from chasing you off to eating you. After all," she went on gleefully as she headed for his Wrangler, "you know how intimidating large dogs can be."

# Eleven

❧

T he next morning, Connor was startled from his dreams by a
loud clanging.

Sitting bolt upright in bed, he looked around wildly,
wondering where the train was. He blinked at the unfamiliar
surroundings, his mind struggling to make sense of the rude
assault.

With an in-drawn breath, memory returned, he fell back
against the mattress. He was at Galloway Glen, settled into a
cozy cabin—one bedroom and a bathroom. He closed his eyes,
reviewing what Taylor had told him yesterday. He was to mend
fences and help renovate and update the small retreat cabins
while Taylor's brother and father were gone on some rafting
trip. In addition to this work, they would be scouting out new,
longer riding trails for retreat day trips. And Taylor's mother
would be around on a regular basis—she served as chief cook
and bottle washer during the retreat season and often stayed
with Taylor when her husband was away.

The playful interaction between mother and daughter yesterday had filled him with the desire to talk with his own parents. Connor peered into the darkness, and images flooded his
mind…his mother laughing, his father running alongside him
as he learned how to ride a bike, both of their faces gleaming
with pride when he graduated college, their family devotions

and prayer times. He loved his parents, as they loved him—and one another. And the Lord.

He stretched, filling the queen-sized bed with his tall frame, and one hand barely missed knocking over the lamp on the bedside table. He stared at the digital clock next to the lamp and his eyes widened. Frowning in disbelief, he threw back the comforter and padded to the dresser. Flicking on the small lamp on the top of the dresser, he picked up his watch and peered at the dial, then closed his eyes.

The clock was right. It really was 4:30 in the morning. He went to the window at the front of the cabin, pushed aside the curtains, and peered out into the darkness. Pitch black. The clanging continued, and Connor's eyes finally located the source. Mrs. Camus, decked out in an apron, stood on the lighted porch of the ranch house, clanging a metal spoon on a large, heavy triangle that hung above her.

With a disgusted snort he let the curtains fall back in place, grabbed a towel from the back of the overstuffed easy chair, navigated past a small table with its accompanying chairs, and stalked into the bathroom to shower.


"Your new worker isn't exactly a morning person."

Taylor turned at this pronouncement and went to stand beside her mother, peering out the kitchen window with her. Sure enough, Connor Alexander was heading toward the house, his hair still wet and slightly awry, his stride indicating he was less than pleased to be up and about.

Smothering a grin, Taylor went to finish setting the table.

"I take it you didn't tell him when we start working around here, eh?" her mother inquired mildly.

"I told him we get up early," Taylor replied.

"Hmmm, apparently he didn't believe you. Perhaps this will help." She handed Taylor a steaming cup of strong, black coffee.

Taylor grinned at her and planted a kiss on her cheek. "Thanks, Mom. You're a jewel."

"Of course," her mother quipped, picking up a tray of bacon and setting it on the table.

The door opened and Connor walked in. "Mornin'," he mumbled as he glanced around the kitchen. Taylor, who had moved to stand next to the door, stuck the steaming mug under his nose.

"Looking for this?" she asked with a smile.

He took one whiff and a smile broke out over his face. He lifted his hands, cupped the mug reverently, and took several quick sips. His eyes closed in what Taylor could only describe as ecstasy, and he set the mug down on the table. She cocked an eyebrow at him but didn't comment, then grabbed the carafe and topped off his cup in silence.

He drank more slowly this time, then turned an appreciative smile on her. "Thanks," he said, his voice less rough than when he'd first come in. "I'm starting to feel human again."

She laughed. "Well, that's good. Now have a seat. I've got a whole list of things we need to do after breakfast."

He pulled out a chair and surveyed the breakfast spread before him, his eyes widening a bit. Plates of hot griddlecakes, toast, and fresh biscuits were flanked by platters of eggs, bacon, and sausage. Next to these were bowls of grits, sausage gravy, and hash browns. Pitchers of orange juice and grapefruit juice stood watch over a bowl of large, ripe strawberries.

At his stunned expression, Taylor didn't even try to hide her grin.

"I wasn't sure what you liked, Mr. Alexander," her mother said in a low, gentle voice. She patted him on the shoulder. "So I fixed you a little of everything. Can't have a man facing his first day on the job without a good breakfast, now can we?"

He looked up at her, and Taylor was struck by the sincerely appreciative look in his eyes. "No, ma'am, we can't. Thank you."

"Of course," Taylor added, "you don't have to eat it all."

He fixed her with a look of offended amazement. "A man doesn't get this kind of treatment often, Mrs. Sorensen, and I intend to enjoy as much of it as I can." He leaned forward to help himself to something from every plate, then commenced eating with gusto.

Donelle beamed at him, patted his shoulder again, and went to the sink to start washing dishes, humming as she stuck her hands into the soapy water.

"Well, suit yourself," Taylor retorted. "But don't expect me to go easy on you just because you end up with a stomachache."

He paused, a forkful of eggs halfway to his mouth, and regarded her with twinkling eyes. "I appreciate your concern, Mrs. Sorensen, but I have been blessed with a cast-iron, bottomless pit for a stomach. So I imagine the only thing less likely than me getting a stomachache"—he popped the eggs in his mouth, chewed appreciatively, then finished—"is you going easy on anyone. For any reason."

An appreciative chuckle came from the sink, and Taylor glared at her mother's back. As perceptive as always, Donelle stopped washing dishes and looked at her. Seeing Taylor's displeased look, she merely smiled.

"It's okay, dear. You go ahead and shoot sparks at me, if it makes you feel better." She turned back to the dishes. "I can understand what a terrible shock it is to get as well as you give." She shook her head sympathetically. "And so early in the morning."

"Mother!" Taylor sputtered, and Donelle turned innocent eyes back to her indignant daughter.

"Well, you have to admit, hon; you started it." She smiled at Connor. "And I must say, he finished it well." She nodded approvingly. "You made a good choice, dear. You need a man around here with spunk."

"I need—" Taylor echoed in disbelief, then stood and stared at her mother. "I most certainly do *not* need a man with spunk!"

"Don't be silly, sweetheart. Of course you do. You'd make mincemeat out of—"

"What I *meant* is that I don't need a man! Period! Spunk or otherwise!" That clarified, Taylor stomped to the doorway, pausing only long enough to spin around and pin Connor with a furious glare. "As for *you!* Be at the stables in fifteen minutes!" Then she was gone.

Connor sat staring after her, then he met Donelle Camus's laughing gaze. "Wow," he said, his eyes gleaming appreciatively.

Her mouth twitched with amusement and she nodded. "Indeed." She went back to her dishes, and he finished eating as quickly as he could. When he rose to leave, she stopped him with a quiet question.

"Are you a praying man, Mr. Alexander?"

He looked at her in surprise, then nodded. "Yes, ma'am, I am."

She smiled benignly. "Now would be a good time, don't you think?"

A grin split his face and he laughed. "Actually," he said, reaching out to pat her shoulder, "I've *been* praying since the minute I got this job!"


For the next week, Taylor kept Connor hopping. He would no sooner finish one job than she would give him another. One thing he could say about his new boss: She was true to her word. She was not going easy on him.

In fact, Connor sensed that she was testing him, pushing him to see if he would resist or rebel. So he made it a point to be as accommodating as possible. He accepted each task agreeably, listening carefully as she explained what she wanted and asking questions only when absolutely necessary.

The second day, after completing a job, Connor had walked into the stables, looking around at the stalls lining both sides of the building. Horses were munching away happily at their hay.

"One thing about Taylor," a deep voice said from behind him, "she knows horses. Too bad her knowledge of people isn't as refined."

Connor turned. A tall, dark-haired man stood there, leaning on a shovel. Connor stepped forward and put out a hand. "I'm Connor Alexander, the new ranch hand."

The man stood unmoving, staring at Connor's extended

hand, making no move to accept it. Just then, Taylor came out of one of the stalls. "Oh, Luke, there you are," she said, a warm smile lighting her face. "This is Connor Alexander. He's—"

"The new ranch hand. Yes, so he's told me."

Taylor glanced at Luke, frowning. Then she glanced at Connor. "Connor, this is Luke Narbona. He's the one who keeps things fixed here and there before they fall apart."

Connor extended his hand again, and the older man shook it reluctantly.

"Luke, I was hoping he could work with you today on the back forty fence."

"I'm not going out there today," he said quietly.

Taylor blinked, and Connor watched two spots of pink tinge her cheeks. Suddenly he wanted to reach out and box the man's ears.

"No disrespect intended, Taylor," Luke went on, "but I'd already planned to finish the plumbing job in Cabin Two."

She studied him quietly, then shook her head. "Okay. That's fine."

Luke nodded and moved away.

"But when you're done"—her own tone hardened—"come see me about jobs for you and Connor to do together."

His gaze swiveled back to her, then he gave a curt nod and stomped off.

Taylor turned back to Connor. "So," she said, clearly doing her best to recover gracefully. "How are you at mucking out stalls?"


When Sunday came around, Connor showed up bright and early at the breakfast table. Taylor looked at him in surprise.

"It's Sunday," she said. "You can sleep in."

"I forgot to ask what time you leave for church," he said. "I didn't want to miss it."

"You…want to go to church?" She looked slightly stunned.

He held back his amusement with difficulty. "If that's okay with you."

"Oh. Sure. Of course. I mean, I just didn't realize—"

"That I wasn't a heathen?"

"Ah…well, yes," she admitted with a rueful chuckle. "I suppose that's exactly what I thought."

He smiled. "Well, I'm not. At least not any more so than any other believer who's struggling to do what's right."

She studied him quietly, then nodded. "Okay, then. Drink up your coffee, Mr. Alexander. Dad's not there to preach, but we're still having praise and worship singing. And you won't want to miss the prelude." She grinned at him. "Mrs. Huntsicker plays a mean organ. Foot pedals and everything. Fairly makes the rafters rattle!"

Their time of worshiping together had been peaceful and enjoyable. Connor was pleased to find that Taylor had a sweet alto voice, and she sang the hymns with sincere emotion, as though the lyrics were more than just words. He liked the way their voices blended as they sang. She must have noticed it, too, for she glanced up at him several times during the first hymn.

After that day, Taylor treated him differently—as though she'd begun to trust him. At least a little. Several times he glanced up from his work and found her watching him, a curious expression on her face. When his eyes met hers, she turned away, busying herself with whatever happened to be at hand. He returned to his task with a chuckle.

The days quickly fell into a routine. They would rise with the sun, head out for the day's work—sometimes with Luke, but more often just the two of them—then return in the early evening to clean up for dinner. Mealtime had become one of Connor's favorite events, and not just because of Mrs. Camus's cooking. He enjoyed watching the affectionate, often teasing, exchanges between Taylor and her mother. From the moment he met her, Donelle Camus had made him feel at home, pulling him into comfortable conversation, listening with interest as he talked, and sharing her own insightful views. As he spent time with the older woman, he discovered that she possessed wit, intelligence, and a remarkable ability to put one in one's place when necessary. All traits she had passed on to her daughter. In abundance.

Along with the company of the two women, the feasts Taylor's mom prepared were a grand way to start and end each day. The elegant cook would beam at him as he devoured the food, then pat him on the shoulder as she cleared away his dishes.

Invariably, as he rose to leave, she would give him some word of wisdom: "Patience is the key to victory"; "Soft words turn away wrath."; "The dog that growls the loudest has usually been hurt the most."

The last one had been her comment as he left the kitchen that morning and headed for the stable to meet Taylor. She'd informed him that they were going riding today to check out a new route she wanted to use on trail rides next spring. Once again, Luke had bowed out.

"Got to rewire Cabin Three," he said, and he walked away, leaving Taylor staring after him with a troubled expression.

Donelle's earlier words had stuck in Connor's mind as Taylor watched him silently while he saddled his horse, a sorrel gelding with the unremarkable name of Chestnut. Though he sensed Taylor was waiting for him to make a mistake, he was almost sure she was pleased to see how comfortable he was around the horses. It hadn't taken more than a few minutes, and a carrot stick from Taylor's mom, to make friends with Chestnut.

Now, Connor glanced at Taylor as she rode along beside him in silence. *The dog that growls the most*…He grinned. He would never have equated Taylor with a dog, but she did seem to growl a lot. He wondered if her mother's aphorism were true.

"You know, your mother is quite a lady," he remarked, and Taylor shot him a rueful smile.

"She is that. Sharp, too. She has an almost uncanny ability to tell if someone is trustworthy or not." Her lips tipped in a slight smile. "Apparently you passed muster. In record time, I might add."

Connor nodded, pleased, and turned his head to take in the scenery. They were at the top of a hill, and he could see the jagged peaks of the Tetons to the west.

"Yellowstone is north of here, right?" he asked, trying to get his bearings.

"About forty-five miles. Idaho is across the mountains, twelve miles or so as the crow flies."

Connor stared at the Tetons dubiously. "That'd have to be some crow." He took a deep breath of the crisp, cold air. "So you've lived here all your life?"

Taylor nodded. "It was a great place to grow up," she said, and he heard the sincerity in her voice.

"Pretty remote," he commented.

"Very remote, but I like it that way. It doesn't bother me at all that our nearest neighbor is several miles away." She lifted her shoulders in a self-deprecating shrug. "I'm not exactly what you'd call a social butterfly."

"I've gotten that impression," he said, and she laughed lightly. He watched with interest the way her whole face lit up when she smiled, and he suddenly realized she was a beautiful woman. Not in the typical, fashion-model way, but in an exotic, almost exquisite way. And it was more than her features that stirred him; it was the total, intriguing package that was Taylor Sorensen. In fact, Connor couldn't remember the last time a woman had affected him the way his new boss did. One minute he wanted to throttle her, the next he found himself wondering if her hair was really as silken as it seemed—

*Whoa! Hold on there, Alexander!* He told himself, abashed by the unexpected direction of his thoughts. *You're here to watch wolves, remember?*

"You know," she went on, thankfully oblivious to his inner struggle, "I actually like it that I can go for days without seeing anyone other than my family." She grinned. "And the only reason I see them is that they live about a half-mile from the ranch house, in a cabin they had built several years ago."

"They didn't want to stay in the ranch house?"

"They thought Josh and I needed to have a place of our

own. Ryan and his family have their own place closer to town. And since Josh and I were running the retreats, they offered us the ranch house. I was thrilled." Her eyes had a faraway look in them. "I love that house. I grew up in it, and it's full of wonderful memories. I can see images of my family in nearly every room."

"And your husband?" Connor asked. Mrs. Camus had told him about Josh's death and Taylor's struggle to deal with the loss. He watched the emotions drift across her face, the shadows fill her green eyes.

She nodded slowly. "Yes. Josh, too."

She fell silent, and Connor regretted bringing up the subject. "Are your folks retired?" he asked, hoping to distract her from whatever dark thoughts he'd triggered.

"My mom is retired, from teaching. I think my dad will go on being a pastor until the day he drops." A bemused smile lifted her lips. "His church is small, barely more than fifty members, but they're a lively group." Her smile deepened. "They keep him busy anyway."

"Your parents have been in this area for a long time then?"

"Forever," she said with a chuckle. "Galloway Glen was actually settled by my great-grandfather on my mother's side"— she suddenly developed a lilting, Irish accent—"the good and honorable Riley Galloway, in the late 1800s."

Connor laughed, caught up in her unexpected playfulness. "Let me guess. Big and hard-working, with red hair and emerald green eyes."

"Sure, an' you couldn't be more on target if you'd known the fine fellow!" she crowed with delight, her infectious laughter flowing around him. "Seriously, he did have red hair—"

"Which is where yours came from, I suspect. And the green eyes?"

"Guilty. A definite carryover from the Irish side of the family. I have yet to see a green-eyed Ojibwa."

"Ojibwa?"

"Yup. My great-grandmother, the love of Riley's life. He saw her watching him tend sheep one morning, and it was love at

113

first sight. He found her father, offered for her, and they were married soon after. Between the two of them, they took a few acres and built it to more than two thousand. Small by Wyoming standards, but a decent ranch nonetheless."

"Small?"

Taylor nodded, a small smile tilting her lips. "Any good rancher knows you need close to fifty acres a head when you're raising cattle or sheep. The ranches around here average more than 4,000 acres."

Connor showed his surprise, and Taylor's smile broadened. "That's why Galloway Glen was considered a nice little spread by the other ranchers. But my grandparents weren't really ranchers at heart. They knew the land was their greatest asset, so from time to time they sold sections off." She glanced around them, a smile on her face. "Now Galloway Glen covers a little over 600 acres, about a square mile, most of which is wilderness."

"No more sheep?"

Taylor shook her head. "Only the one the twins raise to show at the county fair. But that's okay. Riley's work and my grandparents' business acumen have left us pretty well set." She shrugged. "Which is why I can afford to run the retreat center. And it's a part of why I do it—to give something back."

"How about wolves?"

Taylor started and gave him a swift, alarmed look. "What?"

"Are there any wolves left in this wilderness?"

"No." Her answer was swift…a little too swift. "They were wiped out sixty years ago. Trappers, hunters, men out for the bounty." She urged Topaz forward, ending the conversation.

"That's too bad," Connor said when he caught up with her. "Galloway Glen seems like the perfect place for wolves."

Again that sharp glance came his way, her eyes searching, as though trying to reach into his thoughts. He kept his expression blank, and she turned away with an impatient shrug.

"I wouldn't know," she said coldly. "I've never seen one." She jabbed her heels into her horse's side and the buckskin bolted forward, as though startled at the forcefulness of the action.

*Now why don't I believe that?* Connor thought. *And why do I get the distinct impression, Taylor Sorensen, that you're running away from the truth?*

"Did you know frowning causes ten times more wrinkles than smiling does, dear?"

At Taylor's intractable look, Donelle Camus smiled slightly. "See there? You just cost your face another ten years or so." She leaned forward, taking her daughter's hand in her own. "Do tell me what's troubling you, Taylor."

"Nothing, Mom. I'm fine. Just tired, I guess." The smile she gave her mother was anemic at best.

"Taylor—" Donelle began, but her daughter rose, muttering something about checking on the horses, and left the house.

Donelle settled back in her chair, cupping her mug of tea, a smile on her lips. It was good to see Taylor so…affected. It had been too long since anyone had gotten close enough to get a rise out of her. With the exception of Ryan—who could send his sister into fits of irritation almost by his mere existence— Taylor seldom let anyone bother her. Anyone outside the family, that was.

Donelle knew it wasn't her daughter's remarkable self-control and patience that allowed her to be untouched by others' foibles; rather, it was that she did not let anyone get close enough to matter. Josh had been the exception, and a delightful one. When he was killed, Donelle's fears that her daughter would sink back into her somewhat reclusive shell had been more or less realized. Oh, Taylor spent time with Duncan, but even with him she seemed to maintain a distance. Donelle wasn't particularly concerned about that. Duncan was a good friend for Taylor, but Donelle wasn't convinced he was the right one to be anything more.

Connor Alexander, on the other hand…

Donelle's smile broadened. There was something about the man that she liked. A great deal, actually. She had learned from their talks that he had a heart for God and that he shared many of Taylor's interests and values. He clearly enjoyed life on a ranch and had a passion for animals. His intelligence was evident, as was his sense of humor. He'd even made a few suggestions on how to incorporate wildlife walks into the retreats to teach the youngsters about God's creative genius. Taylor's eyes had lit up with excitement at the idea. Also, he seemed remarkably patient with her daughter—a trait that almost qualified him for sainthood! And several times Donelle had caught him watching Taylor with some indefinable emotion in those wonderful blue eyes.

*Yes, indeed,* Donelle thought with pleasure as she sipped her tea, *Connor Alexander has definite possibilities.*

# Twelve

❧

I think that's everything." Taylor studied her list, her lips pursed in thought, then nodded. "Yup, we got it all."

"Good thing," Connor remarked dryly. "There's no room left in the truck for anything else."

She laughed and pulled the door open, sliding behind the steering wheel. They had come to Jackson for "a quick supply run," and ended up being there most of the afternoon. Connor had been intrigued with Jackson, what with its wooden sidewalks and Old West appearance.

"I have an idea," Connor said, slanting her a smile. "How 'bout I buy you dinner?"

Taylor looked at him. "Dinner? Why?"

He laughed. "Mainly because I'm starving!"

"Ah, so your altruistic gesture is really self-serving?"

"Entirely."

"I have a better idea," Taylor said.

"Does it involve food?" he asked suspiciously.

"I promise."

"Then lead on, boss lady."

They picked up sandwiches, chips, and soda at the grocery store, then drove to the town square. Connor stared in amazement at the elk-antler arches that stood at the four corners of the tiny park there. He and Taylor sat on a bench, offered grace, and started eating.

"You're right," he said, munching happily. "This is better than a restaurant." He looked around appreciatively. "My mom would love this place. She loves touristy towns with shops and atmosphere to the nth degree."

"I suppose you stand outside while she shops," Taylor remarked.

"Definitely," he agreed. "But she doesn't mind. She just likes to chat as we walk from shop to shop." His smile deepened. "She's the best. My dad, too." He met Taylor's warm gaze. "Your mom reminds me of them, in a way. Always saying good things about people and laughing a lot."

"Do you have any brothers or sisters?" she asked, and he shook his head.

"Only child. Spoiled rotten and loving every minute of it. My folks were older when I was born, and Mom couldn't have any more children. So they poured all their creativity and love into me, and one another. And the Lord. I think I heard every Bible story about a zillion times."

"Me, too," Taylor said, giggling. "And I still love them!"

Connor smiled in response, struck by the picture she made. The red light of the setting sun reflected in gleaming highlights in her hair, and her eyes were lit with the warmth of shared memories. She was at ease, relaxed, and completely captivating.

*I could spend hours talking to her, laughing with her,* he thought. *Maybe days.*

*Maybe forever,* a small inner voice added, startling him.

"You know, I always wanted to have the kind of relationship my parents share," she said. "I didn't think I ever would…but I did. With Josh."

Connor stilled. She'd never discussed her husband with him before.

"We had such a great time together. I was sure we'd go on forever, that we'd have a passel of kids. Maybe even twins, like Ryan and Lisa." She met Connor's gaze, and he saw tears gleaming in her eyes. "Josh loved kids. All ages."

"Your mom told me he was on a trip with the church youth group when he died?"

She nodded. "One of the campers went out on a ledge, and Josh brought him back. He saved the boy's life."

The pain in her eyes struck at him. He wished he could hold her close, ease her hurt.

"It shouldn't have happened." The harshness in her tone surprised him. "It shouldn't have been Josh on that ledge. There was another boy, a senior. Brad Momadey. He was supposed to be watching the younger boys. It's his fault Josh is dead."

Connor put a gentle hand on her arm. "Taylor, it was an accident—"

She pulled away abruptly. "No. It was Brad's fault." She met his concerned gaze. "Brad stopped coming to church. He's all but disappeared. Mom talked with his mother, and she said she hasn't seen him for months…" She blinked rapidly. "He's nineteen years old and he just vanished. But do you know what?" Her voice choked. "I don't care. I hope he never comes back. Because when I see him—and I did catch a glimpse of him in Wilson not long ago—all I can think of is what he did, what he cost me. And all I can feel is hatred."

Connor reached out and took her now-cold hand in his own. They sat in silence, until she turned wide, sorrow-filled eyes to him.

"So now you know what a terrible person I am."

Connor shook his head gently. "You're not terrible." She lifted her gaze, searching his face.

*God, give me wisdom. Show me how to help her.* "You're hurting. I understand that. And if I can understand that, don't you think God does as well?"

She swallowed convulsively, closed her eyes, and sat in silence. After a moment, she withdrew her hand and stood. "Well, we've been gone a lot longer than I thought we would be. We'd better head back."

He grinned. "Before Luke sends out the state troopers, right?"

"Exactly," she said, mustering a smile, and he stood to follow her to the truck.

"Taylor, can I talk to you?"

Taylor turned from where she was mending a halter. Luke stood in the doorway of the barn, concern etched in his weathered features.

"Of course," she said, moving toward him. "What's wrong, Luke?"

He shifted from one foot to another, but his gaze never strayed from her face. "Yazhi, what do you know about this man you've hired?"

She hesitated. "About as much as I know when I hire anyone," she replied slowly, scanning his expression, wondering what had him so bothered. It was unusual for Luke to question her decisions. "Why?"

Luke studied her face for a moment, then shrugged. "I don't like him."

Taylor couldn't hide her surprise, and Luke looked away. She moved to touch his arm gently. "Has he said something to offend you? Because if he has—"

He was shaking his head before she could finish. "No, no. Nothing like that. It's…actually, I'm not sure what it is. But there's something about him, Yazhi, something I don't quite trust. Sometimes people are far different inside than they seem on the surface."

Taylor bit her lip. Connor had been at Galloway Glen for a week and a half now, and he'd been the picture of trustworthiness and hard work. And he'd been nothing but kind and understanding that day when she talked about Josh and Brad. Still, she trusted Luke. He'd always acted in her best interests. So why did she sense that he wasn't being completely honest with her now? That there was something going on beneath the surface, something Luke wasn't willing to share with her.

The thought that her longtime friend might be concealing something troubled her far more than his apparent dislike of her new ranch hand.

"I'll talk with Mom," she said after a moment. "She has good instincts. I'll see if she shares your concerns."

Luke nodded and turned to leave.

"Luke," Taylor said, and he paused. "You know you can talk to me about anything."

"Yes, Yazhi," he said, his dark gaze not quite meeting hers. "I know."

And as he turned to leave, Taylor had the distinct impression that he didn't believe that at all.


Taylor did as she promised. She talked with her mother about Connor that afternoon.

"I don't understand it, dear," her mother said after Taylor told her of Luke's concerns. "Connor seems like a nice man. Kind. Honest."

Taylor shrugged. "I know. It just doesn't make any sense."

"Actually, it might."

Taylor looked at her mother curiously.

"Taylor, you know I think the world of Luke, but he has a definite tendency to treat you as though you belong to him. It might be that he's feeling a bit, well, threatened."

"Threatened? By Connor?"

"By anyone who isn't a part of Galloway Glen. Remember how long it took Luke to warm up to Josh?"

Taylor nodded thoughtfully. "You're right. I'd forgotten about that."

Her mother patted her arm. "Luke is a good friend to you, Taylor. And we're told that 'many counselors make a man wise.' Keep what he's said in mind, and let's ask God to show you if there is anything about Connor Alexander that should concern you."

Taylor nodded, grateful for her mother's calm perspective.

"And while we're at it," her mother added, her eyes twinkling, "we just might ask him to bring your father back in one piece. Ryan and the twins could be leading him on a merry chase."

A few days later, during yet another of her mother's marathon breakfast feasts, Taylor announced to Connor that they would be heading for the "back forty" to repair several sections of a paddock.

"The back forty?" Connor repeated.

She nodded. "We take the retreat families out there as a day trip," Taylor explained. "It's about a three-hour ride on horseback through some really pretty terrain. Mom goes out there ahead of us with the truck, and when the group arrives she's got a picnic lunch all set out and ready to go."

Connor surveyed the breakfast fixings and grinned. "I take it she fixes more than egg-salad sandwiches."

"Count on it," Taylor replied, laughing. "We usually eat the leftovers for the next three nights." She reached for a buttermilk biscuit. "Of course, that's not exactly a hardship," she went on, spreading homemade jelly on the biscuit and taking a hearty bite. "You haven't really lived until you've tasted my mother's fried chicken. Hot or cold, it beats Colonel Kentucky any day!"

After breakfast, they loaded the truck with poles and tools, then drove westward, toward the mountains. As always, Connor was captivated by the beauty of the ranch and the ever-changing terrain. They drove across fields dotted with wildflowers, past stands of evergreens, and around rocky outcroppings. In the distance, the jagged peaks of the Tetons jutted toward the crystalline sky.

They rode in a comfortable silence, something Connor couldn't remember ever experiencing with a woman before. Taylor would speak up from time to time, pointing out landmarks or spots of interest, but for the most part she simply drove without talking, relaxed and competent.

They had just rounded another small stand of trees when she leaned forward and pointed. "There it is."

Connor saw a small cabin of rough logs in front of them. Other than a picture window and the ever-present rocking chairs standing guard on the porch, the cabin looked as though it could have been in that spot for a hundred years.

"This used to be a sheepherder's cabin," Taylor remarked. "We updated it a bit, but tried to keep the authentic, rustic feel."

She pulled up next to a small paddock located at the side of the cabin and shut off the ignition. Near the enclosure were three picnic tables.

"Here's our project for today," she said as they climbed out of the truck.

Several of the main support timbers around the paddock needed to be replaced, and the two went right to work, quickly and smoothly, like a finely tuned team, each understanding what the other needed almost before he or she asked. Connor would no sooner glance around for a tool than Taylor would hand it to him. She would just open her mouth to ask for help when he would stop what he was doing and offer an extra set of hands—or muscle.

Several times, however, Connor noticed Taylor pausing to glance around, a bemused look on her face. After the fourth or fifth time, he said, "What's up, Taylor?"

She bit her lip, giving him a somewhat sheepish look. "Nothing," she said, brushing his question aside.

He set down the hammer he'd been using. "Uh-uh. Not good enough. You've been looking over your shoulder like a highwayman watching for a posse. What's the matter?"

She leaned on the fence. "It's happening again."

He frowned. "It?"

She sighed. "I can't explain it, can't even give you a good reason for it, but I'm positive we're being watched." She shook her head. "I know it sounds silly, but the feeling's so strong it's making me as nervous as a three-legged frog on the highway."

Connor turned to scan the surrounding woods, then turned back to her. "Do you want me to take a ride around? Check things out?"

Quick gratitude swept through her at his accepting attitude, relief that he didn't merely dismiss her feelings or try to talk her out of them.

"No, never mind." She turned to stare into the distance. "Truth be known, if someone is out there, I'd rather have you stay close by."

She turned back to him, then paused at the odd look in his eyes. Something shimmered in the blue depths of his gaze, something protective and so purely male that she felt a sudden tingling in the pit of her stomach. For a moment, the very air around them seemed to snap with electricity. And then he looked away from her and the spell was broken.

She stood, struggling to get her emotions under control, as he turned to pick up the hammer. As she drew a steadying breath and moved forward to help him, she found herself wondering if the man beside her wasn't far more dangerous—to her peace of mind, if nothing else—than anyone who might be lurking in the woods.

"Maybe it was one of those wolves the ranchers have been talking about," Connor said.

Taylor looked at him in alarm. "What?"

"When I first came to town, I overheard a group of ranchers at the general store talking about wolves. They said they'd been seen in the area."

"Not seen," Taylor corrected, pounding a nail more viciously than was necessary. "Heard. There have been a couple of reports about wolves howling." She reached for another nail. "But if you ask me, it's all a bunch of exaggerated nonsense." She positioned the nail and brought the hammer down, then added in a low voice, "I just hope these guys come to that conclusion, too, before somebody gets hurt."

Connor fixed her with an curious look. "Hurt? Why would someone get hurt?"

She shrugged, concentrating on the nail.

"Taylor?" he pressed, and she let out a frustrated puff of air. She leaned her arms on the top of the fence and regarded him, debating how much she could safely say.

"You don't know these people like I do," she began. "They're good men, Connor. But talk about wolves and they get stone cold." She sighed again. "They hate wolves. They call them killers, and vermin, and wouldn't think twice about gunning one down or putting poison out for it."

"Even though it's illegal to do so?" he asked quietly.

"They don't care. What matters most to them is their livestock, which is understandable. I mean, it's their livelihood..." her voice trailed off, and he sat back, watching her.

"What do you think of wolves?"

The question startled her. Her eyes flew to his face, but she saw nothing there other than mild interest...and, oddly enough, compassion.

She bit her lip, staring unseeingly into the distance. "When I was a little girl, my grandmother used to tell me the stories and legends of her people, the Ojibwa. She told me how the Ojibwa believed each of the animals had a unique power, an attribute that belonged to it alone. Do you know what the wolf's attribute was?"

"Cunning?"

"Fidelity. Loyalty. From the time she was a small girl, my grandmother was taught that the wolf was a wonderful creature. She often showed me her grandfather's warrior band. It bore a wolf totem for perseverance and guardianship. In their creation story, a wolf befriended and cared for Nanabojo, one of the four most important spirits in the Ojibwa religion. She told me time and again that her people revered the wolf as an example of high family values." She gave a mirthless laugh. "Can you see the ranchers buying into *that*?"

"Let's just say the odds aren't real high."

"Let's just say they're nonexistent. But for me"—she paused, searching for the right words—"for me, wolves have always been a source of wonder. They're remarkably caring and loving to their family members, to the others in the pack. And they seem to find a great delight in living. Sometimes they almost seem to be smiling."

"You sound as though you've seen them," he said, and she looked at him in alarm.

"I've seen pictures," she said quickly.

He scanned her face, as though seeking to delve into her

thoughts, to understand what she was trying to share with him. "You're drawn to their loyalty," he said after a moment. "I can see that. Loyalty, faithfulness, they're important to you. And they're a part of you."

She looked at him. "What do you mean?"

"Anyone who spends time around you can see that you're loyal to the people you love and the ideals you hold dear. Look at the way you are with your mother, the tone of your voice when you talk about your grandmother. And about God."

His words both pleased and embarrassed her. Once again she had the sense of something passing between them, something powerful and magnetic. She felt her cheeks grow warm and turned away, not sure how to respond. A gentle touch on her arm brought her eyes back to him.

He stood beside her, and the look in his eyes seemed to wrap her in an invisible warmth. It was as though her entire being was filled with waiting, with anticipation.

"Taylor, I want—I need to tell you—"

But whatever he'd been about to say was cut off by the sound of an approaching vehicle. They turned as one to look in the direction of the engine noise.

When Taylor spotted a Blazer heading toward them, her eyes widened in surprise. "It's Duncan."

"Duncan?"

She nodded. "Duncan MacEwen. He's a neighbor. And a...friend." She frowned slightly at the hesitation. Duncan was more than just a friend, wasn't he? So why was she hesitant to say so?

"Must be coming to check up on the work," Connor said as he knelt to put the tools back in the toolbox.

"Or on the workers," she muttered under her breath.

The Blazer pulled up, the engine was cut off, and Duncan stepped out, pushing his hat back off his head as he did so. "Hey there, beautiful," he called.

"I assume he's talking to you, not to me," Connor remarked dryly, and Taylor felt a surge of red creep into her cheeks.

"Yes, well, probably," she muttered.

Duncan came over and slipped his arms around Taylor, giving her a quick kiss. She was so surprised, she didn't stop him. Then he turned to Connor, one arm around Taylor's shoulders, hugging her possessively to his side, and held out his free hand. "Duncan MacEwen, at your service, sir."

Connor shook his hand. "Connor Alexander, resident gofer. For the time being, anyway."

Taylor wondered fleetingly at the odd expression of displeasure in his eyes. *Maybe he's jealous,* she thought, then dismissed the idea along with the inordinate sense of delight it had triggered. What did she care if Connor Alexander was jealous? The man was nothing more than a temporary employee.

*A very attractive, extremely intriguing, ridiculously appealing temporary employee,* an inner voice pointed out.

"Shut up," she muttered under her breath.

"Did you say something, darlin'?" Duncan turned to her, and she shook her head. "Well then, put me to work, lass. I've come to offer my services," he said with a cocky grin.

"Much appreciated," Connor replied, "but we're all done." He straightened, the toolbox clenched in his hand. "Looks like your trip was a waste of time."

Duncan's eyes flashed, but the amiable smile never faltered. "Not a bit of it!" he shot back, squeezing Taylor. "It's always worth any effort to see my darlin' girl."

"Well, now that you're here," she said, easing her way out of his arm, "you can help us load the extra poles back into the truck."

"With pleasure," Duncan said, moving to lift one end of the pole Connor had grabbed. "Anything for you, lass." He cast a knowing grin at Connor. "On the count of three?" he asked, and Connor gave him a curt nod.

Together they lifted the timber and walked to the truck. As they slid it into the bed of the vehicle, Duncan gave Connor a casual look. "Ever heard of the caber toss?"

"Duncan—" Taylor started to protest, but the two men ignored her.

"Isn't that a contest of strength you Scotsmen indulge in

while you're wearing skirts?" Connor inquired, turning a wide and innocent gaze on the man beside him.

Duncan's eyes snapped. "Those are kilts, mon. Not skirts."

"Ah. Of course," Connor replied, though his tone said he was clearly unconvinced.

"But, then, it takes a man confident in his masculinity to wear one, so I can see how you'd be a bit wary of them," Duncan said smoothly as he sauntered back to the pile of poles.

"For heaven's sake, you two!" Taylor said, clearly irked. She might as well have been invisible for all the attention they paid her.

"Well, now," Connor drawled, bending to grasp the end of the pole. "Since you're such a confident man, why don't you just show me the ropes on this caber game."

Duncan fixed his adversary with a stony glance. "Toss, mon. Caber *toss*." He straightened. "It's a test of strength and mettle, not a game."

Connor made no reply. He merely fixed the other man with an amused glance.

Duncan's eyes narrowed, and he tilted his head toward an open area in front of the cabin. "Head that way," he said between clenched teeth.

Connor complied, and he could hear the Scot muttering under his breath the entire way. The grin that split Connor's face was one of pure relish.

"Hello? Anyone want to hear my opinion of this little event?" Taylor asked in even, deliberately controlled tones. "Anyone even care that I'm alive?" When neither man responded, she turned with a furious huff, stomped over to pull open the door of the truck, climbed into the seat, and closed the door with a satisfying slam.

The sound of the slamming door brought another grin to Connor's face. Ooooh, she wasn't happy at all. But that was okay. More than okay, since it meant Duncan's inopportune arrival was a source of irritation for her. Why exactly that

128

should delight him so, Connor wasn't prepared to analyze. All he knew was that he didn't care for the Scotsman's proprietary air where Taylor was concerned.

"Well, are you ready?" Duncan asked.

"As I'll ever be. You show me how it's done, and I'll follow suit."

Duncan gave a brusque nod, then moved so his back was to the cabin. "Set your end of the pole down, then," he said.

Connor did as instructed and stepped back. Duncan walked forward, pushing the pole, which was a good two feet longer than he was tall, up on end in front of him. That done, he crouched, slid his hands beneath the end of the pole, blew out a few deep breaths, then stood, lifting the pole with his hands cupped beneath it.

Leaning one shoulder into the timber to keep it balanced in front of him, Duncan shuffled his feet quickly, as though dancing with the pole. Then, in one smooth motion, he did a knee bend, tensed, and straightened quickly, throwing his arms up and forward and launching the pole in front of him. The pole rose in a graceful arc, did a complete flip, and landed squarely on its end. It shuddered, then fell with a resounding thud.

"Aye!" Duncan exclaimed, brushing his hands with a proud smile. "Now that was a toss to be proud of!"

"So let me get this straight," Connor said. "You lift and toss the pole so it goes end over end and lands square."

"That's it," Duncan said. "Think you can handle it?"

"No sweat."

*Do not keep talking so proudly or let your mouth speak such arrogance!*

Connor frowned and dismissed the thought. There was no reason for that Scripture to be coming to him now.

*The Lord hates pride and arrogance.*

Connor's frown deepened as the two men walked to the pile, took hold of another timber, and made their way back to the field.

What they were doing wasn't pride or arrogance. They were just having a little fun.

*A wise man's fun is being wise.*

"Ready?" Duncan's question pulled Connor from his thoughts, and he hesitated. A quick, gloating gleam twinkled in Duncan's eyes. "Havin' second thoughts, are you?"

This time it was Connor's face that darkened. "Not a bit!" he exclaimed.

"Fine, then, off with you!" Duncan said, dropping his end with a flourish.

Connor walked forward, pushing the timber up on end. When he had it balanced, he crouched and slid his hands beneath the end as he'd seen Duncan do.

"Remember the rules of lifting, lad," Duncan cautioned. "Take the load with your legs, not your back. I'd hate to have to carry you back to the truck."

Connor didn't dignify the comment with a reply. Instead, he focused on the task at hand, regulating his breathing, tensing his muscles...one, two, THREE!

He stood, lifting the pole in his cupped hands. The weight bore down on his laced fingers and he clenched his teeth.

"Use your shoulder, mon!" Duncan instructed. "Don't let the caber get away from you!"

It was good advice. Unfortunately, Connor had no way of following it. The heavy pole swayed back and forth, then began to gain momentum and fall forward. Connor tried wildly to compensate, which only succeeded in bringing the timber back against his shoulder with too much force. He staggered, then started a wild backpedal as the pole fell backward, throwing him off-balance as it went.

"Throw it, Connor!" Duncan hollered, and with one fierce effort he tensed his muscles and launched the timber over his shoulder. The momentum of his action combined with that of the pole knocked him flat.

Connor slammed onto the hard earth, his head snapping back and smacking the ground with a sickening *thunk*. The air whooshed from his lungs, and he lay there, blinking, every inch of his body encased in pain, wondering when the stars had come out.

Vaguely he was aware of a crash, then voices.

"Connor? Con? Are you okay?"

Ah. He knew that one. It was a woman…her beautiful chestnut hair fell like a silken curtain across her face as she leaned down to him, her moss-green eyes filled with alarm.

"Give him room, lass! The man needs some air."

That would have to be Duncan. The one who got him into this mess. The one he'd have to kill…as soon as he could move again.

Slowly, painfully, awareness filled his mind and he was able to focus.

*A wise man's fun…*

He groaned, and then laughed weakly. "Okay, God, you win," he said, coughing. "You're right. It was a stupid thing to do."

"He's delirious!" Taylor said.

Connor laughed harder and rolled onto his side.

"Maybe you're right." Duncan's voice was filled with uncertainty, which only added to Connor's mirth.

"Maybe you should radio for a doctor—"

Connor cut Taylor off by raising a hand. "No," he managed between hoots of laughter and gulps of air. "No, just give me a minute. I'll be okay."

He pushed himself onto his hands and knees, and Taylor moved to slip her arm around his waist. As he stood, she pulled his arm around her shoulders, steadying him.

He looked down at her, amazed that someone so small and slim could be so strong.

"Well, your toss landed, true enough, Alexander," Duncan said.

Connor followed the Scotsman's gaze—and cringed. The timber was lying half in, half out of the cabin. It had gone through the front window as cleanly as an arrow shot from a giant's bow. Regret washed over him, then relief that neither Duncan nor Taylor had been hurt.

"Taylor, I'm sorry," he muttered.

"The cabin's not a big deal, Con." Her voice was husky with

concern, and Connor looked at her in surprise.

He started to straighten, to move away from her support. "I'm okay, Taylor," he assured her. Then a movement caught his eye, and he glanced behind her to catch a dark look of displeasure on Duncan's face. Connor quickly bit his lip to keep from grinning with delight. Oh, this was too good to be true. He wouldn't have to kill the man after all. He could have his revenge in a much more enjoyable way.

"Then again..." he said in a weak voice, and she tightened her hold on his waist. He sagged against her, leaning his forehead against the top of her head and speaking into her fragrant hair. "Maybe I do need some help after all."

Duncan sputtered and moved toward them, but Taylor didn't even notice. She moved toward the truck, still supporting Connor and making sympathetic sounds. He cast a waggish look over his shoulder at the Scotsman.

The sight of Duncan MacEwen standing there, looking ready to explode, almost made the whole escapade worth the pain he knew he'd be experiencing for the next week.

"What are you looking at?" Taylor asked, and he met her look, startled, feeling a guilty flush creeping into his face.

"Um, well..."

She glanced back over her shoulder, took in Duncan's stormy expression, then brought her eyes back to Connor. Before he could formulate a believable explanation, she stopped cold. Caught unaware, he toppled forward, landing again in a pile on the ground.

She stood over him, hands planted firmly on her hips, her face thunderous. "I was worried about you!"

"Taylor—"

"I knew if you were asking for help you must really be hurt!"

"I—"

"Forget it!" she snapped.

"Darlin'..." Duncan reached out to put his hand on her arm, but she shrugged him off, angry tears glimmering in her eyes. She pinned him with a glare. He fell silent, which Connor thought was remarkably wise.

She held out her hand to Duncan. "Give me your keys." He didn't even bother to argue—again, a wise move.

"In the ignition," he said.

She spun on her heel, stomped to the Blazer, and climbed in. As soon as the engine came to life, she threw the vehicle into drive and stomped on the gas. Gravel flew in all directions, and Connor and Duncan dove for cover.

"Well, laddie," Duncan said after a moment, "looks like we've got a window to fix."

"Aye," Connor said, standing up and brushing off his jeans. He watched the Blazer disappear around a hill.

*And that's just the beginning of the repairs I need to do,* he thought with a sigh.

# *Thirteen*

Donelle Camus was just starting to sip her tea when the kitchen door slammed open. She looked up with a start to see her daughter storm into the room, stomp over to a cupboard, and jerk a glass from the shelf. Muttering the entire time about "ridiculous louts," and "brainless dolts," she flipped on the tap, filled the glass with water, then spun around to stomp out of the room.

Raising her delicate eyebrows with interest, Donelle smiled complacently.

Ah, love. Wasn't it grand?

Later that evening, after a bath full of Epsom salts, Connor started to think he might actually be able to move again someday without grimacing in pain.

He dropped carefully into the oversized chair and leaned his head back. "I blew it, Lord," he said.

*Your words are truth…*

"Very funny," he muttered, recognizing the verse from 2 Samuel. Rolling his sore shoulders, he rested his elbows on his knees, then pushed himself out of the chair.

No point in putting this off any longer.

Taylor had just settled into her favorite chair and taken a sip of her hot chocolate topped with miniature marshmallows when the knock came at the door.

She looked at Sasha and pulled a face. "Guess who that is," she said. The knock sounded again. "He knows he's in trouble, so he won't come in until I open the door."

Sasha tilted her head, her ears perked, as a third knock sounded, this one a bit more forceful. Taylor leaned back in her chair, giving the husky a pondering look.

"What do you say, girl? Do we let him in?"

Sasha yawned, her pink tongue curling, and then lowered her head to her paws.

Taylor smiled. "I couldn't agree more," she said with satisfaction. She stood, went to the door, and, with a sharp twist of her wrist, threw the dead bolt. That done, she padded back to her chair, folded her slippered feet beneath her, and snuggled into the soft cushions.

*Take that, Alexander.*

Standing on the porch, Connor heard the dead bolt latch. He turned the doorknob, just to be sure he'd really heard what he thought he had. The door was locked.

"Fine! She doesn't want to talk, we don't talk!" he muttered as he turned and began to stomp back to his cabin.

"Well, I must admit I'm disappointed. You give up far more easily than I would have expected."

He spun around. Donelle Camus sat in one of the rockers on the porch, watching him with a bemused smile on her face. He knew he should say something polite, but he was too frustrated.

Her eyes filled with compassion. "I know, dear. She can be a bit trying." She frowned delicately. "Sometimes she gets a bit…well…dramatic."

Connor snorted indelicately, and she smiled.

"Yes, I can see you understand. Well, never fear. There are ways around that stubborn streak, which I'm quite certain she gets from her father."

Connor cocked an eyebrow, but he was no fool. No way was he going to argue the point.

She stood and took his arm. "Come along, Connor."

Wordlessly he let her lead him back to the front door.

"Stand right there, if you please," she said, giving him a gentle push so that he was off to the side of the door. Then she reached out and gave a quick knock and turned the doorknob. At Connor's surprised look, she smiled. "She knows I'd knock and just come in," she said. "To do anything different now would seem odd, wouldn't it?"

Before he could answer, Taylor's muffled, wrath-filled voice shot out. "Go away!"

"Taylor, it's Mom." She glanced at Connor and smiled serenely. "Why is the door locked, dear?"

Connor felt a grin break over his face as he heard scuffling inside, as though Taylor had bolted from her chair and hurried to the door. Within seconds, the dead bolt sounded and the door opened.

Taylor stood there, mortification on her face. "Oh, Mom! I'm sorry! I thought it was—"

"Thank you, dear," she said, reaching out one manicured hand to take hold of Connor's sleeve and pull him forward with surprising strength. "Connor needed to talk with you, and I simply couldn't believe you meant to lock the door."

Taylor stared at her mother, stunned. She began to sputter and protest as Donelle propelled Connor into the house.

"Have fun, you two," she said as she pulled the door shut.

As he stood there in the entryway, Connor could hear her bell-like laughter floating on the breeze.


Taylor was so angry she was shaking. Her own mother! A traitor!

She swiveled quickly, presenting Connor with her back, and returned to her chair.

"Taylor…"

She was not going to speak to him. Not a word.

"Taylor, please." He came to stand in front of her chair.

She stared right through him.

With a sigh he knelt in front of her, taking her hands in his. The touch of his hands sent an alarming jolt through her, and Taylor finally met his eyes. They were brimming with remorse. "Taylor, I was wrong. I'm sorry."

*Ohhhhh, he had to be sincere, didn't he?*

She let out her breath and sagged back in the chair, her hands still held captive. "You were both silly nits," she said.

He hung his head and nodded. "I know."

A smile twitched at her lips. "And you destroyed the window in the cabin."

"It's all boarded up, and as soon as we can get the glass, I'll go back and replace it." He raised his head and met her eyes with a slightly hopeful look.

"So that makes it okay?" she demanded, doing her best to maintain a stern voice.

"No. Not at all. But I believe you are a merciful woman—"

She rolled her eyes heavenward.

"—and you recognize true contrition when you see it." He gave her a hangdog look, his eyes wide and sorrowful, his mouth drooped and quivering, and she laughed. She couldn't help it. He really was appealing when he groveled.

"Okay, okay, you can keep your head," she conceded, and he bent forward to touch his forehead to her hands. Her breath caught in her throat and her heart felt as though it somersaulted.

"Thank you, milady."

He rose, and she leaned back in her chair. When their gazes met, the expression in his eyes sent her breathing haywire again.

"I discovered something interesting today," he said as he sat in the chair next to her. His low voice seemed to vibrate around her.

"Oh?" Not very original, but it was all she could muster at the moment.

He nodded, reaching out to take her hand. She wove her fingers into his, surprised—and yet not surprised—at how well their hands fit together.

"I don't like it when I hurt you."

The gentle words wrapped around her and sudden tears sprang to her eyes. *Father, what's happening here?* she wondered.

As though aware of her confusion, he released her hand and leaned forward, his gaze coming to rest on the old, leather-bound book that was open on the table in front of her.

"May I?" he asked, and she nodded.

"Looks like an antique." He turned the timeworn pages with great care.

"My grandfather's journal. I like to read through it. It's very soothing." She leaned forward and handed it to him. "He had a real talent for putting images down on paper. You can almost see his life taking place as you read."

He scanned the elaborate script, and she could tell by his rapt expression that he was soon engrossed. He settled back in his chair and continued to read.

*Amazing how comfortable silence can be with some people,* she thought as she curled her feet beneath her. Sasha stretched and yawned from her spot on the floor, and Taylor smiled in contentment. This felt good.

"Listen to this," Connor said, his voice filled with emotion. "'I did not understand this change of heart, this sudden affection some now claimed they felt for wolves. Could they not see these beast were killers? They cared not that they destroyed God's glorious creation? So I thought, until that day in the woods. I had laid my traps well, hopeful of capturing the killers. And my hopes were realized.

"'As I neared the line, I saw a gray mass, a furry form lying on the stark, cold earth. Good! I thought. And I hurried forward, anxious to see the end of such evil. I drew near, cautious. Ever I have believed the soul is reflected in the eyes, and so I determined to look into its golden stare, thereby to determine for myself that this was evil. And so I knelt. And so I looked. And what I saw chilled me to the core.

"'The beast lived indeed. And there, in those golden depths, I found such emotion! Confusion, pain, and the deepest of sorrow, sorrow so deep as to break the heart. And I understood, as though struck with a lance, that the sorrow was not for himself, but for me, for what I had become. I saw myself, reflected in those fading eyes. It was I who was evil. A killer. Cold-hearted. This majestic animal, this creation of the Almighty's hand, was not the beast. I was. God help me, I was. But by God's grace, I will never be so again.'"

They sat, silent, absorbing the words, and Taylor's heart all but melted when she saw tears reflected in Connor's eyes.

"Wow," he whispered. "Talk about a revelation."

Taylor nodded, her throat choked with emotion. "From that day forward my grandfather did all he could to preserve the wolves." Hopelessness swept over her. "Not that it did any good. But he tried." She stood abruptly and went to stare out the window, looking through the darkness toward Reunion.

Were her wolves safe? Was there a pack? Were they healthy? Would they suffer the same fate as the wolves her grandfather tried to save?

She heard Connor move, felt him come to stand beside her. "That's all any of us can do, Taylor. Try." He slid a comforting arm around her shoulders, and she leaned against him.

They stood in silence—until Taylor felt a shiver travel down her spine. There it was again! That sense of being watched.

"Cold?" Connor asked, but she shook her head and looked at him.

"Have you ever felt as though someone was...out there?"

He raised a dark eyebrow. "'Out there'?"

"You know," she turned from his slightly confused expression to look toward the dark window again. "Watching." She wrapped her arms around herself. "It's the oddest thing, but ever since Josh's death, I have times when I get the distinct feeling there's someone, just beyond my line of vision, watching me." Good heavens. She sounded positively paranoid! She gave an uneasy laugh. "Who knows, maybe I've got a second shadow."

Thankfully, Connor didn't make a joke. His eyes were serious as he looked down at her. "Does it frighten you?"

She nodded slowly. "Sometimes." She let the admission out hesitantly. "It's unsettling, I guess. If I knew who it was—"

"Assuming there's really anyone there," he added quietly.

She inclined her head. "Okay, assuming it's something more than my too-active imagination, it would be nice to know it's a friendly shadow."

He turned to peer out the window. "Seems to me if it wasn't, you would have known by now."

The thought surprised her—mostly because it rang true. She'd been feeling this way for over a year, and yet nothing—and no one—had ever threatened her. She bit her lip thoughtfully. "I hadn't considered that."

His smile was quick and easy. "Who knows, maybe what you've got out there is a guardian angel who's new at his job and still needs to learn how to be undetectable."

She laughed, oddly comforted by the idea. "Now *that* would figure. A rookie guardian angel." She nodded. "Well, why not? I suppose I'd be a good case for an angel to cut his wings on, wouldn't I?"

"You'd definitely be a challenge," he said, his eyes twinkling with warm amusement. "But a delightful one."

She looked down, her face growing warm with confusion. She was surprised—and a bit disturbed—at how good his comment made her feel.

"Well," he said, stepping back, "I'd better get some rest. My boss is a regular slave driver. Believes in starting the day at the most unearthly hour."

She grinned. "Terrible the things a working man has to suffer."

"Indeed," he said. "But it's really not all that bad."

"Oh?"

He shook his head, moving closer to her again. "Nope," he said, his eyes roaming her face. "It's not bad at all." He reached one long finger to tilt her chin. "Because she's got the most amazing…" he lowered his head, his warm breath fanning her face.

*He's going to kiss me!* Her eyes widened in startled amazement, and an alarming thrill shot through her.

"Cook," he finished, pressing his lips, with feather softness, to her forehead. Then he stepped back, walked to the door, and left.

She stood frozen to the spot, a bemused smile on her face. *I wonder...*she thought with a sigh. *I wonder if guardian angels are tall and broad-shouldered and have smiles that can melt your insides?*

# Fourteen

❦

Connor grunted as he hefted a large sack of grain from the bed of the truck onto his shoulder.

"Need some help?" a voice from behind him asked. He turned to find Luke Narbona sitting in one of the rocking chairs on the front porch of Taylor's house.

"Sure," Connor answered with a grin. "I never turn down an extra pair of hands."

Luke rose slowly, his gaze resting on Connor in a way that made him feel like a bug under a magnifying glass. Of all the people he'd met at Galloway Glen, Luke was the greatest mystery. The older man had kept a close eye on Connor from the day he'd arrived, but he seldom spoke. He didn't even return Connor's greetings when they encountered one another.

Connor was at a loss as to what he'd done to incur Luke's dislike. Which made the older man's offer of help that much more surprising. And interesting.

Connor carried the bag into the barn and dropped it near the feed bin. As he turned, Luke came in with another bag and dropped it next to the one on the ground. As the Navajo straightened, their glances met and held.

The air was thick with a tension Connor didn't fully understand. He waited. If Luke had something to say, he wanted to give him the chance to say it.

After what seemed like an eternity, Luke said, "Taylor is the closest thing to family that I have."

Connor nodded. "I've seen that."

"I won't stand by and watch anyone hurt her."

Connor nodded again. "If she were my friend, I would feel the same way."

Luke's dark eyes studied him, and then he nodded brusquely. "We understand each other," he said.

"I believe we do," Connor agreed.

"Good. Then let's get to work. That truck won't unload itself."

Connor watched thoughtfully as Luke walked from the barn and back toward the truck. Well, it wasn't exactly a declaration of friendship, but it was as good a place as any to start.

Connor was hard at work later that day, shoveling out the stalls, when he had the sensation he was being watched.

He turned, half-expecting Taylor's guardian angel to be there, and found himself looking at two boys who were exact replicas of one another, from their strawberry-blond hair and bright blue eyes to the smattering of freckles dancing across their noses and cheeks. One of the two stepped forward, gazing up at him with large, solemn eyes. Connor guessed him to be about ten.

"Hi," Connor said, smiling.

The boy returned his smile. "Hi. Are you the crazy loon Dad says has come to work with Aunt Taylor?"

"He doesn't look crazy," the second boy said, and his twin shot him a disdainful look.

"Well, course not. You can't tell someone's crazy just by looking at them." He turned back to Connor, studying his face intently. "Least, I don't think you can."

"Did your father happen to mention exactly why he thought I was crazy?"

The boy nodded vigorously. "Uh huh. He said anyone—"

"Any *man*," his twin corrected, stepping up beside his brother.

The more talkative twin glared at him. "Don't innerupt, Mikey. You know it's not p'lite."

Connor had to look away to hide his sudden grin. The boy's haughty expression and tone were perfect imitations of Donelle Camus, who Connor was willing to bet was this dynamo's grandmother.

"Anyway," the boy said, turning back to Connor, "Dad said any man who was willing to spend every day, day in and day out, being bossed around by Aunt Taylor had to be crazy as a loon."

"An' if he wasn't, he soon would be!" Mikey piped up.

Connor bent over and whispered conspiratorially, "If I tell you a secret, can you keep it?"

Two blond heads inclined toward him; two pairs of blue eyes widened in anticipation. "Sure!" they chorused.

He looked left, then right, then whispered, "It's not that bad."

They looked at him, searching his face as though to determine if he was being honest, then Mikey nodded, a grin breaking out over his face. "I told you so, Mark. I told you Aunt Taylor would be fun to work for."

"Well!" Connor laughed. "I don't know that I'd go *that* far!"

"So you want some help?" Mark inquired.

Connor raised an eyebrow and nodded toward the stalls. "You'd be willing to help with this?"

"Sure, we do it all the time," Mikey replied, going to pull a shovel from the wall hanger. Mark followed suit.

"Right. Dad keeps tellin' us it will help prepare us for what we have to face when we're adults."

Connor's lips twitched again, but the boy's words were so serious and sincere, he kept as straight a face as he could. "I'd say you've got a pretty smart dad," he said, going to join the boys who were already tackling adjacent stalls.

By the end of the afternoon, Connor had two devoted followers. The twins trailed after him from job to job, always willing to lend a hand, always wanting to talk about their Aunt Taylor.

Connor enjoyed listening to them, not only because they were entertaining, but because he learned more about Taylor in that one afternoon than he had the entire two weeks he'd been at Galloway Glen. As they followed Connor to the ranch house in response to the supper bell, the twins finally ran out of revelations about their aunt, so they launched into an animated recounting of the wilderness trip they'd just taken with their father and grandfather.

Connor was still listening and laughing as they entered the kitchen.

"Okay, you two, give the man a break," said a tall cowboy seated at the table.

Connor grinned. "Let me guess, the Marlboro man, right?" he said, and the man laughed.

"Only if I want to receive a sound dressing down from my mother." He cast an affectionate glance at Donelle, who sat across the table from him, then stood and extended his hand to Connor for a firm handshake. "I'm Ryan Camus. And I take it you're our new ranch hand, come to take on all the work we don't want to do."

"Something like that," Connor responded good-naturedly.

Seated next to Donelle, his arm draped across the back of her chair, was an older version of Ryan. He, too, stood and offered his hand to Connor.

"Hey, Grandpa!" Mark chirped, going to perch on the kitchen counter. "This is Mr. Alexander. He's not crazy at all."

"Yeah, Dad," Mikey said, tossing his father a superior look. "He's as normal as you are."

"Poor man," Taylor's father muttered, then introduced himself. "Holden Camus, Mr. Alexander. Welcome to Galloway Glen."

"Thanks," Connor said. "It's been a pleasure so far."

"Uh-huh, right." Ryan's grin was broad and knowing. "I can't think of anything more pleasurable than being bossed around by Taylor—"

"As though anyone would believe you could think," came

the teasing retort from behind him, and Connor glanced up to see Taylor sauntering into the room. He stared at her, taking in the picture she made, and suddenly found he was having trouble breathing. She was surrounded by her family, and happiness glowed in her eyes, giving her a radiance that seemed to shimmer around her. Her high, exotic cheekbones were tinged with pink, and her easy laughter rippled through the air. Connor found his gaze drawn to her lips, which were relaxed and smiling. She was stunning. Gorgeous.

*What I wouldn't give to have a woman look like that because of me,* he thought in wistful amazement.

"Are you okay, Mr. Alexander? You look like you swallowed a bug."

There was a moment of silence following this concerned proclamation from Mark, then the room exploded with laughter. Connor shook his head, smiling wryly, and his eyes met Taylor's for a moment.

A spark flew between them—a surge of awareness—and the pink on her cheeks deepened to a dusty rose. She looked away and went to hug her father, while Connor moved to take a chair as Donelle got up and began setting food on the table.

The meals with Taylor and her mother had always been enjoyable, calm affairs. Not so this particular dinner. Things started out calmly enough, with everyone holding hands and Taylor's father offering the blessing, but the moment the "Amen" was over, everyone launched into animated discussion. It quickly became clear to Connor that every member of the Camus family was blessed with a quick wit and a clever tongue. Yet underlying the teasing and jesting was a warm, deep affection. These people truly loved and respected each other.

Connor found himself struggling with a lump in his throat. His childhood had been fairly typical: hard-working parents who spent whatever time they could with their only child. But what he saw around this dinner table was something remarkable, something rare. And he was grateful he was getting to share in it.

*I wonder how welcome you'd be if they knew what you were really up to?* The thought struck at him, dimming his enjoyment of the nonstop chatter around him. The food, which had tasted so good only a second before, now tasted like sawdust. He took a long swallow of water, then set down his fork.

"Well," he said with forced cheerfulness, "time for this working boy to get some shut-eye."

They tried to coax him to stay longer, but he just smiled, shook his head, and made his way out the door.

*I hate this, Father,* he thought angrily as he walked toward his cabin. *I hate deceiving such good people.*

"Connor?"

He paused, then turned. Taylor had followed him out. She walked up to him now, concern in her green eyes.

"Are you okay? You seemed…well, you just left so suddenly." Her cheeks flushed slightly and she shifted uncomfortably. "I don't want to pry," she said quickly. "I was just…uh, well…" She shook her head impatiently. "Oh, never mind."

Before she could spin and hurry away, he put out his hand and caught her arm gently. She stopped, and those beautiful eyes came to rest on his face again.

"Thanks," he said softly, his heart pounding a rapid beat in his chest. "I'm fine. I just need some time alone."

Her expression softened with understanding. "They can be a bit much, I suppose."

He shook his head in quick denial. "Not at all. I think your family is amazing. I haven't enjoyed a meal that much in ages."

The smile that lifted her features warmed him from head to toe. "They are pretty wonderful, aren't they," she said with an infectious giggle.

"They really are," he said, gazing at her, filled with a sudden, intense longing to reach out and pull her close. Instead, he settled for lifting one hand to smooth an errant wisp of hair from her face. "And so are you."

Her eyes flew to lock with his, and he saw a multitude of emotions reflected there: surprise, awareness, pleasure. She bit her lip, and he smiled, tracing the line of her face with tender fingers.

Leaning forward, he brushed a gentle kiss across her lips—at least, that's what he intended to do. But it seemed so right when his mouth touched hers that he moved forward, slipping his arms around her, cradling her against him.

She fit in his arms perfectly. Like she was made for him. And the realization sent his emotions reeling. When he finally raised his head, he felt dazed, as though he'd been spun in circles and turned upside-down. He looked down into her face. From the look in her eyes, she was in much the same condition. She didn't move, didn't step away; she merely looked up at him with a faraway smile—and a sharp pang of guilt pierced him. What was he doing? He didn't have the right to do this!

Self-loathing filled him, and he stepped back, dropping his arms to his sides. The look of startled confusion on Taylor's face only compounded the accusing voices hammering at him from within.

"I'm sorry, Taylor," he said hoarsely. "I—" He broke off.

What could he say? *I shouldn't have kissed you because you don't really know me? I don't deserve to have you care about me because I'm not who you think I am?* How about simple and to the point. *I'm a liar. I'm only here for the wolves. I'm using you.* Clenching his teeth, shaking his head helplessly, he took another step away from her.

"Good night," he croaked, then he turned and walked away into the darkness.


Donelle leaned against the sink, watching out the kitchen window, her face furrowed with concern.

"If you caught one of the kids spying on someone, you'd have their head," her husband's voice came from behind her. She turned and went to sit beside him.

His eyes roamed her face. Then he leaned forward to touch her cheek tenderly. "Trouble in paradise, love?"

She nodded. "I'm afraid so." She shook her head, puzzled. Something just wasn't making sense. "Holden, it's painfully clear that those two are drawn to each other."

"And?"

"And though they haven't known each other long, it feels right for them to be together. There's just something about Connor Alexander..." her voice trailed off, and she put her elbows on the table and rested her chin in her hands. "I'm certain he's trustworthy. But I get the oddest feeling that—"

"That he's hiding something?"

Her eyes met his in surprise. "You think so, too?"

He nodded. "At the beginning of dinner he was fine. In fact, I think he was enjoying himself. Then, just before he left, it was as though a cloud passed over his face."

"Exactly!" Donelle agreed, relieved it hadn't just been her imagination. "He looked upset, almost angry. And then he left."

Holden leaned back in his chair. "So, what if it's true. What if he is hiding something?"

"I don't know. I haven't any idea how we could find out."

"Well, I'm certainly not Sam Spade, and neither are you."

Donelle's lips twitched. "Sam Spade? Good heavens, dear, you're dating yourself."

"I'd far rather date you," he replied, reaching for her hand.

She entwined her fingers with his, loving the warmth and familiarity of his clasp. He leaned forward, brushing a gentle kiss across her lips.

"It will work out, my love. We've seen God's protective hand at work in Taylor's life more than once. He's not going to stop now."

She smiled in gratitude, and they bowed their heads, taking their concerns and confusion to the One they knew could make all things right.

*I am such a fool.*

The thought kept going through Taylor's mind as she got ready for bed, her movements stiff, almost mechanical. She felt like a spring that had been wound too tightly—ready to come completely, totally undone.

Tears threatened, but she refused to cry. She'd given all the tears she intended to give for Josh. No one else was going to get them. Her heart had closed itself off the day Josh died, and she had no intention of letting it open again. No one else was getting in, no matter how tantalizing he might be.

*Liar,* the voice in her head mocked. *Liar. He's already there.*

"No," she whispered, startled at the agony in her voice. "No!" she said again, more firmly, swallowing the lump of painful emotions. She dropped onto the bed. Pulling her knees to her chest and circling them with her arms, she buried her face.

*You believed what his eyes were saying. You wanted to believe he cared.*

"No." She saw again the look in Connor's eyes as he stepped away from her after kissing her...repulsion, disgust, rejection.

*You trusted him. You let him in.*

"No," she repeated, not even aware she'd lost the battle with humiliation and pain and that hot tears coursed down her cheeks. All she knew was that tomorrow would be different. Tomorrow she would remember her vow, and her heart would remain safely closed.

No one—not Connor Alexander with his tantalizing smile, not Duncan MacEwen with his assurances of friendship, not Brad Momadey with his burning, haunted eyes—was going to hurt her again.

# Fifteen

W ylie Marsten, you're a thief of the first order."

Wylie laughed and rang up the purchase. "Maybe so, MacEwen, but since I own this general store and I'm pretty much the only game in town, I guess that means I can make the rules. Now, hand over your wallet."

Duncan grinned and did as Wylie commanded. As the older man pulled the appropriate bills from the wallet, Duncan thought again of Taylor.

He'd called her to see if she wanted to come to town with him, but she'd told him she and Connor had already been to town. To say he'd been less than pleased would be an understatement. Connor Alexander was becoming a definite nuisance.

Duncan hoisted his bag of groceries and headed for the door, only to run headlong into two small torpedoes as they burst through the door.

"Oops!" Mark Camus exclaimed, stepping back to give the Scotsman a sheepish look. "Sorry, Duncan!"

"Yeah, sorry," Mikey echoed.

"No problem, lads. It's clear you were on a mission of great importance."

Two heads nodded vigorously. "We're buying supplies for Mr. Alexander!" Mark said.

Duncan's lips thinned. Alexander again! "Are you, now?" he asked, trying to keep his tone amiable.

"Yup!" Mark said, turning to glance at the aisle with hand tools. "And we gotta hurry, 'cuz if we get back soon enough he's gonna show us how to build a birdhouse."

"Is he, now?" Duncan said, but his dry tone was lost on the boys. They just beamed up at him.

"Isn't Mr. Alexander the best, Duncan?" Mikey said, adoration evident in his young eyes.

"He sure is," Mark echoed, grabbing his twin's sleeve and tugging him toward the tool shelves. "C'mon, Mikey, I don't want to be late."

They drifted away, and Duncan walked out of the store, an oddly sour taste in his mouth.

"Aye, he's just a peach of a man, I'm sure," he muttered through clenched teeth. "A true gem! Why, it should be an honor that the fine Connor Alexander is tryin' to steal my woman!" He pulled open the door of his Blazer with a fierce motion, tossed his package inside, then slammed the door.

He leaned against the door with a disgruntled air and stood there, thinking. Just what exactly did he know about Connor Alexander? The longer he thought, the deeper his frown grew. Realization dawned, and suddenly he straightened.

He didn't know much. Not much at all. And that just wasn't acceptable. Duncan had learned long ago that the only way to deal effectively with an adversary was to know all you could about him. He turned and started down the sidewalk. It was time to pay a friendly, unofficial visit to his deputy friend, Amos Erdrich.

And maybe he'd just ask Amos to do some friendly, unofficial checking on Mr. Connor—"the best"—Alexander.

# Sixteen

The answer to Donelle's prayers came much sooner than she'd anticipated. Oh, she'd believed God would answer, but she'd never dreamed he would do it so quickly—or in such an unexpected way.

It happened several mornings later. Donelle had decided to spend the morning in bed, getting caught up on her reading. She had just settled under the covers, her tea on the bedside table, a pile of magazines stacked beside her. She was thumbing through the pile, trying to decide which one to read first, when a cover caught her eye.

It was a wildlife magazine, one of her favorites. The articles almost always presented a balanced view of the issues, which she greatly appreciated. On the cover of this particular issue was a stunning picture of a timber wolf. The title of the article, which was printed on the cover in big bold letters, was, "Wolf: Victim or Villain—or a Little of Both?"

She arched her eyebrows. That was certainly a timely topic, considering the ever-increasing debates among their friends and neighbors regarding the rumored return of wolves to the area. She flipped open the magazine to the page indicated in the contents, settled back in her pillows, and began to read.

Soon she was absorbed, caught in the writer's skillful work

and the beautiful photographs accompanying the article. When she finished reading, she turned back to the first page of the article. Suddenly her eyes widened slightly, and her mouth opened into a silent "Oh."

She laid the magazine down and leaned back against her pillows, closing her eyes, a gentle smile dancing across her lips.

*Thank you, Father,* she prayed. Her heart overflowed with both gratitude and understanding. *You are a wonder.*


Connor wanted to hit something. At the very least, he wanted to go someplace isolated and remote and scream his lungs out.

Since the night he had kissed Taylor, she had treated him as though he had some contagious disease. Or as though he *were* one. Oh, she continued to work with him, even beside him from time to time, but in almost complete silence. Any conversation with her was stilted and awkward. She answered his questions with curt responses and seldom met his eyes. The easy camaraderie they'd shared had vanished as quickly as snow in August.

It was driving him crazy. At first he'd refused to believe her reserve could last. But it had been four days now and, try as he might, he couldn't break through the wall she'd erected around herself. Couldn't even chip it.

Today, she was holding the ladder as he climbed to remove storm windows from one of the cabins and replace them with screens. He'd already made several efforts at conversation, and she'd squelched them. Well, he wasn't done yet. If the subtle approach wasn't going to do the trick, then he'd just have to be more direct.

"Where do you keep your rifles?" he asked and felt a flash of satisfaction when she looked at him with a startled expression.

"I beg your pardon?"

"Your rifles." He kept his voice light, unconcerned. He handed her a window, then took the screen she lifted to him and turned to the window. "I mean, I figure you keep them in the house." He snapped the screen in place, fastened it, and started down the ladder. "I was just wondering in which room."

"They're locked in a cabinet in the den," she said, clearly confused. "Why?"

He lifted the ladder and walked to the last window, where he set the ladder in place with a great deal more precision than was necessary.

"Connor," she said as he took the screen from her. Her voice had grown just a bit testy. That was fine. Anything was better than that inaccessible, remote tone she'd been using.

"Connor," she repeated, temper clearly rising. He snapped another screen in place, his back to her, and indulged in a slight smile. Her rigid control was slipping.

"Connor Alexander!" she finally exploded. "Will you kindly answer my question?"

"Hmmm?" he asked, giving her a bland look as he made his way down the ladder. "Did you ask me something?"

She planted herself directly in his path, her expression murderous, her hands on her hips. Her eyes were burning with frustration, and the color in her cheeks had heightened from a slight pink to an exasperated red.

Now this was more like it! His stormy, exhilarating Taylor was back, for the moment at least. It was all Connor could do not to laugh out loud with relief.

"You know very well I asked you why you wanted to know where I keep my rifles!" she snapped.

"Oh," he said mildly. "That. No reason, really." *Other than getting a rise out of you, that is,* he thought with satisfaction. He stepped around her deftly, heading for the barn. "I'll put the ladder away." He let his grin loose now that she couldn't see him.

But suddenly she was there, in front of him, her narrowed eyes glowing with a dangerous light. "How dare you turn your back on me!"

He jerked to a halt, taken aback by the fury in her tone. "Taylor—" he began, but she wasn't having any of it.

"How dare you treat me this way! I thought we were becoming friends. I thought—"

She broke off abruptly, and at the catch in her voice, he set the ladder down and took a step forward.

Immediately she backed away. "Don't!" The desperate sound of the word froze him in his tracks. "Don't you dare come near me," she hissed. "And from now on, *Mister* Alexander, keep this in mind. When I ask an employee a question, I expect an answer."

Her tone was clearly insulting, clearly condescending, and Connor's anger ignited in response. "Is that so, *Mrs.* Sorensen?" he asked in carefully measured tones.

"Unless, of course, you have a problem with that," she said, her voice tight.

He started to respond, but she cut him off. "Because if you do, then maybe it's time to find yourself another boss."

He stared at her, his eyes blazing. "Actually, Mrs. Sorensen," he said with a deceptively mild tone "I don't have a problem with your request." He took a step closer bringing them almost nose to nose. "However I do have a problem with you."

He wasn't sure what kind of response he'd expected—a kick to the shins wouldn't have surprised him—but what happened next did. She met his glare and held it for several seconds. Then a sob caught in her throat, and suddenly there were tears running down her face. She whipped around and fled from him, as though running for her life.

Everything within him screamed to follow her, to stop her and work through what had happened between them...not just today, but over the past few weeks. He wanted, needed, to understand what she was feeling. What *he* was feeling. But now was not the time. He had to give her a chance to recover, to get her emotions under control.

And then he had to tell her the truth.

So he stood there, watching her run, and as the sound of her sobs drifted back to him, his lips compressed into a thin line. *The deceit ends here, Lord,* he vowed. *Tomorrow I tell her why I'm here. It's up to you where it goes from there.*

He put his hands in his pockets and walked toward his cabin. *She'll probably hate me,* he thought glumly. *I wouldn't blame her if she told me to pack my bags. If she does, I'll just have to respect her wishes.* He dropped into one of the old-fashioned rocking chairs outside his cabin door and stared up at the sky. *I can do that, Father. I can leave. This is nothing more than an assignment. If I fail, I fail. Regrettable, but not the end of the world.*

He believed the reassurance, was convinced it was true. So he found it especially confusing, and irritating, that the thought of losing Taylor left his throat dry and his heart constricted with sudden, blinding fear.

# Seventeen

It was still dark the next morning when Connor emerged from his cabin. He rolled his aching shoulder muscles gingerly, stretching his neck one way and then the other as he walked. The dull pain that rewarded every movement brought a grimace to his face.

He'd spent most of the night tossing and turning, which hadn't improved his state of mind. Even Taylor's crack-of-dawn mom wouldn't be up this early, so there wouldn't be a warm breakfast to greet him.

*Please, God, at least let the coffee be brewing,* he thought wistfully.

He entered the still-dark kitchen and turned on the light over the sink. Glancing around, he spotted the coffee maker, already brewing a pot of the elixir of life, thanks to the timer Taylor had set.

*God bless your socks off, Taylor,* he thought with a grateful smile, starting to feel uplifted. God was, indeed, merciful. He sniffed the air appreciatively and rummaged in the cupboards for a mug. He finally found a "man-sized" one and set it on the counter, waiting impatiently. Coffee makers were never fast enough.

He eyed the filling carafe, then grasped the handle with one hand and held the big mug right next to it with the other. With one quick movement he whipped the carafe out from under the stream of coffee and replaced it with the mug.

*Didn't miss a drop,* he thought with a smug smile.

"Bravo, Connor. That was masterfully done."

He turned in surprise to find Taylor's mother watching him from the doorway.

"Morning," he said sheepishly. "I, ah…I wasn't expecting anyone else up so early."

"Oh, I had some trouble sleeping last night," she replied. "Too much on my mind, I suppose. And you?"

"The same," he admitted. She nodded as though she understood. If only she did. He caught her glance at the rapidly filling mug he still held under the coffee maker. "Uh, it was taking too long…" his explanation trailed off when her face broke into an amused grin.

"Of course it was," she said, coming forward to set several magazines on the table. Her eyes twinkled with amusement. "Anyone knows that three minutes is far too long to wait for one's first cup of coffee."

"Actually," he admitted, as he switched the carafe back under the drip, "it was more like a minute and a half, since the pot was about half full."

She filled the cream pitcher from the carton in the fridge and set it, along with the ceramic sugar bowl, on the table.

"Either way, I agree. It was ridiculous to wait. Though my first preference is tea, I have suffered from the occasional taste for coffee. On such occasions, I find a mug works quite well."

"Ahhh," he said conspiratorially. "So you've done the same thing, eh?"

She looked at him around the edge of the cupboard door as she got down her own mug, and he almost burst out laughing at the mischievous gleam in her emerald eyes. For a brief moment Connor had the feeling he was looking into Taylor's green gaze.

"Let's just say that while I strive to be the very epitome of restraint and self-control, patience is not my strongest virtue," she said as she poured a mug of coffee from the now partially filled carafe, then came to sit next to him at the table.

He nodded, sipping his coffee. "I understand. Far better than I care to admit," he said with a low chuckle.

"Indeed?" she asked, watching him carefully. "So you share my struggle with impatience, Connor?"

He considered her for a moment, and the look in her clear eyes told him there was some vague undercurrent to the question. He inclined his head slightly.

"And do you struggle with other virtues as well?" His eyebrows shot up at the unexpected question, but before he could compose an appropriate response, she went on. Her tone was casual and relaxed, as though she were discussing something completely commonplace, like the weather. "I find that integrity can be most troublesome at times, don't you? Somehow it so often seems as though honesty is…well, risky, at best. Hazardous, at worst."

Connor shifted uncomfortably in his seat but kept his expression blank, trying not to look as though he were squirming.

"Isn't it odd?" she continued conversationally, cupping her mug with both hands. "For all that God directs us to use honesty, it's remarkable how much easier it seems to be to act with caution, perhaps even a touch of deception." Her gentle smile was filled with compassion, and he felt an unfamiliar heat in his face.

This couldn't be happening! He couldn't be sitting here blushing!

"Oh, not true deception, of course," she continued with amiable ruthlessness. "Nothing cruel or evil. Just a small, harmless deception, one in which the entire truth isn't told. That way, a person could—" she frowned slightly. "What *is* that term Ryan uses? Oh, yes! Scope out! That's it!" She regarded him triumphantly. "Not revealing hurtful or difficult facts might give one time to *scope out* a situation, to evaluate how those involved might react to the entire truth." She tilted her head and regarded him quizzically. "Don't you think so?"

"I suppose it's possible," he said slowly.

"Hmmm." She nodded thoughtfully. "Yes, I'm sure that seems wise, perhaps even kind, to most people." Her eyes met his, her look direct. "It is a shame we can't use such tools, isn't it? I mean, if we're to follow God's leading in our interactions with each other."

Connor was fairly certain this was how bugs felt when captured and skewered by entomologists. He'd never considered the practice unkind before, but if those insects felt a fraction as uncomfortable as he did, he would write his congressman tomorrow to stop the senseless suffering. He swallowed hard, trying to manage a feeble answer, but she didn't give him a chance. She just went on as though totally oblivious to the fact that she was driving darts of doubt and uncertainty deep into his conscience.

"I am thoroughly convinced that you are as devoted to honoring God as we are, Connor."

Her smile was positively beatific, and he floundered before the brilliance of that look. "I...well...Mrs. Camus..." he stammered, but the words died in his throat when she reached across to pat his arm gently.

"Of course you are. I can tell by your eyes. I know you understand, as I do, that it's best, easier even, to deal in the truth from the very beginning. There are no lies to remember, no fabrications to cover. No relationships to mend."

He felt as though a tidal wave of emotion had come crashing down on him, grinding him into the dirt. Chief among the sensations was a deep sense of regret. And shame.

"My," she said with a contented sigh, "this is good coffee."

He blinked, dumbfounded at the abrupt change of topic. His eyes narrowed slightly, and he studied her sweetly smiling countenance—and at that moment understanding dawned. Donelle Camus's wide-eyed innocence was merely a smoke screen. Beneath that guileless facade was the shrewd mind and well-honed instincts of an experienced hunter, one who recognized vulnerability and opportunity at a glance—and used them to perfection.

"Would you like more?"

The simple question hit him like a semi, and his eyes flew to meet hers. He cleared his throat with difficulty. "More?" he rasped.

She held up her mug. "More coffee?"

"Ah." He shook his head slightly, feeling entirely out of his league. This woman was a master. "No. Thank you. I…uh…I think I've had plenty." He pushed back his chair and went to set his empty mug in the sink. "I should be heading out, anyway. There's a lot of work to do, and I figure I can get a good bit done if I start before breakfast."

"Whatever you think is best," she said quietly.

He nodded curtly and started for the door.

"Oh, Connor."

He paused, his hand on the knob. He'd come so close. Two more steps and he'd have been gone. With a sigh of resignation he turned to face her. "Yes, Mrs. Camus?"

She rose and came to him, holding out the magazines she'd brought in with her. "I read the most interesting articles last night in a few of our wildlife magazines. I thought you might enjoy them as well."

He accepted the magazines and glanced at them—then stood there stunned, shaken. He recognized both of the magazines. Each carried an article on wolves. Articles he had written.

"I particularly enjoyed the articles on wolves. The author is quite good," she said quietly, and once again he met her eyes. He expected to see anger, accusation. Instead, there was only kindness. "His passion comes across clearly, as does his intelligence. He presents a balanced perspective on the issues. I daresay he would be most convincing in person, particularly if a person were already predisposed to his views." She smiled again, and the warmth of her expression enveloped him. "Or predisposed to the man himself."

He nodded wordlessly, unable to speak around the lump in his throat.

She patted his arm. "Now, off with you. As you've already said, there's a good deal of work waiting for you. And for me."

He turned and went out the door, the magazines clutched in his hands, his heart beating a rapid, pained rhythm.

Donelle turned and found her husband leaning in the doorway, his head cocked, a pensive smile on his generous lips.

"So, think you got through?"

"The issue isn't whether I've gotten through, dear," she said, going to the fridge and pulling the door open. "It's whether God gets through. And I'm sure he will. Connor merely needed a little push in the right direction."

She pulled a carton of eggs and a package of bacon off the shelf, balanced a loaf of bread and tub of butter on top, and stepped back, bumping the door shut with her hip.

"Hmmm," her husband said, his lips twitching.

"Oh, please, Holden. Don't 'hmmm' me!" She set the food down with a thud on the counter and turned her back on the love of her life.

"Yes, dear," he said, his smile broadening.

"I just couldn't sit there and watch this charade continue."

"No, dear." He moved from the doorway.

"But if I had told Taylor the truth about her 'handyman,' she would never have given him a chance to explain himself. I swear, I don't know *where* that girl gets her temper!"

"Yes, dear." The laughing response came from just behind her ear, and strong arms slipped around her waist and pressed her close. She sighed and leaned back against her husband, loving the warm familiarity of his embrace. He tucked her tight against him, resting his chin on the top of her head.

"She loves him, Holden. I don't think she even knows it yet, but I see it every time she looks at him. And I think he loves her."

"I think you're right," he said. "And I think you did the right thing."

Quick tears pricked Donelle's eyes, and she turned to slip her arms around her husband's still-trim waist. She buried her face against the soft flannel of his shirt.

"I want her to be happy," she mumbled, her words slightly muffled.

He reached out to tip her chin up. Their eyes met, and they smiled.

"As happy as God has made us," he agreed, kissing her softly, his eyes glowing. "You've done your part, my love. The rest is in God's hands. We need to wait and watch. He won't let us, or our girl, down." His eyes drifted to the counter, and he waggled his eyebrows at her. "Now, how 'bout some grub, woman? Your man is here and he's hungry!"

Thoughts raced through Connor's mind as he walked toward his cabin. He pulled the door open and went inside, flicking on the light and tossing the magazines on his bed. Then he sank into the overstuffed chair and leaned his head back wearily.

*God, I've messed this up royal,* he prayed, swallowing again the bitter reality that he was in a mess of his own making. *How do I make this right, Lord? How do I tell Taylor the truth without hurting her?* The image of her jade-green eyes, blazing with anger, floated before him. *O God, she's going to hate me. And I deserve it, Father. How can I find a way to be worthy of her trust…and the trust her mother just showed me?*

Silence answered him, and he stood restlessly, going to stare out the window. The sun was just beginning to peek over the mountains, its red glow coloring the sky in brilliant hues and tones. But the beauty was lost on Connor. His eyes focused unseeingly on the landscape, then came back to scan the room. He needed guidance, direction, something that would give him some glimmer of hope.

*God, I know you don't drop answers from heaven on a string, but could you give me a hand here?* The desperation in his muttered request surprised him, and a heavy realization cloaked him.

There was much more at stake here than the wolves. For the first time in years, the animals weren't his first concern. Taylor was. Though he was determined to protect the wolves, their importance paled when compared with hurting Taylor. He'd be angry, upset, disappointed if he lost the pack, but if he lost Taylor…

His reaction to that thought was even fiercer than it had been last night. It was frightening—and exalting. His heart thudded in his chest as the devastating truth hit him squarely: Somewhere between wanting to shake Taylor until her teeth rattled and discovering the wonder of who she was in all of her unpredictable, irrational, infuriating glory, he'd fallen in love.

He stared blankly around the room. He was in love. One side of his mouth twitched, then quirked up, as though drawn by an invisible string. *He* was in love. Suddenly he was sure of himself and his rightful place in the universe. He would go to Taylor and tell her how he felt. He'd fold her in his arms, cradling her against his chest, and gaze down into her beautiful face. And she would look up at him and…and…

He frowned. She'd look up at him and welcome his pronouncement of lifelong devotion with a sucker punch right in the gut, *that's* what she'd do!

"O Father," he groaned, raking his hands through his hair. "Father God, help me." He sat down on the bed with a defeated sigh and reached for his Bible. Then his eyes fixed on a small plaque on the wall just above the table.

Curious, his heart beating with an anticipation he didn't entirely understand, he moved closer and read the beautifully scripted words: "Do not let kindness and truth leave you; bind them around your neck, write them on the tablet of your heart. So you will find favor and good repute in the sight of God and man."

The words washed over him, easing the self-recriminations and anger he'd been allowing into his heart. He read the plaque again, then opened his Bible to the reference, Proverbs 3:3, and settled back against the pillows to read and to prepare.

Before the day was out, he would tell Taylor the truth.

# Eighteen

❦

Several hours later, Connor headed for the kitchen for the second time that morning. This time, however, he was filled with resolve and the confidence that everything would work out. He would trust in God and in Taylor and in the love he believed they shared.

He pulled the door open, walked in, then stopped in his tracks. Taylor sat at the table, deep in what was clearly a heated discussion with Duncan MacEwen. They looked up as he entered the room, and the expression on Duncan's face when he saw Connor could only be described as predatory. Warning bells sounded softly in Connor's head.

"Connor. I'm glad you're here."

At Taylor's carefully controlled words, the warning bells went from soft to blaring. Her eyes raked him, and he saw deep hurt and disbelief reflected on her face. His heart sank, and he knew that he wasn't going to have the chance to tell Taylor anything.

The Scotsman had done it for him.

"Duncan has the most interesting bit of information," Taylor said as Connor pulled out a chair and sat down. He drew a breath and met her eyes squarely, waiting. "It seems there's a gentleman who works for an organization, the Wildlife Awareness Coalition, I believe"—she glanced at Duncan and he nodded—"a wildlife biologist. He's a field representative, apparently. When Duncan spoke with a secretary at the organization, she said this man is on an assignment. Something to do with wolves in Wyoming. But the most interesting fact is that…he has the same name as you do."

Connor's gaze didn't waver.

"Duncan is sure this man is you. That you're here under false pretenses. That you weren't looking for a job at all, but for wolves. On Galloway Glen."

The slight tremor in her voice as she spoke those words pierced Connor. *Oh, Taylor…I'm so sorry.*

"He's right." His words were calm, steady, not giving any indication that they cost him everything.

Taylor's face drained of color. He started to rise, to go to her, but she held up a shaking hand, halting him. Her eyes, which had never left his face, now blazed with contempt.

He eased back into his chair. *Lord Jesus…please. What do I say?*

"I see."

He hadn't realized how cold—how dead—two words could be.

She rose from her chair and walked to the doorway of the kitchen. She paused for a moment, her back to him.

"I want you gone," she said. "As soon as possible. And I don't ever want to see you again." She spun back around, her eyes large and dark in her white face, and hurled words at him. "I *trusted* you! Believed in you! I even let myself care—" She broke off, closing her eyes against him.

And her heart. He knew it as surely as if he'd heard a door slam shut and a key turn in a lock.

She walked from the room, her back stiff and straight.

Connor sat there, silent, absorbing what had just happened. He wanted to hate Duncan, wanted to jump up and beat the man to within an inch of his life…but he couldn't deny the fact that all Duncan had done was reveal the truth.

Without giving the Scotsman a glance, Connor stood and left the house. He walked to his cabin, his steps slow and heavy.

He had lost her. Before he'd even had a chance to tell her he loved her.

He'd never felt so sick in his life.

Taylor sat in the living room, in her favorite chair, curled into a ball. Her face was awash with bitter tears.

*Stupid, stupid, stupid! How could you trust him? How could you trust anyone like that?*

Footsteps sounded behind her, and Duncan came to kneel in front of her. He looked into her face, searching.

"I was a fool," she said.

"No, Taylor. You were trusting. That's all."

"I should have known better. You can't trust anyone, not if you don't want to be hurt."

There was a flicker of emotion in his dark eyes. "Did he mean so much to you, then, lass?" he asked in a soft voice.

She couldn't answer. She closed her eyes against the tears that threatened to overwhelm her. Oh, yes. Yes, he'd meant that much to her.

A gentle touch on her face brought her attention back to Duncan, and when their gazes met, she saw sadness—and loss—in his mahogany eyes. Remorse swept over her.

"Oh," she whispered brokenly. "Oh, Duncan, I'm sorry. I didn't mean—"

He stopped her words with a slight shake of his head. "Taylor, it's okay." He took her hand in his, his gaze studying her face, taking in the feelings she couldn't hide. "It's sure you are then?"

Tears slipped down her cheeks. "I don't know. I wish I did. All I know is that he matters. A lot."

He sighed slowly, as though breathing were painful. "So. Your heart has chosen, lass."

His eyes were dark with emotion, and she wanted to reach out to him, but she couldn't. She was the source of his pain.

After a moment, he went on. "It's not exactly what I would have wished for, truth be known. But I trust God to lead you to the right decision." His expression grew more tender. "And the right man. If you're meant to be with me, you will be. But first I think you need to find out what this man really means to you. And you to him."

"I can't mean too much," she whispered brokenly, "otherwise he wouldn't have lied to me." A sob rose in her throat, and Duncan reached out to gather her close, cradling her against his broad chest. She leaned against him, giving in to the grief that washed over her in bruising waves.

"It's okay, darlin'," he said, his arms tight and protective around her. "It's okay."

But it wasn't. It couldn't be. Not when she had just sent away the man she loved. Despite his deceit, despite the sense of betrayal that swept over her, she could no longer deny what her heart had been telling her for weeks.

She was in love with Connor Alexander.

And it would never be okay again.

"Sasha, you idiot dog! Where are you!"

Taylor seldom got angry with the husky, but she couldn't hold back her irritation. Sasha *would* pick tonight of all nights to disappear. It wasn't enough that Connor was gone. Now the Siberian was as well.

*What do you want from me, God?* she wondered angrily.

She stomped out of the house, calling the dog's name, peering into the darkness. The moon was high in the sky, and the stars painted the gloom with twinkling light. Taylor stepped off the porch, moving toward the cabins. Maybe Sasha was with Luke.

She started to pass Connor's empty cabin, then paused. The door was ajar.

Her heart thudded in her chest at the possibility that Connor might still be there, and a sudden, wild joy surged through her. She moved forward, pushing the door open and turning on the light as she entered.

Sasha blinked at her from where she lay on the empty bed.

Keen disappointment filled Taylor, and she went to sit beside the husky, circling the dog's thick neck with her arms. As she buried her face in the dog's soft fur, she felt the tears begin again.

Prayer poured from her heart. For strength, for guidance, for understanding...and for Connor. And before she could stop herself, a plea slipped from her heart and flew heavenward.

*Bring him back, Father. Please, bring him back.*

# *Nineteen*

❧

The wind blew in warm gusts as the man trudged along, his traps dangling from his long, lean hands.

He had considered using poison instead of the traps, but that would risk killing other predators unintentionally. Besides, he wanted to be sure there was as little chance as possible that Sasha would become an unwitting victim. If he used poison, Taylor's beloved dog could be drawn to the scent of the meat. He shuddered at the thought.

No, the traps were safer. Less indiscriminate.

He set the traps, glancing around periodically, reassuring himself he was undetected. He'd done his best to ensure that Taylor had no idea what he was doing. When he knew he would be hunting the next day, he made it a point to talk with her, to find out where she planned to spend the coming day. Then he would give that location a wide berth. Just to be sure he wouldn't be recognized, he wore a handkerchief tied around the lower part of his face.

He'd been hunting the wolves for weeks, covering acre after acre of land on the ranch, watching for any small sign. But without the assistance of snow, it was a difficult proposition at best. Sometimes he stayed out all night, forcing himself to stay awake until dawn, listening, straining his ears for the faintest howl. But the sound had come only once since he'd first heard it, carried to him on the wind. He had guessed at its source, traveled there the next day, and found nothing.

No prints. No scat. Nothing that indicated wolves were—or ever had been—there.

He'd set out a line of traps, just to be sure. But he couldn't leave them out long, couldn't chance Taylor coming across them.

So far, when he retrieved the traps he'd set, he'd found them empty, mocking him, laughing at him for his ineptness. But let them mock. He would not give up.

One day his enemy would make a fatal error.

# Twenty

❧

Connor walked down the sidewalk, hammer in hand, flyers tucked securely under his arm. He had been posting the notices about the town meeting everywhere he could think of. Area stores had been surprisingly cooperative. As had the officials at the town hall.

When Connor had first phoned Harry to tell him of his failure, the older man's booming voice had reached out to reassure him. "Don't sweat it, buddy. There's more than one way to deal with this issue. If you can't find the wolves themselves, at least you can hold a town meeting to discuss the wolves and what's happening with restoration. Let the locals know we're aware of the reports, maybe make 'em a little less likely to take a shot if they happen to see a wolf. And you can give the ranchers a chance to air their concerns."

It sounded like about as much fun as a root canal. Connor knew he would be considered the enemy, the target for any shots from those who were angry or unhappy about the wolves. Still, Harry was right. It was a place to start.

So he went to the town hall, talked with the officials, and got their okay. Now all he had to do was post the notices. The meeting was set for Thursday night. That gave him four days to get ready.

He paused by a telephone pole, pulled out a flyer, situated the nail, and started pounding. He leaned back to survey his handiwork. The flyer was designed to catch attention. A large drawing of a wolf head was at the top, just below the words "PUBLIC NOTICE." A brief explanation of the purpose and topic followed, along with the date, time, and location. "Any and all are welcome to attend" was the final proclamation.

"So you're not hiding what you're here for any longer?"

Connor turned to find Duncan standing behind him, looking at the flyer. A brief jolt of anger shot through him, then it was gone. Duncan had only done what he thought was best for Taylor.

"I've had enough of coming in the back door, Duncan," he said quietly.

"As have we all," Duncan replied.

Connor inclined his head. He turned to leave, then paused. "Is…how's Taylor?"

Duncan's brows raised, and he regarded Connor in silence. Connor turned away. He hadn't really expected a response anyway.

"She's goin' on, livin' her life."

Connor winced. He'd hoped he would be harder to get over than that.

"But she's like a woman walkin' in her sleep."

Connor faced the other man, and the expression in the Scot's eyes made him pause. He'd expected the anger, though it was so intense he thought it would reach out and strike him. But what surprised him was the pain, deep and bruising, reflected in Duncan's dark eyes.

"I never meant to hurt her," Connor said.

"Aye, but hurt her you did," he replied harshly. "Deeply." His eyes hardened. "You've cost her dearly, Alexander. You've taken a heart that was wounded to begin with and cut it to the core. And it's like she's lost now, and can't get back from whatever cold, dark place her heart has taken her."

The words struck hard, and Connor closed his eyes.

"Aye, the truth is far from pretty, isn't it?" The bitterness in the Scotsman's voice slapped at Connor. "You see where your lies have brought you? What a pity you didn't go there alone. But you've taken Taylor along for the ride, mon. So the least you can do is face her and see this through to its conclusion, whatever that may be."

Connor opened his eyes. Was Duncan saying what he thought he was saying? "See it through?" he asked.

Duncan's voice snapped at him. "Believe me, if I had my way, you'd be run out of town and never allowed back. I'll do anything I can to keep Taylor from being hurt, to protect her. From you. Even from herself."

Connor's eyebrows arched. "From herself?"

Duncan's hard gaze never wavered. "If need be. Sometimes those you love are too close to something to realize it will hurt them."

"A bit arrogant, don't you think?"

A mirthless smile lifted the corners of Duncan's mouth. "Perhaps." The smile died. "But there are some things I can't protect her from. What I've seen in the past few days has made one fact painfully clear."

"And that is?"

"Taylor loves you. Or she thinks she does."

A disbelieving sound escaped Connor, and Duncan fixed him with a steely gaze. "You've been a fool once, Alexander. Don't be one again. Trust what I tell you, mon. It's true. And as much as it galls me to tell you so, you will have a chance to redeem yourself. I see it in her eyes." He gave a wry smile. "It won't be easy, by any means. But I'd count any trial worth the effort to gain a woman like Taylor Sorensen."

"Why are you telling me this?" Connor asked, fighting off the wild hope that was beginning to form deep within him.

"One reason, and one alone. Because I love Taylor and want her to be happy." The Scotsman moved to stand directly in front of Connor, his eyes narrowed. "I give you fair warning, though. Hurt her again and it's over. You won't get another opportunity. I'll do everything in my power to make her forget you. And I will succeed."

Connor held Duncan's dark gaze, and the hope he'd been trying to ignore suddenly flared to life within him. *Jesus, merciful Jesus, let him be right. Please give me the opportunity to make this up to Taylor.*

"I give you my word, I won't hurt her again. Not if I can help it."

Duncan stared at him a moment longer, then nodded curtly, stepped around him, and walked away without another word. But what he'd said rang in Connor's mind for the rest of the day, then echoed in his dreams during the night.

*"You will have a chance to redeem yourself…Taylor loves you…it won't be easy…any trial is worth the effort…."*

By the time he rolled out of bed the next morning, Connor knew what he had to do.

Taylor stood near the edge of the pool at Reunion, staring into the clear water.

"I miss you, Josh. I wish you were here to tell me what to do." The incongruity of her statement hit her and she grinned. "Of course, if you were here, none of this would be happening," she amended, "so I guess, in a way, it's all your fault."

She sat down, drew her knees close to her chest, and leaned her arms on them. "Thanks a lot," she muttered dryly. "You know, it was bad enough when you died, but this bit about falling in love again is really for the birds." She looked across the pool at the grass and the wildflowers. A tender smile crossed her face. "Funny thing is, I'm pretty sure you'd like Connor. You two are a lot alike." Tilting her head and resting her cheek on her crossed arms, she sniffed. "You're both funny, and sincere, and strong, and honest—"

She broke off, tears springing to her eyes. "Okay, so *you* were honest," she said in frustration, rubbing the wetness from her cheeks. "The least he could have done was tell me who he was! But he didn't even give me a chance. He just came in under false pretenses, and he made me believe in him and he made me love him…"—her voice was choked with tears. "Why couldn't he have been honest? Why did he have to let me down? Like you—"

She stopped, afraid of what she'd been about to say. But not saying the words didn't change what she felt—that Josh had let her down. He had promised to come back, but he didn't. She shouldn't have trusted...not Josh, not Connor, not anyone.

*Trust in the Lord with all your heart, and lean not on your own understanding.*

"I know, Lord, I know," she muttered. "But I can't."

*Can't...or won't, child?*

"I *can't!* I try! But every time I do, I remember that you let Josh die!" Her tears flowed freely now. "I asked you to take care of him! Asked you to bring him home. And you let him die. Why, God? For Brad Momadey? Then it was wasted. For nothing! Brad doesn't even care, Lord. He doesn't even care!"

The image of Brad's face—his eyes dark with torment, his cheeks drawn and pale—floated in front of her.

*Get rid of all bitterness, rage, and anger...be kind and compassionate...forgiving...just as in Christ God forgave you.*

"So it's my fault I can't trust?" Anger boiled within her. "It's my bitterness that's keeping me from trusting you?" She jumped to her feet. "I don't buy it, God. Brad killed Josh. And I'm not supposed to be angry?"

*Anyone who hates his brother is a murderer.*

She turned, wrapped her arms about herself, and lowered her head. "Then I am a murderer, Lord." The quiet words seemed to hang in the still air, and she knelt on the soft grass. "God," she whispered, "help me."

She knelt in silence, waiting, longing for release but unable to let go of the bitterness that had settled into her heart like a giant boulder. She was caught. Trapped. And unable to free herself. *Father, help me. I don't know how to get beyond this...how to let go. Help me.* Her mind felt congested with doubts and fears. And a haunting sense of loneliness. *Lord, are you even listening? Am I as alone in this as I feel?*

A soft sound came from behind her, and she turned, startled. "Oh!" she breathed in amazed wonder.

The wolf stood there, just across the pool, at the entrance to the cave. His ancient, golden gaze was fixed on her, looking for all the world as though he'd been listening to her words and her thoughts.

"Oh," she whispered again, delight filling her. "You're still here!"

He was as beautiful as she remembered. His powerful form and erect posture exuded authority.

"Hi," she said in a gentle tone, and the wolf's sharp ears turned toward her. "It's good to see you again."

As he stared at her with that tawny gaze, a sense of peace surrounded her, settled over her, and she smiled. She wasn't alone. Even here, in the midst of the wilderness, the Creator was present. And he had stamped his creation with such wonder—like this marvelous creature.

The wolf tilted his gray head as though studying her, then stood and paced back and forth several times, keeping his attention focused on her. He seemed to be telling her something, but she didn't have the vaguest idea what he wanted. When she didn't move, he suddenly sprang up into the air—as though his long, spindly legs were tightly wound springs—then came down again to crouch, his front paws extended out in front of him, his hind end up in the air. His long, bushy tail waved back and forth playfully, and Taylor had the distinct impression he was trying to coax her to cross the pool and come for a romp.

She giggled. "Okay, so you're a wolf," she said. "But that doesn't mean I can't consider you a friend." An idea dawned, and her smile broadened. "That's what I'll call you. Sikis. According to Luke, *sik'is* is Navajo for 'friend.' What do you think?"

The wolf stood, regarded her thoughtfully, waved his long tail back and forth, then turned and trotted into the cave.

Taylor laughed again. "I'll take that as a sign of approval." She rose and walked back toward Topaz, feeling lighter than she'd felt in days.

She wasn't free yet, but she would be. She didn't know how God would do it, but she believed he would, somehow, help her out of the hole she'd crawled into. All she had to do was wait and listen…and respond.

She swung into the saddle and turned Topaz toward home.


Several hours later, Taylor returned to the ranch, refreshed and relaxed. She walked Topaz into the barn, then slid from his back and removed the saddle with the ease of years of experience. The buckskin whinnied when the air hit his damp back, twitching his muscles happily.

"Feels good when the weight comes off, doesn't it, boy," Taylor said, grinning. She led the horse into his spacious stall, refilled his water and oats, then reached for the curry comb. She'd made a couple of long strokes when Sasha came bounding up, thrilled to see her mistress had returned from her ride.

"Well, hello there," Taylor said, scratching the dog between the ears. "You missed a great ride this morning. Where were you?"

"I'm afraid she was with me."

Taylor spun around, staring. A tall, male form was silhouetted in the doorway of the barn, but with the sun at his back she couldn't see his face. Still, she recognized the deep, resonant voice.

Connor.

As he drew closer, she saw that his face was gaunt and there were shadows beneath his eyes. He looked like he hadn't slept in a week.

Well, it served him right!

Indignant anger rose in her, and all thoughts of waiting and listening—to Connor or to God—were gone in a heated rush.

"Get off my ranch!" she stormed.

"Not until we talk."

She snorted in a most unladylike fashion. "Talk? You want to talk?" She stomped out of the stall, brandishing the curry comb like a weapon. "I don't think so."

"Taylor, I'm not leaving until you sit down and listen to what I have to say."

Her jaw jutted out stubbornly. "Do you seriously think I'd

believe you?" He winced, but she didn't care. "I know you'll say anything, *do* anything, to get to the wolves. Even romance me!"

His eyes blazed. "That's not true and you know it!"

"How should I know *what's* true with you?"

"Ask."

The quiet response took her by surprise, and she paused. *Ask? Just like that? Okay. Fine.*

"Why did you come here?"

"I saw your name on all the wolf books at the library. I figured anyone who was that interested had either seen the wolves or hoped to. Then I remembered seeing your name in the paper. When I found the ad, I knew where to start my investigation."

"I suppose you expect me to believe you care about me as much as you do the wolves?"

"I care about you a great deal more," he responded softly, "but I don't expect you to believe that right now."

"Smart man," she sniped.

"What I do expect you to believe is that I want to help the wolves. And I think you do, too." He stepped closer. "Please, Taylor, if you've seen them, tell me. I'll do my best to protect them. WAC will do everything in its power to do the same. None of us wants to put the wolves, if they really are here, at risk. I promise. You can believe me."

Sudden tears blinded her eyes and choked her voice. "Right. Just like I could believe Josh. You're all so quick to make promises you can't keep. Josh couldn't control the ledge he stood on. Do you think you can do any better with the ranchers? Well, I don't. And I don't know anything about your wolves, *Mister* Alexander. And even if I did, I certainly wouldn't entrust their care to you!"

"To whom, then? To you? You don't even know what you're doing! You've got some naïve notion that you can keep them safe, but I'd be willing to bet some of your fine neighbors have already come onto your land."

"My neighbors, unlike some people, can be trusted! They wouldn't trespass."

"Taylor, get real. The ranchers are as determined to kill these animals as I am to keep them alive."

"You're not touching my wolves!"

His eyebrows arched. *"Your* wolves? Taylor, if you keep going this way, you're going to get them killed! Have you ever seen a wolf in a trap? Or after it's been poisoned? Have you seen what some ranchers will do to a wolf to kill it? The tortures they inflict on it? Well, you will. Count on it. Unless you let me help."

His words struck home, but she refused to let him see the anxiety they had stirred within her. The image of her beautiful friend in pain, being mistreated, was almost more than she could bear. Anger joined with fear within her, and she gave willing vent to it.

"I have a better idea," she said sweetly. "Why don't you let *me* help *you*"—a quick, hopeful light sparked in his eyes—"get off my ranch?" She snapped her fingers at Sasha, who looked suddenly alert, and commanded, "Sasha, protect!"

The husky hesitated, looking from Connor to her mistress as though to say, "You're kidding, right?"

Taylor repeated the command firmly. "Sasha! Protect!"

Galvanized by the conviction in her mistress's voice, Sasha moved toward Connor, her usually benevolent features disappearing into a vicious snarl.

Startled, Connor took several steps backward. "What are—"

Taylor smiled smugly. "Say hello to a well-trained dog." She moved to stand next to Sasha, who continued snarling. Taylor's tone hardened. "Now get off my ranch."

Connor backed out of the doorway cautiously, moved to his Jeep, and slid inside.

"Sasha, release," Taylor murmured as Connor turned to look at her one more time before driving away. The husky immediately became her affable self and padded over to sit beside her mistress, looking up at her with curious eyes.

"Good girl, Sasha," Taylor said in a tear-choked voice. "You're a good girl." She stared after the Jeep, watching it grow smaller in the distance. "And you're extremely lucky that you're a dog and not a human." She turned to head for the house. "Believe me, it's not all it's cracked up to be."

# Twenty-One

Thursday night, Connor stood at the front of the high school auditorium, watching the townspeople come in and take their seats. His heart warmed when he saw Taylor and her family slip into seats at the back of the room. Even the sight of Duncan MacEwen sliding into the chair next to Taylor didn't bother him.

Whatever they thought of him, he considered them all friends. It helped to know he wasn't on his own here.

The turnout was decent. Thirty or forty people filled the chairs set up before him. Now if he could just get through the night without somebody shooting him.

The head of the town council introduced him, and he stepped up to the podium. "Thank you all for coming tonight. I hope you all feel free to take part. This is an open forum, and all questions or comments are welcome."

"Even 'Go home, Scumball'?" one man asked, and appreciative laughter traveled around the room.

Connor smiled good-naturedly. "If it gets the ball rolling, sure."

"C'mon, Frank. Give the man a chance."

Connor cast an appreciative glance at the middle-aged man who had spoken up.

"Name's Amos Winkler," the man said. "And I for one am interested in what you have to tell us, Mr. Alexander."

An older gentleman seated at the back of the room stood, his hat in his hands. "I have a question."

"Yes, sir?" Connor asked.

"I just want to know why this all matters so much to you people? This isn't your land. Or your livestock. You talk about 'reintroduction' and 'natural regulation,' but you keep coming out here and sticking your nose in where it isn't welcome." Sounds of agreement came from around the room. "Why can't you just leave us and the wolves be? Whatever comes of this will be plenty natural."

Another man jumped up. "I agree with Booth. I mean, what you people want to do is crazy, plain and simple! Bringing wolves into populated areas makes as much sense as bringing back smallpox! There just isn't enough natural prey around here to support bringing wolves back. You all talk about the 'wild ungulate populations' like they're unlimited. But those deer and elk have been replaced by livestock. *Our* livestock. Our livelihood! It's hard enough to make a living out here, without having to fight some crafty, four-footed killing machine that's got the government on its side! There just isn't any room here for wolves."

"Here! Here!"s and "Amen!"s rang out, and Connor nodded. "I understand your concerns, but I admit I'm a bit confused."

"You're a lot confused, son!"

Connor smiled placidly. "What I mean is, why do you think the ungulate populations are too small to support natural predators like wolves? When's the last time you went through Yellowstone in late February? There are records of more than 20,000 elk and 800 bison crowding the winter range in the northern part of the park."

"That's Yellowstone!"

"True enough, but if wolves are in this area, Yellowstone will be a part of their hunting range. And there are healthy herds of ungulates around here as well. What's more, unless the wolves learn to recognize livestock as prey, they generally don't seem to know what to do with them. Studies have shown they actually prefer their natural prey."

"What you're saying makes sense," Amos Winkler said. "But I think what people here really want to know is, what will happen if the wolves do kill our animals?"

Connor nodded. "That's a fair question. The Wolf Compensation Fund has been set up for a number of years now. It's been a dependable source of money for reimbursing ranchers who lose livestock to predation. If a wolf is found to be a repeated problem, the state wildlife managers will do their best to capture and move it."

"And if they can't?" Amos asked.

Connor inclined his head. "Then the wolf would be destroyed. But only as a last resort, and only when it's been proven that it's a repeat offender."

"What about our kids?" a woman up front demanded. "There are a lot of remote school bus stops out here. I don't know about you, but I'm not inclined to risk my little girl's life just so some wolf can survive."

"I'd be worried, too, if wolves were known to attack people. But it's a fact that, in all of North America, there's never been a verified case of a wild wolf seriously injuring a person."

Scattered boos and hisses sounded, and a wave of grumbling started.

"How's a man s'posed to make a verified report if he's been eaten by wolves?"

"Not willing to have my kid be the first!"

"Bunch of bureaucratic gobbledygook!"

Connor took a couple of deep breaths to calm himself. If he wasn't careful, he was going to lose them entirely. Just then, a tall, tanned man stood up in the center of the room. He scanned the people seated around him with concerned eyes.

"Listen to what you're saying. We aren't talking about government reintroduction programs here. These wolves have come here on their own. They've returned to the land they lived on long before you or I or any of our ancestors came here." He looked from one face to another. "You are my neigh-

184

bors. I have known many of you since we were children. But these animals are my neighbors, too. I haven't seen them; they're too wise to come out. But I've seen their tracks, heard their howls. They're here already. And we have to learn how to survive together."

"I'll tell you how we'll survive!" one young man spouted. "I shoot every one of those killers I can. *Then* we'll survive. And no environmentalist"—Connor grimaced; the kid made it sound like a dirty word—"is gonna tell me otherwise."

"I more than heard 'em," another man in his late twenties said. "I seen 'em." Everyone started speaking at once, shooting questions. The man stood and turned to glare at Taylor and her family. "I seen one, anyway. A big one. And he was on Galloway Glen."

Taylor jumped to her feet, her eyes blazing. Connor restrained a smile. He knew that combative look well.

"What are you saying, Roy?"

"I'm saying the wolves are on your land, Taylor. And you know it."

"And are you also saying that you trespassed? Came onto my land without asking me if you could do so?"

A dull red swath of color started to creep up the man's throat and into his face. "Well, I was tracking—"

"So you did." Taylor's voice was positively frigid. "And you think that's right?"

"As right as protecting them killers!" the man retorted, and several others voiced agreement.

"Taylor's got a point, Roy." Amos Winkler's tone was harder than Connor had heard it all night. "You had no right to trespass."

"Come on, Amos," the man called Booth spoke up again. "You know as well as I do wolves don't belong here. Even Taylor's grandfather knew it. He killed a mess of 'em in his day. My daddy told me he was one of the best wolf hunters in the region."

Duncan broke in then, and Connor was surprised at his words. "I have to agree with Booth, Taylor. My uncle has told me stories about your grandfather and all the wolves he brought in. He felt the wolves were a threat. As these men do."

"Do you think that, too?" she demanded.

Duncan tilted his head. "From what I've heard here, they've turned your neighbors against you. There seems to be some threat in that."

"I would like to say something, please."

The quiet request came from Taylor's mother. Connor inclined his head. "Go ahead, Mrs. Camus."

Donelle and Holden Camus both rose and walked to the front of the room to stand beside Connor. Donelle laid a gentle hand on his arm, and he was struck by the compassion in her eyes.

"May we?" she asked, indicating the podium.

He stepped aside. "Of course."

The two moved to stand behind the podium, and Connor was struck by the way Taylor's father stood next to his wife. Though he didn't touch her, he was clearly a protective presence. *That's one team I'd hate to mess with,* Connor thought as Mrs. Camus began speaking.

"You're partially right, Booth." She nodded at the man. "But what many of you seem to be forgetting is that my father changed his mind on the day he met a wolf. A wolf he had killed."

"The only kind of wolf to meet!" a woman asserted, then sank in her chair at the quelling looks she received from several of those around her.

Donelle regarded her with compassion. "I certainly understand your feelings, Hazel. I've heard them expressed since I was a child. But I can't help but wonder if you would be less sure of that if you saw what my father did. If you ever met one of these creatures instead of basing your opinions on stories told from fright rather than knowledge." She moved her eyes from face to face before her. "Yes, my father hated wolves, until he actually met one. What he saw in the creature's eyes was powerful enough to change his mind. And his heart. He saw he was wrong. As many of us are wrong."

"What do you think, Reverend?" someone asked.

Holden Camus tilted his head, his eyes thoughtful. "I think this is an issue that doesn't have any easy answers." Agreement sounded throughout the audience. "Like Donelle, I've heard the stories and the concerns for most of my life, but there's something else that troubles me." He smiled. "The last thing I want to do here is preach a sermon—"

"Here, here!" someone shouted, and laughter rippled through the room.

Holden's smile deepened, but his eyes were somber. "Still, I can't get away from what I see in God's Word. God made man ruler over all the earth. In Psalm 8:7 it specifically tells us we're rulers over even the beasts of the field."

"So if we want to rid ourselves of these beasts, it's our right!" Roy said, a smug smile on his face.

"That's not what the reverend is saying, Roy," a man said.

"No, it's not," Holden confirmed slowly. "We are given dominion over the earth, but what we aren't given is ownership. Look at it this way: God has loaned us his world. He put everything in it for our use, to help us survive and thrive. But as often as he tells us we're in charge, he also tells us we have to rule wisely, with kindness and truth."

"Are you tellin' me God cares how we treat a mangy wolf?" said the woman who'd been shushed by the crowd.

"I'm telling you we're given strict instructions on not being abusive to animals. And we're all very fond of reminding each other that God's eye is on the sparrow, that he watches over and cares for even the smallest of his creatures. Why, then, would he not be equally interested in and concerned about a wolf? Or a cougar? Or any animal?"

"So if one of these killers comes after my livestock or my family, I should just step aside and let it do what it wants?"

"Of course not. We're told to subdue the earth, to use it well and wisely. But there's a huge gap between subduing and abusing. If a wolf is killing livestock, it has to be stopped. Certainly if it attacks a human, it must be destroyed. But we will be held accountable to the Creator for the way we treat his world. And nowhere does he condone senseless destruction. Or torture."

Connor was watching the reactions in the crowd with interest. Several faces were tinged with red, though whether from embarrassment or anger he wasn't sure. Others were listening intently, even nodding in agreement.

Holden's advocate stood again. "I think the reverend's hit the nail on the head, folks. I don't know about you, but I want to be sure, when I stand before the good Lord, that I can stand tall"—his face creased into a grin—"well, as tall as any sinner can stand before God." He shook his head, chuckling. "But I don't want to have to answer to the charge of cruelty or abuse. Not to humans nor to animals."

"Ruling the earth is a two-edged sword," Donelle added. "We are to use and subdue it, but we are also called to care for it, to keep it well for its true Owner. We're not suggesting that you put yourselves or your families, or even your livestock, at risk. But I do think it is simple wisdom to act out of knowledge, not out of fear. How many of you have ever encountered a wolf? Ever seen one up close or studied their behavior?" No one answered. "Then how can we be so certain we know the truth?"

Connor watched her with deepening admiration. She had them all listening. They might not be believing her, but at least they were listening.

"Well, I'm sure not going to trust some bleeding-heart environmentalist for the truth!" Booth sputtered.

"Course not!" Amos retorted. "But you know as well as the rest of us, Booth, that there are other sources. Scientists, biologists, all kinds of folks have studied wolves and their interactions with livestock and with humans. I know this ain't a simple issue, not by a long shot. And I sure ain't convinced the environmentalists or wildlife managers have all the answers. But we gotta start working together, or we're all going to come out losers. You can count on it. And so will our kids."

"At least try to get the facts before you start shooting," Donelle urged. "Let Mr. Alexander and his people tell us what they know. At least your decisions will be based on some reality, not on myth."

She looked at her husband, and he shrugged. "I suppose it's

time to pass the offering plates." He grinned, and laughter followed the two of them as they returned to their seats.

Connor stepped back to the podium, glancing at Taylor as he did so. Pride glowed in her eyes as she watched her parents. Then he looked out over the crowd. "Our time is about up," he said. "Any other comments or questions?"

"I got one," a teenage boy remarked, jumping to his feet. "What's the best kind of ammo to use on these critters?"

Some snorts of laughter met this comment, but Connor was relieved to see that just as many people scolded the boy and told him to sit down. Maybe they were making some progress after all.


"Well, that was...interesting."

Taylor glanced at her father and grimaced. "I suppose so. I'm always surprised, though, at how quick people are to be afraid and how slow they are to listen to the facts. But the one who really surprised me was Duncan."

Her father slipped his arm around her mother's shoulders. "Facts can be skewed, Taylor. We all know that. And Duncan cares about you a great deal. It's not that unusual that he would be concerned when he sees people who've known you all your life turning on you. The biggest issue these people have is trusting." His eyes rested on her face. "Now that's something I think you might be able to relate to."

She lowered her eyes and nodded. He was right. The facts hadn't made a lot of difference for her when Connor came to the ranch two days ago.

"Nice bit of preaching, Reverend," a voice spoke from behind them. They turned to see Booth standing there, flanked by four other ranchers. "But it won't make a hill o' beans worth of difference. Wolves are wolves, and there's no room for them around us." His eyes came to rest on Taylor. "I'm disappointed in you, Taylor. I thought you were one of us, that you would understand what's really important."

Anger flared in her, and she opened her mouth to blast the

man, but her father's gentle hand on her arm stilled the caustic response she had ready. She glanced at him, and he shook his head.

*A soft answer*…she could almost hear him say.

"I'm sorry you feel that way, Booth," she finally said to the burly rancher. "And I hope you believe I have no desire to hurt or anger you. But Galloway Glen is my ranch. If I want to let the wolves come on it, I have as much right as you do to keep them off of yours." She met his steely stare without flinching. "I won't tell you and your friends how to run your ranches"—her gaze hardened—"and I won't come onto your land without permission." Her eyes swept the circle of men, noting how several of them dropped their gazes uncomfortably. "I'd appreciate the same courtesy."

"Your wolves set one paw near my land and they're rugs," one of the men muttered defiantly.

She swallowed the rage that threatened to overwhelm her. "You can do whatever you want on your own land." She stepped closer to him, facing him down. "But not on mine." Her eyes pinned him, and he had the grace to look ashamed. "Not on Galloway Glen. I'd like your word on that, Henry."

The man's lips thinned, but he gave a curt nod. "I won't trespass. I give my word."

She looked at the others, her gaze coldly expectant. One by one they conceded. Finally her eyes came back to Booth. "I've always considered you a man of integrity, Booth. I'd hate to find out I was wrong."

His burning gaze held hers, and Taylor knew the lines had been drawn and she was in the enemy camp.

"Just keep your wolves away from our land, Taylor, and we won't have any problems."

A wave of despair washed over her. She couldn't control the wolves. They'd go where they wanted. But she didn't voice her concerns. She just nodded curtly, then watched in silence as the ranchers turned and walked away, their backs rigid.

"You handled that well, Taylor." Her mother's voice was filled with quiet pride.

Taylor looked at her, tears glistening in her eyes. "Maybe so, but we all know I can't stop the wolves from going where they want, Mom. They'll go on Booth's ranch as easily as they came on Galloway Glen. And they'll die for it." She looked away, brushing the wetness from her cheeks.

"You can only do your best, Taylor," her father comforted her.

She stood silent, thinking, then lifted her eyes to his. "You're right." She nodded. "And I think I know what the best thing is for the wolves." She glanced around quickly. "Did you see where Connor went?"

"I believe he was walking with a man toward his Wrangler," her father replied. "Maybe he hasn't left yet, if you'd like to catch him."

"Thanks, Dad." She started toward the parking lot. "I'll meet you at the car."

She ran across the blacktop, and when she spotted Connor's tall frame she called his name. He turned in surprise, his eyes narrowing as she approached.

"Where's your guard dog?" he asked dryly.

She felt the blush rise in her cheeks. "She's at home. Still trying to figure out what I was so upset about, I think."

"I understood."

She fell silent, unsure about how to respond. "You were pretty good in there," she finally said, and he grinned.

"Not bad for fighting off a bunch of hostiles."

She smiled in response. "Not bad at all. And that's what I want to talk to you about."

He leaned against the door of his Jeep. "Shoot." At the look on her face, he laughed. "Figuratively speaking, of course."

"Of course." She hesitated, then plunged in. "Connor, I'm sorry. For a lot of things. And I want you to come back to the ranch."

To say he was stunned would be an understatement. He stared at her as though she'd just sprouted a second head.

"If your offer is still open, that is."

"My offer?"

At his obtuse question she wanted to kick him in the shins. He wasn't making this any easier. "To observe the wolves, to photograph them. To keep WAC informed about their whereabouts." He had straightened quickly when she started explaining, and now his eyes were roaming her face, and the expression she saw in them made her heart pound.

"I want you to get the best photos anyone has ever seen," she said in a rush, emotion surging through her. "I want everyone to see the first wolves to come back to Wyoming. I want people to know how beautiful, how incredible they are. Then maybe they'll have a chance. If enough people hear about them, Booth and his cronies might back off." She smiled grimly. "Even they wouldn't like being known as the cold-hearted killers of the majestic Wyoming wolf." She stepped closer, holding out a hand in entreaty. "Please come back, Connor. Help me protect the wolves."

He didn't reply, and her throat constricted. He had every right to turn her down, every right to walk away. She'd insulted him, raged at him, told him she never wanted to see him again...and all the time he'd just been trying to protect something precious.

The anger she had felt at his deception dimmed and melted away in the light of sudden understanding. *He didn't know if he could trust me, Lord. He couldn't put the wolves at risk. Please,* she prayed. *Please let him forgive me.*

His eyes studied her, intent, seeking, seeming to reach into her thoughts. She stood there, not hiding anything, letting him see in her eyes all she was feeling. Then he reached out to close his strong, warm hand over hers.

"I'll come. But not because of the wolves." His gaze captured hers, and her breathing grew shallow. "I'll come for you."

Relief swept over her, and she moved, almost without thought, into the circle of his arms, burying her face against the softness of his shirt and the hardness of his chest.

She didn't care if anyone saw them. Not her parents. Not Duncan. All that mattered was that Connor was going to help her.

He was coming back.

# Twenty-Two

❧

When Connor called Harry Crowley to tell him Taylor had asked him to return to the ranch, the president of WAC whooped and hollered with glee.

"See there? You're just too charming to resist! Now get out there and find those wolves."

Connor returned to the ranch the next morning, and he and Taylor spent the day discussing their plans. Harry had asked Connor to observe the wolf—since Taylor had told him she'd seen only the one—for at least a month. They agreed to use the ranch as their base, going out during the day to track and observe.

"I'd like to start out by staying in this valley of yours for a couple of days and nights. Since your wolf has come there twice now, it seems like a good place to find him. I've got a yurt tent in the Jeep," Connor told her, "so I can set it up without any trouble."

"I want to come, too," Taylor said. She could help him with the wolves for a few weeks and still be ready for the retreat season. "I can set up my own tent—"

"You don't need to. The yurt is large enough for several people, and we can section off individual rooms." Connor smiled. "It's a regular home away from home."

Taylor nodded, but she didn't return his smile. Though she'd obviously taken a big step in asking him to come back, Connor sensed her caution and reserve.

*She changed her mind because she knows I'm her best bet for keeping the wolves safe,* he thought. *Not because she trusts me.* Well, he had the time now to change that.

"I don't know if it will make a difference." Taylor's expression held uncertainty. "But maybe if I'm there he'll be more inclined to show up."

Connor nodded. Going there together suited him just fine.

Two days later, they loaded the tent and other equipment into Taylor's truck and headed for Reunion. Within a few hours, they had unloaded their supplies and had set up the tent in a clearing among the trees on the south side of the pond, a good distance from the cave and as unobtrusive as possible among the tall evergreens.

Constructed of heavy white canvas, the yurt was octagonal, domed, and stretched over a collapsible lattice framework of sturdy wood. It had a hinged door, and windows of heavy plastic. Canvas flaps could be secured over the windows to make the tent as weatherproof as possible. Inside, it actually felt like a small house. A wood cooking stove sat near a small table and two chairs, along with a small generator-powered refrigerator for their food. A gas stove was pushed to the side in case it was needed for heat. And true to his word, Connor had set up individual rooms using canvas and poles from the ranch.

As Taylor surveyed the result of their work, she smiled. It wasn't the Waldorf, but the spacious tent was far nicer than she had expected. They each had a small bedroom compartment complete with a cot and lanterns. The area they would share for cooking, eating, and studying their notes was fairly large, at least twenty feet across.

"All set?" Connor asked from behind her.

She turned and nodded. They secured the tent, then climbed the path back to the truck and returned to the ranch.

There, they saddled Topaz and Chestnut for the ride back to Reunion, then started out. Sasha loped along beside them.

Taylor was glad the husky was coming along. She'd asked Connor if the husky would be a deterrent to the wolves.

"No," he said. "They generally aren't bothered by domestic dogs, especially the nonterritorial ones like Sasha. She'll be fine."

They made it to Reunion in record time, just under two hours. As they crested the rise, the sun was beginning to set. They tethered the horses next to the tent, pulled off the saddles and saddlebags, and got ready for the night. After a quiet dinner, Taylor slipped into her bedroom, Sasha at her side, and lay down on the cot with a sigh.

Connor had wanted to talk; she'd seen it in his eyes as she stood and walked from the table. But she wasn't ready for that yet. Didn't know if she'd ever be. She didn't want to talk about emotions, or hurt, or trust. She didn't want to debate forgiveness.

For now, all she wanted to do was concentrate on the wolf.


For several days and nights there was no sign of Taylor's wolf. Connor told her the animal could be as much as fifty miles away, for wolves had been known to travel that far while hunting. Or he could just be watching them from a safe distance—and waiting.

"Waiting? For what?" she asked, and his mouth curved in amusement.

"To see if we'll get out of his territory. Or to size us up. Wolves are highly intelligent and equally skittish. He won't come around us until he's sure we're not a threat. Maybe not even then. It's actually pretty rare to see a wolf in the wild."

"And I've seen Sikis twice."

He gave a thoughtful nod. "Could be you've used up your quota."

A quick glance told her he was teasing, and she stuck her tongue out at him. It was the most relaxed exchange they'd had since his return to Galloway Glen, and she felt almost buoyant. Maybe things were going to work out after all.

Then, early the next morning, Connor left the tent. Within moments he was back, his eyes shining with excitement. "Taylor! Come out here!" he whispered urgently.

She hurried from the tent and followed him to the edge of the pool, where he stood and pointed to a spot on the other side.

Across the pond was a meadow full of waving grasses, and just beyond that a small stand of trees. And there, lying in the lush meadow grass, looking comfortable and relaxed, was the large gray wolf—and with him were four other wolves!

Taylor watched in amazement as one of them, a slim, medium-sized black wolf, crawled along the ground toward Sikis, its head on the ground, whimpering and wagging its entire body.

"The black one is probably a young male," Connor whispered as the wolf reached Sikis and licked repeatedly at the larger wolf's chin and mouth.

Sikis put up with this groveling with regal inattention. The other three wolves were larger than the black wolf, but smaller than Sikis. One was gray, like its leader, and it paced back and forth behind Sikis, watching him intently, as though ready for the slightest signal. The other gray wolf had a much lighter coat, and this one danced back and forth, making friendly advances toward Sikis, trotting toward him, then darting away if he flinched or twitched. The fourth wolf was a buff-tan color with a darker brown head.

The attention of the entire pack was focused on Sikis, who lay there, his head high, his velvety ears erect, accepting the homage of his followers. The other four kept their tails low, their ears flattened against their heads, and whined with an almost pathetic appeal as they nibbled at Sikis's muzzle, looking like eager children. Taylor could have sworn Sikis's mouth, which was partly open, was curved into a majestic, munificent smile.

"Apparently your friend is the alpha," Connor remarked.

"And loving every minute of it, from what I can see. Typical male."

Connor grinned at her. "That's as it should be," he quipped, then headed for the tent. He emerged within minutes, his photography equipment in tow.

"Are they still there?" He came to stand beside her, and she nodded.

"It's like they've come for a photo shoot."

He grinned again. "Well, far be it from me to disappoint them!"

The wolves put on quite a show. They stayed in the meadow for nearly an hour, playing or lazing or just sitting and watching Connor and Taylor with cautious interest. Sikis was the least nervous of the group; the black wolf the least confident. Every time Connor clicked the shutter or Taylor shifted positions, the black wolf would crouch, his head spinning to stare at them, his body already leaning away.

A couple of times Taylor was tempted to holler "Boo!" just to see what the animal would do. But she didn't want to scare the wolf or hinder the growing trust they seemed to be building. Nor did she want to spoil Connor's chances to get his photos. She glanced at him, taking in the excitement that was evident in his stance and his face. His eyes shone, a slight smile tipped his lips, and his golden brown hair blew gently in the early morning breeze. If Taylor had been honest with herself, she would have admitted she enjoyed watching him as much as she enjoyed watching the wolves.

But she wasn't ready to be quite that honest.


The next morning, Taylor was awakened by someone shaking her shoulder. She blinked sleepily until her surroundings came into focus.

Above her, Connor's eyes glowed with excitement. "Get up! I have an idea."

With that he left her room, and she rubbed her eyes, then slipped from beneath the covers. She was already dressed—it was cool enough at night that she slept in her clothes—so she pulled on a jacket and went to see what was happening.

"We'll need to leave Sasha here," Connor said.

Taylor started to question him, then shrugged. "Sasha, down," she commanded, and the husky stared at her for a moment, as though trying to determine if she was serious. Taylor grinned. No matter how well-trained the Siberian was, she still had a stubborn streak. Maybe that was why they got along so well.

"Down," she repeated, and Sasha turned, walked over to the table, circled a few times, then plopped down with an exaggerated air of offense.

"Ham," Taylor muttered, then told the dog to stay.

"Come on," Connor urged quietly, and she followed him, brimming with curiosity. Outside the tent, he grabbed her hand and tugged her along behind him. He led her to the far end of the valley, around the pool, then toward the spot where the wolves had frolicked the day before. Taylor looked at him, confused. His grin just widened.

"We're going to see if our friends will come say hello."

She stared at him in wide-eyed disbelief. "Come…say hello?" she echoed.

He nodded briskly. "Sit here." He gently pushed her onto the ground. She landed with a slight thud, but before she could yell at him, he had moved to sit behind her so that their backs were together. "Okay, now we wait. If they're out there, if they're watching, they just might pay a visit."

Taylor sat there, the early morning dampness soaking through the seat of her jeans, feeling completely ridiculous. Not to mention nervous.

"Connor!" she hissed, but he shushed her.

"Be patient!" he responded. Then he turned his head to look at her, and the plea in his eyes was clear. "Trust me. You won't be sorry."

She turned back around, biting her lip. She didn't know what made her more uneasy: the idea of actually coming in contact with a pack of wolves, or trusting Connor.

"They're here!" Connor's hushed voice was filled with jubilation, and Taylor turned her head.

At first all she could see were the trees. Then she realized there were glowing pairs of eyes peering inquisitively from behind the thick trunks.

Alarm shot through her, and she must have tensed, because Connor's hand reached to clasp hers where she had it planted firmly on the ground beside her. "Don't be afraid." His voice was low but confident. "Just stare at your feet as they approach. Don't make eye contact or they'll feel challenged."

Her eyes flew to her boots, and she studied them intently, then dared to peek out of the corner of her eye. One by one, the wolves emerged from the woods, taking cautious, tentative steps toward the two intruders, ready to retreat at the slightest motion.

Taylor swallowed convulsively as the wolves started to circle them. She'd read the books; she knew what the experts said: Healthy wolves don't attack people.

*God, please don't let us prove them wrong!*

Finally, Sikis came right up to Taylor's feet, sniffing cautiously at her boots and then he dropped down into a crouch and started to rub his head all over them, back and forth, with vigorous movements. The light gray wolf approached her next, leaning into her shoulder and rubbing against her, like a grizzly trying to get a backscratch on a gnarly old tree.

Taylor started to giggle. It was the most amazing feeling! She heard Connor's laugh behind her and figured he was getting the same treatment. Soon all five wolves were leaning against them, rubbing their heads and shoulders against them, wagging their shaggy bodies with enthusiasm.

Then Sikis jumped away, gave a sharp bark, and bounded back into the woods. The rest of the pack followed him in a flash, and Connor and Taylor were left to themselves, sitting there, still laughing.

Without thinking about what she was doing, Taylor spun to Connor. He was there, his arms open, and she hugged him tightly.

"That was incredible!" she said with awe, leaning back to look up into his beaming face. "Thank you, Connor."

He studied her face for a moment, and she saw a deep tenderness in his expression. "Thank you for trusting me." He let her go and stepped back. "I know you took a risk in asking me to come back. I don't know if you've forgiven me for deceiving you—" She started to speak, but he shook his head and continued. "I just want you to know that I was wrong. I should have been honest with you from the start. That would have been the right thing...the godly thing to do."

"You did what you thought you had to."

"Yes, at the time. But it wasn't easy, Taylor." He glanced away. "You may find this hard to believe, but my goal in life isn't protecting wildlife. It's honoring God." He looked at her, regret reflected in his eyes. "Deceiving you wasn't in line with that goal. I want you to know that, from this moment on, I will be honest with you. I will treat you the way God calls me to, with respect and truth." He reached out to touch her face, and the tenderness in his warm fingers stirred her deeply. "Taylor, you mean a great deal to me. I want you to trust me. And I'm willing to do whatever it takes to earn that trust."

She didn't know how to respond. She wasn't ready yet to give her trust to God, so how could she give it to Connor? She decided the truth was the best thing she could give him. "I want to trust you, but I don't know if I can."

He nodded. "I've seen that something holds you back," he said as he tilted his head, "something that I don't think involves me. It's always there, in your eyes. Something...hard. Painful."

She fought against the tightening of her throat and turned away. "I don't want to talk about this."

"It's Josh, isn't it? And that boy. Brad—isn't that his name?"

She spun back to face him. "I said I don't want to talk about it!"

His eyes held a gentle warning. "If what's holding you back from me is something I've done, then I can accept that and deal with it. But I won't let someone else keep us apart, Taylor. That wouldn't be fair to either of us." He reached out to touch her face, and she batted his hand away angrily.

"Do me a favor, Alexander. Keep your hands to yourself."

She swept past him, pausing only long enough to turn around and snarl, "And stick to wolves. You stink as a psychologist." With that, she spun around and headed for the tent.

That night they sat around a low campfire in silence. Usually they spent the evenings reviewing what had happened during the day. Tonight they had nothing to say. The silence was heavy and tense.

They had pulled two folding camp chairs outside and set them on either side of the fire. Taylor slouched in hers, deep in gloomy thought. One hand was cupped around a metal camping mug full of cocoa, and the other rested on Sasha's head, scratching the dog's ears. Taylor found comfort in the contact. At least Sasha accepted her as she was, without expecting her to make some huge strides toward forgiveness.

"I'm sure the light gray wolf is the alpha female," Connor remarked quietly, gazing into the fire. His eyes came to rest on Taylor, as though debating something. Then he said, "She looks pregnant."

Taylor's eyes widened and she sat up in her chair. "You're kidding!" She leaned forward and set her mug on the edge of the ring of stones they'd built around the fire.

He nodded. "Wolves usually breed by February, so unless I miss my guess, she's nearing the end of her gestation. She'll be looking for a denning area soon."

"I would have thought the time for pups was past," Taylor remarked.

Connor shook his head. "Wolves usually breed in late winter, but they've been known to do so as late as April. So they could be right on schedule."

"Just think of it," she sighed, "Nokomis surrounded by pups." She leaned back, feeling suddenly happy, then noticed that Connor was looking at her with an amused expression.

"Nokomis?" he inquired mildly.

She shot him a cheeky grin. "That's what I've named the light gray one, the female. It means 'grandmother.' I figure she's going to be the mother of this pack, so it's appropriate."

"I suppose you have names for the others, too?"

She tossed her head. "As a matter of fact, I do. The black one is Ayasha, 'little one,' because he's the smallest and youngest. The tan one is Tala, for wolf. The other gray is Mingan."

"Which means?"

She grinned again. "'Gray wolf,' of course."

He rolled his eyes, chuckling. "Of course. At any rate, if Nokomis is going to have a litter, my guess is it will be soon. Which means we probably ought to make ourselves scarce."

Disappointment, sharp and quick, pierced Taylor. "You mean leave?" He nodded, and she saw regret in his eyes as well. "But we just got the tent up a few days ago! Do we have to take it down already?"

He shook his head. "Not at all. The tent can stay up. We'll be coming out here from time to time, so we'll just leave it here. You said no one else knows about this place, right?"

"Not as far as I know."

"Then it should be fine. We'll take what's left of the food with us, but everything else can stay." He rose and stretched. "I'll pack the nonperishables up now so we don't have to mess with it in the morning."

"So we're leaving tomorrow?"

He fixed her with a compassionate look. "I think it would be best. We've got to give them plenty of room. There can be a lot of tension when a female births. She gets snappy, irritable"—he broke off and a broad grin stretched across his features—"kind of like someone else I know."

"Ha ha," Taylor responded, and Connor turned away with a chuckle.

He paused at the door to the tent. "You coming?"

She shook her head. "Not yet." He nodded and went inside.

Taylor leaned back in her chair, feeling depressed. She should be happy to be going back to the ranch. She'd be with her family again, have the chance to tell them all the amazing things that had happened. And she'd be able to see Duncan... but for some reason, that thought only depressed her more.

She'd expected Duncan to be very much against her coming out here with Connor. Instead, he'd kept his dark eyes on her face, an odd emotion floating in their depths, and listened quietly when she told him what they were going to do.

"I'll see you when you get back," he'd said at last, then rose to leave. Not exactly a warm parting.

Taylor bit her lip and fought off the tears that stung her eyes. She stared at the stars glittering overhead and wondered why life had to be so ridiculously complicated.

The song began slowly, with a single, mournful howl rising on the wind and drifting to float all around them. It was so subtle, so faint at first, that Taylor wasn't even conscious of it. But Sasha was.

The husky shifted, then raised her head, her velvety ears cocked. Taylor noted the dog's movement and looked at her curiously.

"Sash?" she asked, but the usually responsive husky didn't even look at her. Taylor glanced around uneasily; clearly the dog heard something.

Sasha stood and stretched her throat out, reaching toward the sky with her muzzle. Taylor frowned and went to kneel beside the dog. She laid a gentle hand on Sasha's neck, burying her fingers in the thick fur. Sasha glanced at her briefly, and Taylor was startled at the intense, faraway look in the animal's ice-blue eyes.

Sasha looked back to the sky, closed her eyes, tilted her chin up. After a moment, and a quick look around to assure her Connor was nowhere in sight, Taylor followed suit.

She could tell Sasha wasn't alarmed, but something had caught her attention. Taylor was determined to find out what that something was. She closed her eyes and concentrated on the night sounds.

At first all she heard was Sasha's steady breathing and the myriad crickets and frogs sending messages to each other. Drawing a deep breath, Taylor tried to focus.

The low, keening sound came to her then, and a thrill of wonder raced through her. The sound was deep and resonant. Pure and vibrant, it seemed almost a tangible thing as it drifted all around her.

A wolf was howling. But this time, instead of it being some sound that floated to her from a distance, she knew he was there, in the meadow, just across the pond. And the very air vibrated with his mournful song.

The single howl sounded again, rising, changing pitch at least four or five times. Then a second voice joined in, also changing pitch, creating an eerie harmony that seemed to come from all directions.

Tears pricked Taylor's eyes at the beauty of the sound. Before long, more wolf voices joined in, until the night was immersed in a symphony as ancient and as majestic as the mountains and forests around them.

Suddenly the night fell silent, as though the wolves were pausing, listening, hoping for some response. Taylor looked at Sasha. The dog's eyes were half-closed, as though in heartfelt contemplation of what she'd just heard.

"You could join in, you know," Taylor whispered, and Sasha turned to meet her gaze. "For that matter," Taylor said, "we both could." With a grin, Taylor closed her eyes, lifted her chin, and howled, doing her best to copy the rising and falling dance of the wolf voices.

Seconds after Taylor began howling, Sasha followed suit. The two of them sang to the night and a shiver of delight surged through Taylor when the wolves once again lifted their voices, as though in response. The eerie beauty of the discordant chorus continued for a few minutes, and then the sound slowly died away.

Taylor sat there, her eyes closed, awash in wonder.

"I don't know about Sasha, but I think you're a bit off the beam."

The deep voice came so unexpectedly that Taylor leaped to her feet, startled. Sasha merely loped over to welcome Connor back to the fire.

That traitorous act, though, wasn't nearly as irritating as the gleam of amusement in Connor's eyes or the cocky grin on his face.

"I thought you went to bed," she remarked dryly.

"Nope. Just to pack things up. When I heard the symphony begin, I came back out. And what a show it was!" His grin was filled with teasing. "You're lucky you didn't kill the howl," he finished, sinking into his chair and resting his hand on Sasha's head as she sat beside him.

Taylor raised an imperious eyebrow. "Kill the howl?" she inquired in overly sweet tones. "And how would I have done that, pray tell, O Wise One?"

"Your howl was the most pitiful thing I've ever heard, and I've heard some awful ones. So I'm sure the wolves were less than impressed. Maybe even insulted."

"Har dee har," Taylor muttered as she moved to snatch her cup of cocoa from where it rested on the fire ring.

"I wouldn't—" Connor began in alarm, but he was too late. With a yelp that sent Sasha heading for the shadows, Taylor jerked her hand back in pain, sending the metal cup—and its scalding contents—flying.

Tears sprang to her eyes for the second time that night, but this time they were caused by physical pain. Before she could move, Connor had hold of her arm and was leading her to the nearest seat. For once she didn't argue. The sight of the angry red skin filled her with frustration. She knew better. Even an amateur camper knew you didn't grab anything metal that was near the fire. Not barehanded. She shook her head, silent recriminations flying, and her pain was only compounded by the knowledge that Connor would have a heyday with this act of stupidity.

But Connor seemed too busy dousing a towel in cold water to yell at her. When he came back to her side, the concern on his chiseled features warmed her. He didn't meet her gaze, but concentrated on the burn, wrapping her hand in the cold, wet material and holding it gently.

Taylor hadn't realized tears were streaming down her face

until Connor looked at her, then reached out with that same gentleness to wipe her damp cheeks. Their eyes met.

Neither spoke. Taylor couldn't have if she tried, her throat was so dry. All the churning emotions she'd been feeling, all the love she felt for Connor and the depth of her hurt, filled her eyes. She was sure he could see it all, could see her heart, but she couldn't stop it. It just poured out of her.

His eyes widened slightly, and she swayed toward him. For an instant she felt as though she were falling, as though her senses were caught in a spinning vortex, and then the spell was broken when Connor vaulted to his feet and stepped away from her as though she'd suddenly grown fangs and hissed at him.

She blinked once. Twice. Then anger swept over her. "For heaven's sake, Connor, I don't bite!"

He moved to stand near the fire, staring down into the flames, his expression troubled. After a moment of silence, he looked at her again. "I'm just trying to honor your request to keep my hands to myself." He angled a look at her. "Unless, of course, you've changed your mind. Again."

She jumped to her feet, careful to keep her swaddled hand clutched close to her chest. "If I live to be a hundred years old, I will never understand men." Her tone was low and furious. "And I especially will never understand you!" She walked away, heading for the tent to hunt up the first-aid kit. It would have burn ointment.

And, if she were lucky, pest repellent.

Connor watched as Taylor jerked the tent door open and disappeared inside. She slammed the door shut, but because of the tent material, the sound was far less than satisfying. Had it been a normal door, Connor was sure his ears would be ringing with the sound of her fury. He chuckled for a moment, then sank down into the chair. Sasha came over to sit beside him, looking at him with a bewildered expression.

He shook his head and shrugged. "Don't look at me, girl.

I'm just the wolf expert. I sure can't explain women."

Sasha let out a huff of air and lay down, curling into a circle, resting her head on her paws and covering her nose with her tail.

Connor leaned forward and gazed into the dwindling fire, his elbows propped on his knees and his chin in his hands. "I'm just a man. If you ask me, the only one who really understands the fairer sex is God. He made 'em. He must know what makes 'em tick." He looked at Sasha in exasperation. "You're a female. You explain this to me. Here I am, trying to give her space, trying to give her time to build up trust in me again… and she looks at me with those beautiful green eyes all full of emotion. How's a man supposed to respond?"

The Siberian didn't move; she just looked up at him in mute eloquence. But Connor didn't need an answer. He had one already. A man responded the way he had: with an overwhelming urge to pull her close, to enfold her, cradle her against him, and keep her safe.

Either that, or shake the stuffing out of her.

CHAPTER

# Twenty-Three

❧

Taylor was unusually quiet the next morning, and Connor wondered if her hand was hurting. After a breakfast of coffee and rolls, she stood at the edge of the pool, looking across at the meadow. The wolves were nowhere in sight.

He walked toward her, wondering if he was risking his head in doing so. But when he drew close, he saw the dejected droop of her shoulders and heard a small sniff. Moving forward, he placed a gentle hand on her shoulder. She tensed momentarily, then relaxed.

When she looked at him, tears glimmered in her eyes. "I'm sorry I got angry, Con."

"I'm sorry I acted like a jerk," he replied, and won a watery smile.

"Well, we seem to be trading off where that role is concerned." She looked back toward the meadow. "Do you think they'll miss us?"

He sighed. "Maybe. I hope so. At least a little."

She turned to head for the tent, then paused, turning her focus back to the cave. He saw surprise dawn on her features, and he followed her gaze.

The wolves stood outside the cave, pacing back and forth, whining and scratching at the ground in front of the entrance.

Taylor looked at him quickly. "Is something wrong?"

But Connor was grinning broadly, and in his excitement he reached to encircle her with his arms, hugging her to his chest. *"Nothing's* wrong! Something's right! The female must be denning. In the cave." He looked down at her, his eyes glowing. "Sikis and Nokomis are going to be parents."

Her head spun to stare at the pack again, then she gave a squeal and threw her arms around Connor.

"When will it happen?" she asked, and he laughed down at her, struggling to catch his breath—in part because she'd hugged him so tightly, and in part because she was so beautiful and so close.

"A few days. Right now the pack is staying close. When the birth happens, the female won't let them inside, and the alpha—"

"Sikis," she inserted.

"Right, Sikis will be extremely protective of the den." He hugged her again, then set her away from him.

"Can't we stay, Connor?" Her eyes pled with him, but he shook his head.

"No, but I'll make you a deal."

"A deal?"

"We'll come back in a few weeks—"

"Weeks!" she wailed.

"The pups won't venture out of the den before that, Taylor. The last thing we want to do is make the pack nervous or give Nokomis reason to move her brood."

Despite the pretty pout on her face, he knew she understood. "Okay," she said grudgingly. "Three weeks. But no longer."

He laughed, threw his arm around her shoulders, and nodded. "You got it." They walked toward the tent. "And it will go quickly, I promise."

"Right," she responded, her voice dismal. "Mom and Dad used to tell me the same thing about my birthday and Christmas. But they always took forever to come." She cast a glance back over her shoulder.

"Well, it will be worth—"

She shot him a dangerous look. "If you tell me it will be worth the wait," she threatened, "I'll scream."

He clamped his mouth shut. That was exactly what he had planned to say.

She read his guilt on his face and her lips twitched. "I get it. You've decided to exercise the wisdom of the ages and remain silent in the face of a woman's impending fury."

He nodded.

"See there, Sasha?" she remarked to the dog walking along beside them. "I *told* you he was smarter than he looked!"

# Twenty-Four

Contrary to her gloomy prediction, Taylor was amazed at how quickly the next three weeks flew by. There was still work to be done on the retreat cabins, as well as brainstorming for retreat activities. And they spent several days riding around the ranch, looking for places for Connor to take his photos. Galloway Glen was exploding with color. From sunflowers to lupine to phlox and wild irises, the meadows were alive with blossoms.

The warm days and the increase in color and fragrance filled Taylor with a renewed appreciation of God's creative genius. "How can anyone look at this and deny there's a God?" she said as they stood in her living room, enjoying the view.

Connor shook his head. "You've got me. I figure it takes a whole lot more faith to believe this all came about by some cosmic accident than it does to believe in an almighty, all-loving Creator."

Taylor looked at him and grinned. "Two more days and we get to see the pups!" she said, her eyes shining with anticipation.

"Taylor." His voice held a gentle but firm warning. "It's entirely possible we won't see Nokomis or the pups. I keep telling you that."

"We'll see them," she asserted, her tone filled with confidence. "I know we will."

He shook his head, his lips tilted in a tender smile. Taylor turned to look out the window again, fully aware that he thought her a daydreaming optimist. But she didn't care. They were going to see the pups. She was sure of it.

"I think I'd like to get some shots of the sunrise tomorrow." Connor's words broke into her thoughts.

She turned to him eagerly. "Oh, Con! I know the perfect place! But it will mean getting up awfully early. I'd like to go on horseback, and it's a bit of a ride."

"No problem!" Connor said, clearly caught up in her enthusiasm.

She just gave him a placid smile. *We'll see about that,* she thought, *when 3:00 A.M. rolls around.*

"Connor."

The soft voice broke into his dreams, trying to coax him away from the comforting darkness. He rolled over and resisted.

"Connor, wake up."

This time it was accompanied by a slight tugging on his arm. He mumbled something uncomplimentary and pulled the covers over his head.

There was blessed silence for a second, and then a huge THING pounced on him, landing in the middle of his chest and punching him in the stomach. Connor sat up with a roar, and Sasha—who happened to be standing on top of him—quickly jumped off and ran for the hills.

Blinking in the sudden light from the bedside lamp, his mind still fuzzy from sleep, he stared at Taylor in disbelief.

"And a happy good morning to you, too," she said in response to his glower. "Now, get up. If you want pictures of the sunrise, it's past time to be on our way."

She strode from the cabin, and he fell back against the mattress with a groan. He had to admit the idea was far less appealing this morning than it had sounded last night. He threw back the covers, shivering in the cold. Fortunately the camera and equipment he needed were already stowed safely in a large duffel bag. He pulled on his clothes, then hauled the bag outside. He found Taylor in the barn. She already had both horses saddled. He tied the duffel to the back of his saddle.

"All set?" Taylor asked as she slid her foot into the stirrup and swung herself into the saddle with a smooth, effortless movement.

"Lead on," he said, his eyes following her in the morning darkness as she urged Topaz forward.

They rode in silence, turning east toward the Wind River mountain range.

As he settled into the saddle, Connor found himself studying Taylor, taking in the picture she made. Even in the dim light he could see that she sat upon her horse with a natural ease and grace. Woman and beast moved in a delicate, barely discernible harmony. Topaz was finely tuned to his rider, responding to the merest touch of Taylor's heels, the slightest lean in the saddle, the barest tug on the reins. As he watched them, Connor wondered vaguely what it was like to be so connected to someone…to Taylor.

He shook his head slightly, feeling foolish and just a bit embarrassed. Was this what being in love did to you? Made you think goofy, flowery thoughts? *Heaven help me,* he thought, dismayed. *Get your mind on your business, Alexander,* he scolded himself. *You need to think about focus and f-stops, not Taylor—no matter how appealing she may be.*

Appealing. That was certainly an appropriate term for Taylor. As was delightful. Captivating. Enchanting. Guileless. Utterly charming—

*Knock it off!* He cut into his train of thought angrily. *You're pathetic! Can't you think about something else? Anything else!*

He focused his attention on the deft manner in which his horse was navigating the woods they had entered, on the stunning scenery surrounding them, on anything but the woman riding in front of him. But his traitorous eyes drifted toward her once again, as though she were too compelling, too magnetic to resist.

The first subdued light of morning glinted off her hair, turning it a rich copper. Her eyes, when she glanced at him, shone with excitement; he had the impression she could hardly wait to reveal whatever treasure she had in store.

She was so natural, so beautiful, so filled with grace and a childlike eagerness, that watching her brought a lump of emotion to Connor's throat. Every day they spent together, the pull he felt toward her grew stronger; he had the sensation of being carried along on the rapids of a river, terrified and exhilarated all at the same time.

*Okay, God, how much longer until I can tell her how I feel?* he asked with a sudden fierceness.

"We're here!" Taylor's triumphant voice broke into his rueful thoughts, and he looked around. They had emerged from the woods and now stood on the edge of a beautiful meadow. Tall grasses swayed in the wind; wildflowers of all kinds and colors created a natural quilt of color and texture. Several tall lodgepole pines stood beside a bubbling stream, which meandered merrily through the meadow. On the opposite side of the stream, 150 feet away, the ground rose to become a small, rocky hill. The grass and flowers gave way at the top of the gradual rise to hard, dirt-packed earth topped with large boulders.

"It's incredible," he said with excitement. "Absolutely incredible."

She beamed at him, pleasure gleaming in her forest-colored eyes. "We can tether the horses to one of the trees and walk over to the hill. You'll get some great shots of the sunrise behind the trees that way."

He glanced up. The rising sun was just beginning to tint the sky with brilliant reds and oranges. If he hurried, he could get set up in time to take full advantage of the color changes as the sun came up.

"Let's do it," he said, excitement filling him with energy and anticipation.

They rode to one of the trees on the edge of the creek, dismounted, and secured the horses. Lifting his duffel bag from his horse's back, he turned and followed Taylor as she leaped from rock to rock to cross the bubbling water and made for the hill. It didn't take long to reach the summit and locate a good vantage point.

As Connor pulled the tripod, camera, and filters from the bag, setting them up with quick, efficient motions, Taylor perched on a nearby boulder, watching him with interest. It didn't seem to bother her a bit that he was entirely focused on the task at hand. She seemed content to merely sit and watch.

*Amazing. That's another word that fits,* he thought as he bent to peer through the viewfinder. *Independent, confident,* his mind went on as he reached forward to adjust the focus. *Creative, adventurous—*

It hit him like a sharp slap that he'd done it again, gotten caught up in his fascination with the woman who was watching him. He heaved a heavy, defeated sigh, resting his forehead against the camera.

"Connor, are you okay?"

Taylor's question brought his head up, and he turned to look at her.

*No. Definitely not,* his mind answered.

"Sure, I'm fine. Just…thinking." *What a laugh.*

She nodded, smiled, and hopped off the boulder. "You'd better start snapping. You're running out of sunrise."

He turned back to the camera, made the needed adjustments, and "started snapping." The first roll was shot in record time, and he popped it out to replace it. He knelt to the bag and reached inside, then froze.

A low, horrific sound filled the air around them. He lifted startled eyes to Taylor, saw the same alarm on her face that he knew must have shone on his. It was the most bone-chilling thing Connor had ever heard.

"What in the world…?"

The noise sounded again, and Connor felt the hair on the back of his neck rise. The sound was unearthly. If Duncan had been with them, Connor was sure the Scotsman would say it was a banshee. Part growl, part scream, it was the stuff of nightmares.

215

Suddenly another sound caught Connor's attention. The horses. They were screaming in fear. Connor looked at Taylor in alarm, then glanced around cautiously, eyes scanning the area, seeking the source of the ghastly sound.

Nothing. There was nothing there but rocks.

Taylor stepped toward him. "Con, I think we'd better get out of here."

"I think you're right." He grabbed his equipment and started to dismantle it, when Taylor uttered a muffled scream. He spun to look at her. Her face was pale, her eyes wide and staring. He followed her gaze, and his eyes widened in disbelief.

There, perched on a boulder about thirty-five feet away, was a cougar. Its lips curled back in a threatening snarl, revealing vicious fangs. Tiny, pointed ears lay flat against its round skull, and it crouched with tense, twitching muscles. Its throat rumbled with its banshee scream as it kept its piercing gaze fixed on them.

"God help us," Taylor whispered.

Connor closed his eyes for a second, the image of his rifle, still in its saddle scabbard, dancing in his mind. He'd been in such a hurry to catch the sunrise, he hadn't thought to bring it.

He studied the cougar, noting the way it watched them but didn't advance. *God, you created this monster,* he prayed desperately. *Please, please hold it back.*

"We have to get to the horses, Taylor," Connor told her in a low, hoarse voice. "It's our only chance."

She swallowed, then gave a quick, slight nod.

"Step back, hon. Come toward me. Slowly. Carefully." He watched, his heart pounding in his chest, as she moved. His eyes went from her to the screaming cat and back again. If nothing else, he would put himself between Taylor and the beast. He would do everything he could to give Taylor time to reach Topaz.

When Taylor reached him, he moved as slowly as he dared, positioning himself as a barrier. At his movement, the cougar tensed, as though readying to lunge.

*"Memories, all alone in the moonlight..."*

216

Connor looked at Taylor, stunned. She was singing!

"What—" he started to ask, but she just shook her head and kept on. He glanced back at the cougar. It looked about as taken aback as he was.

Connor stepped backward, keeping himself in front of Taylor who kept singing as they moved. The cougar watched them, still angry, still snarling—and, apparently, still flummoxed. It didn't lunge, didn't advance. It just watched them with those wrathful, ebony eyes as they eased away.

Suddenly Connor became aware that Taylor was no longer singing lyrics, but was singing to him.

*"I've heard stories of people stopping grizzlies with songs. It was all I could think off, to give us time."*

"Fine, great," he hissed. "But *Cats*? What if he hates musicals?"

*"It just seemed right…"*

After what seemed like an eternity, they finally moved out of the cat's line of vision. Connor grabbed Taylor's arm, cutting off her singing abruptly and spinning her around. With a shove he propelled her forward.

"Run!" he ordered fiercely. He didn't have to order twice. She exploded into action, and they raced down the hill and across the meadow, toward the panicking horses.

*God! God, save Taylor!* The prayer flew through his mind, over and over. *Please, Father, please!*

Another horrendous yowl sounded from behind them, and Connor threw a glance over his shoulder. *O Lord, no!* The cat was coming, running with an almost careless grace, his long legs loping across the ground after them.

Connor looked ahead. They were about a hundred feet from the creek, and the woods were more than a hundred yards beyond that. The horses were pulling at their restraints frantically, eyes wide with terror.

*You and me both, guys!* Connor thought, a hysterical laugh bubbling up inside him. He assessed the distance left to safety and his heart sank. They weren't going to make it.

"Taylor, keep running!" he barked. "No matter what, don't stop!"

She looked at him in alarm, and he shouted in her face. "RUN!" Without watching to see if she obeyed, he veered off, heading away from the tree where the horses were tied.

*Please, God. Let it come after me!*

"Connor! No!" Taylor's scream echoed in his mind, but he didn't pause. He glanced behind only long enough to see what the cougar was doing, and satisfaction mixed with terror shot through him when he saw it was behind him. Apparently he was the more appetizing prey.

He vaulted across the creek, then sprinted toward the woods, his feet pounding the ground. His breath burned in his lungs, the blood pounded in his temples, and all he could think, over and over, was, *God! God! Help us!*

Taylor watched in horror as Connor led the cougar away. She forced herself forward, splashing through the brook and racing to Topaz's side.

The buckskin was screaming, tossing its huge head in a desperate attempt to break loose and run. Taylor knew she could mount him, but not without a fight. And Connor was running out of time.

She grabbed at the saddle, screaming at the horse and slapping him on the neck to get his attention. He danced in terror, his eyes wild, jerking the saddle from her hands. She lunged at him, grabbed a hank of mane, and pulled for all she was worth, screaming again. Topaz hesitated for a second, and that was all the opening she needed. She grabbed her rifle, jerked it from the leather scabbard, then whirled to run after Connor.

*God! Let me be in time!* she prayed, but one look told her the awful truth. Though Connor was no more than ten feet from the woods, the cat was almost on top of him. He'd never make it.

"No!" she screamed, stopping abruptly and bringing the rifle to her shoulder, knowing even as she did so that it would take a miracle to save the man she'd come to love.

She sighted the cougar—and a terrible realization filled her. Connor and the cat were perfectly aligned. If she shot at the cougar and missed, odds were good she'd hit Connor. A sob escaped her lips. "What do I do, God?" she whispered desperately.

The sound of a gunshot ripped through the air.

Someone else was shooting!

Taylor watched in stunned amazement as a rock near the running cougar splintered, sending shards flying. The cat uttered a pain-filled scream and jerked to a halt, coiling its sleek body and roaring out its rage.

Taylor was scanning the woods, seeking the source of the shot, when another sounded, and the rock splintered again, peppering the cat with tiny projectiles. It recoiled in fury and pain, raising one huge paw to claw at the air. A third shot sounded, and Taylor felt a cheer rise in her throat.

Who cared who was shooting? The cat had had enough! He turned and raced away, heading across the meadow, away from where Connor had raced into the woods, away from where Taylor stood in stunned amazement.

They were safe.

Suddenly her legs seemed to be made of rubber, and she sank to the ground. She knelt there, her rifle propped up in front of her, leaning her forehead against the cool barrel, willing herself to stop shaking.

Within moments strong hands slid under her arms and lifted her to her feet.

Connor. She opened her eyes and, at the sight of him, her rifle slipped from her fingers and she threw her arms around his neck. He drew her close, engulfing her in his embrace, clamping her in an iron grip that told her he wasn't going to release her any time soon. And that was absolutely fine with her.

"Are you okay?" he asked, his voice hoarse.

She nodded as best she could with her face pressed against his chest. Then his hands cupped her face, and she leaned back to look at him. When their eyes met, her heart swelled with the tenderness of his expression.

"Thank God," he said, searching her face with anxious eyes. "Thank you, God." His grateful prayer was breathed against her lips as he lowered his head and his mouth covered hers. And suddenly it was as though she came alive. Truly, fully alive for the first time since Josh's death.

Instinctively, moved by a deep and indefinable need, she leaned into him. When at last they drew apart, Connor's eyes were dark and burning—and slightly dazed.

She brought her hand to his face, laid it gently against his cheek. "You saved my life," she said, amazement sweeping her again at the risk he had taken for her.

He took her hand in his and pressed his lips to it. "All I could think of was leading the cougar away from you." His eyes darkened. "Taylor, I know you don't want to hear this, but I have to say it. I love you. I don't ever want to leave you, to live without you. You are my life." His voice caught, and she was stunned to see tears in his eyes. "The thought of you being hurt was more than I could stand." He smiled weakly. "I've never prayed so hard in my life."

She smiled suddenly, feeling almost giddy, though whether from their escape or Connor's words, she wasn't sure. "I was praying like crazy myself."

He looked down into her eyes, and she felt enveloped in warmth. "Well, he answered. And he guided your aim, too. That was some kind of shooting."

She nodded. "It was indeed, but it wasn't mine."

"Wasn't yours?" He looked at her in confusion, and she shook her head, snuggling closer into the warm circle of his embrace.

"I sighted the cougar, but you were in the line of fire." She looked at him, remembering the wave of despair that had washed over her. "I was afraid to shoot. Afraid I would miss the cat and hit you."

He looked toward the spot where the cougar had stopped, and a slight frown creased his brow. "If you didn't do the shooting," he began, turning to look at her, "then who did?"

She shook her head. "I don't know. I can't imagine who would be out here...or why he didn't come over after the cougar left. But I don't really care. All that matters is that God gave us a miracle."

His eyes twinkled suddenly. "Maybe it was your guardian angel."

She tilted her head, slanting a look up at him. "Who knows? I mean, somebody was watching out for us. But it would be the first time I've ever heard of an angel carrying a gun!"

"Not me," he said, giving her a squeeze. "I see one right now."

She blushed and leaned her forehead against his chest. "Connor, I care about you, too. I think…" She paused, searching for the right words, and he waited patiently. "I think I love you." She looked up. "At least, I want to. I know I don't want to lose you, no matter what happens with the wolves." The light in her eyes dimmed a bit. "But I'm…I'm just not ready yet to give my heart to you. To anyone."

He leaned down, pressed a gentle kiss to her forehead, then stepped away from her. She felt suddenly cold, bereft, but his smile warmed her. "I understand, Taylor. I can wait." He moved to pick up her rifle, then held his hand out to her. "Let's get the camera equipment and go home."

She grasped his hand, and they walked back toward the horses.


The sun was just setting that evening as Taylor sat in one of the rockers on the porch, pushing back and forth gently. She loved this time of day, when the sky was exploding with color and the evening darkness crept over everything. She leaned her head back against the chair, drawing a deep breath of the clean, spring air.

Images of the day drifted through her mind…the meadow, the cougar, the kiss she and Connor had shared…

A warm flush washed over her at that last memory, and she hugged her arms around herself. Something was happening here. Something good and right. Between her and Connor. She wasn't sure where it was leading, but she was ready to find out.

"What brings you such pleasure, *Yazhi*, that your face shines with it?"

She turned slightly to look at Luke, who was coming up the steps of the porch. He pulled one of the rockers over next to her and lowered himself into it, his gaze resting on her face.

She shrugged, wishing Luke weren't so set against Connor. "I don't know, Luke. Just life, I guess."

"It has been a long time since you've had such a look in your eyes. Not since you came home with Josh in tow."

She felt the traitorous color flood her cheeks and glanced down at her lap. Luke's large, work-toughened fingers reached to cover her hand where it lay on the arm of the rocking chair.

"Taylor, you know I love you as the daughter I never had."

She nodded. "Yes."

"And you know I want only what is best for you."

She nodded again.

"I see what this man has become to you, how you feel about him, how he feels about you."

Her eyebrows arched. "How he feels about me?"

Luke smiled, mild amusement dancing in his usually sober eyes. "A person would have to be blind to miss the affection he feels for you. But that should not surprise you. Connor Alexander has spent a great deal of time with you these past weeks. It was unavoidable that he would come to love you."

Taylor chuckled, shaking her head. "Oh, Luke, you're so good for my ego."

His hand squeezed hers. "I speak what I know, *Yazhi*." His eyes darkened with concern. "And that is what makes me uneasy. I do not know who this man is. What he wants from you. From Galloway Glen."

She looked at him thoughtfully. "I won't pretend I know, Luke. Not entirely. I'm still learning who Connor is. But there are a few things that I think are true. He's committed to following God, and he's determined to protect the wolves. And he's become—" She broke off, her voice choked with sudden emotion. "He's become very special to me. I can't explain it, but it's true. I care for Connor a great deal."

Luke stared into the growing night around them. When he spoke again, the coldness in his voice surprised Taylor. "I do not want you to go back into the wilderness with him."

"Luke—"

His gaze captured hers, and she was startled by the intensity of the distrust she saw there. "You are too far away. I cannot protect you."

She shook her head. "I don't need protection. Connor won't hurt me—"

"He has before."

Irritation rose within her, and she pushed it down. Getting angry wasn't going to help. *Father, what can I say to help him understand?*

Her mother's words came back to her. *"It might be that he's feeling...threatened."*

Gently she turned her hand palm-up to weave her fingers with his. "You are my dear friend, Luke," she said, "and nothing will change that. Josh didn't. And Connor won't. You are a part of my life, a part of Galloway Glen, and you always will be. I am not replacing your part in my life with Connor." She met Luke's gaze, willing him to hear her. "But God brought Connor here for a reason, and he has become a part of my life, too. I don't know what he means to me, what he will mean in the future. All I know is that I care for him. A great deal."

Luke stared down at their entwined hands, then looked up at her with a weary sigh. "I hear your heart, *Yazhi*. I will do my best to see this man as you do."

"That's all I ask, Luke. Just give Connor a chance. I think you'll find you have a lot more in common than you realize."

He nodded silently, squeezed her hand once more, than rose and walked down the stairs and into the night.

With a sigh, Taylor closed her eyes. Luke wanted to please her, she knew that. But the dislike she'd seen in his eyes when he talked about Connor was clear and intense. And she felt a sharp pang of sadness that one who had shared her life and dreams for so long suddenly seemed very far away.

# Twenty-Five

Taylor's heart was pounding as she slid from the saddle the next morning. It was early yet, barely after dawn. She waited for Connor to dismount and gather his photography equipment. Then together they walked through the trees and went to stand at the edge of the pool.

At first, there didn't seem to be a wolf anywhere around. Taylor looked up at Connor in disappointment, but he smiled at her as he set up his tripod and fitted a camera on the top. "Give them some time."

She nodded and sank down on the lush green carpet beneath them. She plucked at blades of grass with restless movements. A small patch of lupine was beside her, so she picked several of the lavender flowers and pulled the small bell-like blooms off, one by one.

"I hope the pups show soon," Connor said, laughter in his voice as he came to sit beside her. "Otherwise you're going to trash this place."

She looked up to make a retort, but the words died in her throat. Instead, she stared, wide-eyed, toward the cave. Connor spun around, following the direction of her gaze, then he moved to his camera and started clicking.

A small bundle of fur stood at the edge of the cave mouth,

peering out at them. It shuddered when the cool morning breeze ruffled its downlike fur. Staring at them with curious blue eyes, it took a tentative step forward, only to be run over by another pup from behind. This pup was far more adventurous than its littermate, and it bounded out into the open with a total disregard for any hazards that might be awaiting it.

"Oh, no!" Taylor whispered as the pup ambled to the edge of the ledge and peered at the water below.

"It's okay," Connor told her, still taking shots. "Watch."

The first pup squealed in displeasure, its face in the dirt where it had sprawled. Within moments, Nokomis was at the mouth of the cave, her dark eyes scanning the ledge, locating her offspring. In two quick strides she stood over her audacious infant, then leaned down to gently take the pup's head in her mouth. With tender care, the mother carried the pup back inside the cave.

Taylor sighed with relief, then giggled when the first pup, still sprawled in the dirt, voiced its displeasure in a high-pitched yowl.

"Not much different from human kids, eh?" Connor said, and she laughed.

"They remind me of Mark and Mikey when they were little. Whatever one didn't get into, the other did."

"Oops, here she comes again."

Sure enough, Nokomis was standing over the fallen pup, leaning down to lick at it with her long, pink tongue. The pup suffered the washing, then opened its little mouth in an enormous yawn. Nokomis nudged it with her muzzle, and the pup struggled to its feet and toddled back into the cave. Without a backward glance, Nokomis followed her offspring.

Taylor sat back, clapping her hands with glee. "They're adorable!"

"And I'm sure you'll have names for them in no time," Connor said as he unfastened his camera from the stand.

"Do you think there are more?"

"Probably. Wolves generally have litters of five to seven pups, sometimes even more. The others are probably still asleep inside." He tucked his tripod under his arm, slipped the camera strap around his neck, then extended a hand down to her. "And we should probably head out. We've disturbed them enough."

Reluctantly she let him pull her to her feet.

"Okay," she said, none too graciously, "but you owe me something wonderful for not letting me stay longer."

"How 'bout a kiss?" he asked, waggling his eyebrows.

"Something wonderful for *me*," she retorted. "That would be wonderful for you."

# Twenty-Six

⁂

Laden with traps, his gun strapped over his shoulder, the hunter knelt in the loose dirt, inspecting the drying tracks. The print was nearly as large as his hand. He guessed it was from a female, one that was several years old. His eyes narrowed in speculation.

It was the right time of year…

He stood abruptly. He had to find her before the beast could reproduce. Odds were good that she was already pregnant, maybe even denning. If so, he'd find the den and finish off the lot of them.

He tracked her for hours, and it took all his skill and knowledge of the old ways to stay on her trail. She was clever, doubling back and doing all she could to cover herself. But it wasn't enough. No matter how clever they were, they were still just animals.

When he followed the trail to a rock formation, he frowned. Wolves didn't den in the high places. They denned underground, or in a low spot covered by brush and branches. He'd even heard of one female denning in an abandoned beaver dam.

Cursed creatures. They had the most amazing knack for survival.

He studied the trail again. Mud from the recent rain had left a trail of paw prints, and they clearly led up the rocky rise. He hoisted the traps and set them on the ground. The less encumbrance the better. Slipping his gun from his shoulder, he checked the chambers and nodded in satisfaction. If the wolf was there, he was ready for her.

Within moments he was at the top of the rise, and what he saw widened his eyes in amazement. A valley lay below him like a small piece of heaven. Trees, flowers, grasses, and a pool all combined to create a vision of beauty and tranquillity. He couldn't believe his eyes. He thought he'd wandered every acre of Galloway Glen, but he'd never come across this place.

It was then that he spotted the tent at the far end of the valley. Realization dawned and he nodded slightly. So, the biologist was here. Which probably meant Taylor had brought him. Sharp pain squeezed his heart as he thought of her here with Alexander. The sense of betrayal he'd felt the night he first heard the wolves returned, was fed and strengthened by this most recent offense. He and Taylor had never come across this place on their rides because she had made sure they hadn't. She'd kept its existence to herself, willing to share it with no one. Except the intruder.

He glanced down at the tracks. And her wolves.

How could she do this to him?

*Calm down,* he told himself. *She's deceived. She just doesn't realize what's best for her. It's not her fault.*

The reassurances washed over him, easing the heat in his gut. That had to be it. Taylor had been fooled. Now it was up to him to protect her, to help her see the truth. Before it was too late.

His jaw tensed as he thought about Connor Alexander. The man was trying to move in on territory that was already claimed. Well, first he'd take care of the wolves. Then he'd see to Connor Alexander. With him out of the way, Taylor would be able to understand.

A rustling sound from below drew his attention, and he froze. His heart pumped double-time as he watched a slender wolf trotting easily toward a rock ledge beneath him. He thanked the old ones that he was downwind of the beast, or she would have spotted him long before he saw her. He watched her approach the area just below, then examined the ledge more closely. He smiled in satisfaction. A cave. So that was where the creature had denned.

Moving slowly and soundlessly, he brought the gun to his shoulder. When the wolf was in his sights, he closed his eyes for a second against the sheer adrenaline rush that washed over him. He opened his eyes and sighted the wolf again.

*You're mine,* he thought to himself, then pulled the trigger.


The sharp sound of rifle fire echoed on the wind, and Taylor spun in the saddle, looking at Connor in alarm.

"That sounded close!" she exclaimed.

"Too close," he agreed. "Like it came from the valley."

Quick fear suffused Taylor's face with color, then siphoned it off again, leaving her pale and tight-lipped. Without another word she pulled on the reins, spinning Topaz back toward Reunion and urging him to a gallop.


The gray form lay on the ground below, unmoving. The hunter exhaled a long sigh of contentment and stepped forward. Already he heard the whines from the cave. His smile broadened. This was going to be a productive day, indeed.

He made his way down the incline, then stepped cautiously toward the unmoving form of the wolf. No point in taking any chances. He would make sure she was dead before he killed the pups.

Suddenly he was hit from behind. Someone had tackled him, and the two went down in a rolling, struggling heap. Fists flew in his face and several solid punches landed on his nose and his cheeks. Stunned, disoriented, he swung his fist as hard as he could. The satisfying thud and groan that followed told him he'd connected, and his attacker sagged momentarily.

Taking advantage of the moment, he rolled away and staggered to his feet. He wiped at his face, pulled the handkerchief down around his neck, and spit blood and curses. He looked at his attacker and his eyes widened. Lying there, trying to shake off the blow to the side of his temple, was Brad Momadey.

With a snarl of fury, the hunter took his gun in both hands, raised it, and brought the butt down with a sharp motion to connect with the side of Brad's head. The boy stiffened, then his eyes rolled back in his head and he sank, unconscious, to the ground.

Turning toward the cave, the hunter spit again. First he'd take care of the cubs. Then he'd see to this young fool. He glanced at the boy's inert form with disgust.

The sound of pounding hoofbeats halted him, and his mouth twisted into a snarl of frustration. "No!" he roared angrily, looking down at the cave. "These are mine!"

He listened carefully, gauging the distance of the riders, and knew with a sinking certainty that they were too close. He wanted to scream, to race to the cave and finish what he'd started. Instead, he turned quickly, jumped over the fallen boy, and scrambled up the rocky slope. Then he raced down to snatch up his traps and head for the nearest woods.

Brad's head felt as though it was going to explode. He blinked rapidly, willing the spinning world to come to a stop. When it did, he pushed himself up carefully.

Woozy, slightly confused, he looked around, and saw the still form of the wolf. Memory hit him in a wave, and he cried out in grief and rage. Struggling to his feet, he staggered to the wolf's side. He knelt beside her, reaching out to touch her muzzle gently. A soft puff of air against his hand startled him, and he felt a thrill of hope. She was still alive!

Slowly she opened her eyes, her breathing shallow and ragged. "Please," he whispered. "Please don't die!"

But the look he saw in the wolf's eyes was all too familiar. He'd seen it before, just before death came to claim its victim. As he watched, the fierce amber light focused on him, blazed for one wonderful moment, then flickered and died. The wolf's eyes glazed, and she was gone.

A sob tore at Brad and he lowered his head.

He'd failed again.


When Topaz crested the rise, Taylor vaulted from the saddle and ran to look down into the valley. Connor was right behind her, and she felt his hand grip her arm.

"There." His voice was flat and grim. She followed his pointing finger and saw the still, gray form. Her mind was so focused on the wolf that it scarcely registered that someone was kneeling next to the animal.

"No!" A flash of wild grief ripped through her. "Oh, no!"

Wordlessly, Connor mounted his horse and went down the path to the valley floor. Taylor wanted to follow him, but she couldn't make her legs move. It was Nokomis, beautiful, laughing Nokomis.

Taylor felt sick. She leaned against Topaz's side, squeezing her eyes shut, drawing in deep gasps of air, willing her stomach not to reject her lunch. Her head spun and she shook with impotent rage and fear. Then one thought pierced through her misery and spurred her into action: *The pups!*

With a cry, she grasped the saddle horn and swung herself into the saddle. Within minutes, she was down in the valley, off the horse, and circling the pool.

Connor was kneeling next to Nokomis's body, his hand resting in her lush fur, his face ashen. When Taylor came toward him, he looked at her, and his eyes glittered dangerously.

"She's dead," he said, stating in a low, rasping voice what she already knew. She nodded, unable to speak around the knot of grief in her throat. She laid a hand on his shoulder, and he reached up to take it in his. His grip was so hard that it hurt her, but she didn't care.

Then with one lithe movement he was standing, and he pulled her into his arms, as though he desperately needed contact with something warm and alive. He crushed her to him, burying his face in her hair, and she felt him shudder with emotion. She slid her arms around his waist and tried to offer him what silent comfort she could.

At last he drew a ragged breath and set her away from him.

It was then that she became aware of someone else standing there, watching them. She turned, and her grief exploded in fury.

"You!" she hissed. Until that moment she'd never realized one word could be the embodiment of violence. But that was what she felt, what surged through her in waves. Violent rage. Fury.

And all she could think of was making Brad Momadey pay for what he'd done.

# Twenty-Seven

❧

Without thinking, Taylor advanced toward Brad. "Did you do this? Did you?" she demanded shrilly.

Brad flinched as though she'd struck him. "No!" His horrified denial was immediate.

"I don't believe you!" Her hands clenched into fists.

"Taylor, stop." Connor grabbed her arms, holding her firmly.

She struggled against him. "He killed her!" she cried, unaware that tears were streaming down her cheeks.

Connor turned her to face him, shaking her slightly. "No, he didn't." Connor spoke quietly but firmly.

"You don't know," she said hoarsely, a sob in her voice. "You don't know him like I do. He killed Josh!"

Connor's eyes widened at that, and he looked at Brad's strained, pale face.

"It was my fault," the boy said, his words laden with guilt and self-recrimination. "I was supposed to watch the boys and I didn't."

Understanding dawned in Connor's eyes and he nodded slowly. "You're Brad Momadey."

"Yes."

"What are you doing here?" Taylor demanded again. "How dare you come on my land—" she broke off when Connor's grip on her arms tightened. She looked up at him, and shame swept over her at the look in his eyes. Some small part of her knew she was being vicious, shrewish, but she didn't care.

*Forgive us our trespasses, as we forgive those who trespass against us.*

The words echoed faintly in her mind, but she pushed them away. Forgive? How could she forgive this boy for all he'd cost her?

*Forgive as you've been forgiven…*

*No, Lord. I can't.*

"What were you doing here, Brad?" Connor's question was filled with gentleness.

"I was watching over the wolves," Brad responded quietly.

Taylor looked at him suspiciously. "Watching over the wolves? How? Why?"

He looked at her and she was shocked to see how old his eyes looked. Old and weighed down.

"I knew they were here a year ago," he said simply. "I heard their songs, saw their tracks. I've been following them since they arrived, trying to cover their tracks and make sure the ranchers didn't find them. I wanted to protect them. Keep them safe."

Her mind spun with bewilderment. Brad had been on her land, following her wolves, for the past year! How could that be? How could she not have seen—

"It was you!" she breathed, struggling to comprehend what was happening. "You're the one who's been shadowing me. You scared the cougar away—"

At his stiff nod, she crossed her arms and looked away. So this was her guardian angel, her protector, the one who had made her feel so safe at night. This was the one God had sent to watch over her.

"Why?" she asked. Then she directed a clear, probing look at Brad. "Why did you do this?"

Emotions swept over the boy's face. His haunted eyes burned with an inner despair, and Taylor found herself suddenly overwhelmed with the desire to reach out and smooth the anguish from his young face. Stunned by her unexpected feelings, she stiffened and stepped back.

Brad took in her movement and looked away. "I—I wanted to be there...to make sure nothing happened to you, because—because it's my fault you're alone. It's my fault Josh isn't here to take care of you." A sob caught at the words and he closed his eyes, tilting his head back. His jaw was clenched, and his entire body seemed coiled with anguish and tension.

After a moment, he opened his eyes again, and Taylor found herself faced with the rawest grief she'd ever seen. *God, how does he live with that much agony?* Her heart squeezed painfully with the sorrow she felt emanating from him.

"When I saw how much the wolves meant to you, how much you loved them, I swore I'd do everything I could to protect them, too. I knew you were spending every day with him," he said, nodding at Connor, "so you'd be safe. But the wolves were here...alone..." Despair washed over his face as he looked at Nokomis's body. "I've been staying here, sleeping in the tent for a few hours each night. Then I'd go up on the rise and watch from there. Today, I came out of the tent and saw the man standing on the opposite side, saw him sight his rifle on the female. I didn't have time to reach my gun. To reach him." His eyes came back to hers, pleading with her to believe him. "I would have stopped him if I could. But I couldn't save her. I'm sorry..." His words trailed off and he gulped hard, tears slipping down his cheeks.

Connor stepped forward to lay a gentle hand on the boy's shoulder. "You did what you could, Brad. Do you know who he was? Did you see his face?"

The boy shook his head abruptly. "I didn't see his face. I came up behind him when he was going to the female, I think to make sure she was dead. We fought. I caught a glimpse of him, but he was wearing something across his face. Then he hit me with his gun, and all I saw were stars." He looked at Nokomis. "I watched her die." The flat words seemed wrenched from somewhere deep within him. "I saw the light in her eyes go out. She looked at me as though she felt bad for *me*, like she was trying to tell me it was okay, and then she was gone." He moved restlessly, rubbing his temples with shaking fingers. "I'm sorry, Taylor."

Hearing him say her name startled her. She stared at him, more uncertain than ever. Brad just kept talking, as though he couldn't help himself. "I wanted to stop him. I never wanted him to die."

With a shock Taylor realized he was no longer referring to the wolf, but to Josh. Her eyes flew to Connor, and he shook his head. *Let him talk,* his eyes seemed to say. *Let him get it out.* He came to stand beside her, his arm around her waist, offering her his strength, his support.

*God, I can't,* her heart cried. *I can't bear this! You can't ask this of me!*

Brad paced back and forth, his hands clenched at his sides, his movements quick and strained. "I can't get it out of my mind. I keep seeing him fall, keep seeing his face, the look he gave me." He stopped abruptly and looked at Taylor, his face filled with confusion. "He should have hated me! He should have screamed at me! But he just looked at me with such... understanding. Like he wanted to comfort me, tell me it was okay."

Taylor's chest felt as though it would burst. Listening to Brad's voice, she heard the echo of her own pain; looking at his face, she saw the reflection of her own grief and confusion.

His eyes searched her face, as though hoping against hope to find some answer, some reason there for what had happened. "Josh knew he was going to die," he went on, "I could see it in his eyes. And he just looked at me as though *he* was worried about *me.*" The last word was filled with anguish, and Brad sank to the ground, his knees pulled up against his chest, his face buried in his hands. "I can't get that look out of my mind. It haunts me. It's like he won't rest until I understand, but I don't. I can't."

Connor's arm tightened around Taylor's waist, but she pulled away, distracted. She stood poised, ready to flee, yet something held her there. Watching Brad's anguish tore at her heart, and she clamped her lips shut to imprison a sob of her own.

At last, at long last, her enemy was here before her in agony. But there was no joy, no triumph, no sense of victory.

*Why not, Lord? Why not?*

*He is not the enemy.*

Guilt and regret washed over her in great, drowning waves. *God! O God, forgive me!* She'd thought Brad was going on with his life happily, uncaring that Josh was dead or that he had been responsible. She'd pictured him as cold and cruel, painted him a monster without heart or conscience. And all this time, day in and day out for a year and a half, he had been paying penance, living like a wraith, watching over her. He was as imprisoned in his guilt as she was in her hatred and bitterness.

*Father, forgive me. Josh was willing to die for Brad, to give his life so that Brad might find you. And all I've done is hate. And wish him dead. If anyone wasted Josh's life, Lord, it's been me.*

Connor's strong hands gripped her shoulders from behind, and she turned to look into his compassionate eyes. Tears spilled down her cheeks, and she shook her head.

"I was so wrong," she whispered.

He nodded gently toward Brad. "Tell him. He needs to hear. He needs to be set free, and I think you're the only one who can do it."

She held his gaze, drawing strength from the love she saw there, then nodded. She turned and went to kneel beside Brad. Gently, with infinite tenderness, she slid her arms around him.

For a moment he stiffened, and she thought he might bolt. Then, with a broken sob, he sagged against her.

"I'm sorry! I'm so sorry! I never wanted him to die. He was the only one who ever listened to me, who didn't give up on me. And I killed him!"

"You didn't kill him, Brad." *He didn't, did he, Father?* "It was an accident."

"But it was my fault!" He pulled away from her, surging to his feet. Desperation lined his features, and he reminded her of the wolves just before they bolted for the woods. "Billy never would have gone out on that ledge if I'd been watching him. I was too proud, too concerned with showing Josh he couldn't tell me what to do. I wanted to teach him a lesson."

At Brad's words, Taylor waited for the anger and pain to sweep through her, but they didn't. Instead, she felt surrounded with God's peace, cloaked in his presence and forgiveness.

*Forgive, beloved, as you've been forgiven.*

She stood. "Brad, listen to me." Though she didn't move toward him, she caught and held his eyes with her own. *Let him hear me, Father. Please, just let him hear me.*

"You're right," she acknowledged quietly. "It *was* your fault Josh ended up on that ledge." Brad flinched as though she'd struck him, then closed his eyes as though waiting for her to strike a death blow. "I hated you for a long time for that, even wished you had been the one to die—" she broke off, looking away in shame. "I didn't care if you knew God. I even hoped you didn't. I wanted you to suffer for eternity for what you'd done."

Brad opened his eyes, and they were a dark void in his colorless face.

She took a step toward him, extending her hands, palms up. When she spoke, her voice was full of regret. "Please, Brad, will you—can you—forgive me?"

He blinked, stunned, and she smiled in spite of herself.

"You want *me* to forgive *you*?" His husky voice was ripe with disbelief and confusion. His sable eyes clung to hers, and she saw that he wanted to believe her. Wanted it as desperately as she'd wanted to trust God again.

They'd both been in prison, trapped by their emotions.

*No more, Father,* she prayed, filled with a sudden sense of a locked door being thrown wide open. *It's time for us to be free.*

"How can you ask that? I killed your husband! You should hate me!"

"No, Brad. No. Don't you see? We've both been wrong. I forgot that Josh loved you. I forgot that God loves you—"

"God doesn't love me!" His response was immediate and harsh. "He can't! Not after what I've done."

"Yes, he can." She was in front of him now, and she reached out to take his clenched hands. For a moment he kept them clamped, but they began to relax in her warm grasp. "And he does. We've all done terrible things, Brad. Yes, you made a mistake. And yes, Josh died because of it. But it was an *accident.*" She lifted one hand to touch his cheek gently, wiping away a tear. "What I did was far worse. It was intentional. Determined. I let myself blame you. I feasted on my bitterness and nurtured my anger until I hated you."

Pain was alive and glowing in his eyes, and she squeezed his hand in entreaty. "But I was wrong! Christ is clear about that. If I hate you in my heart, then I'm as guilty in God's eyes as if I murdered you." She was crying again, and she wondered vaguely if she'd ever reach the end of her tears. "But that ends here, Brad. Now. The hate ends here." Her voice gained strength. "I forgive you, Brad." A glint of wonder entered his eyes at her words. "I forgive you," she said again, "And I know Josh forgave you, too, before he died. He loved you, Brad." She reached out to place her palm over his heart.

He caught his breath at her touch, as though it were painful.

She understood. It could hurt to the core when your heart started to thaw after a long, long freeze.

"Josh loved you," she repeated. "You said he knew he was going to die. He loved you enough to give up his life so you could have the chance to know Jesus. That's what mattered most to him. And, when it comes down to it, that's what matters most to me, too."

"Why?"

She gave him a watery smile. "Because it's what matters most to God. He died for you, too, Brad. Christ came for you, to die in your place on the cross, because he loves you."

He nodded. "I know. I—I've been reading a Bible my mom gave me. I wanted to believe…wanted to ask God to forgive me, to accept me…" He looked down. "I just figured I wasn't worth it."

"You aren't," Connor said from beside them. Brad looked at him sharply, and Connor smiled. "None of us is. We can't be worthy of God's love. He just gives it because he wants to, not because we deserve it. You don't have to be good enough. All you have to do is say yes."

Brad glanced again at Taylor, and she nodded.

"Will you…will you pray with me?"

A warm glow of praise and gratitude flowed through Taylor. She smiled, and Brad's mouth tipped into a hesitant smile in response.

"Yes, of course," she said. She reached out to take Connor's hand, too. "We both will, if that's okay."

Brad looked at Connor and nodded. "I'd like that."

The three of them knelt there together, and Taylor's heart resonated with delight as she and Connor ushered Brad to the throne room of his heavenly father.

*Josh, you did it! You planted the seeds that he couldn't resist, and now Brad has come home!*

She knew, somewhere up in heaven, Josh was singing.

# Twenty-Eight

❧

It hadn't been hard to find the pups; all five were cowering at the back of the cave, whining piteously for their mother. Taylor couldn't hold back the tears as they gathered the tiny furry bundles and took them back to the tent.

The other wolves were gone. For now at least. The gunshots would have sent them into hiding.

Brad stayed with Taylor and Connor, and all three spent the night feeding the pups every hour, using some dry formula and bottles, supplies Connor had brought in case they were needed.

When he first mixed the powder with water and shook the bottle, Brad wrinkled his nose in distaste. "They're supposed to like this stuff, eh?"

Connor slanted him a knowing grin. "Like it or not, they'll eat it when they get hungry enough."

"I'll believe it when I see it," Brad retorted.

At first the pups seemed to agree with Brad. They resisted the bottles, turning their heads this way and that. After several frustrated efforts at coaxing the small, whining bundles, Connor took the bottles and strode from the tent. When he returned, his face was grim. He handed the bottles to Taylor and ordered, "Try it now."

She did so, amazed when the pup she held latched onto the

nipple greedily, sucking for all it was worth. Taylor looked at Connor curiously.

"You put the mother's scent on them, didn't you?" Brad asked quietly.

Connor nodded. Again tears sprang to Taylor's eyes, but mixed with her grief was gratitude for Connor and his willingness to do what was necessary.

The night wore on, and all the pups but one drank their fill, then dropped off into an exhausted slumber. The last pup, the smallest and weakest, continued to refuse the formula. His whimpers persisted nonstop for several hours, but as grating as that was, it wasn't nearly as alarming as when the pup fell silent.

Taylor held him, petting him tenderly. A large hand covered hers, and she looked up to meet Connor's eyes. "Is he going to die?" she asked.

"I don't know. He might."

"Please? Can't we do something?"

His eyes held hers. "We can pray."

Her heart swelled with love for him, and she leaned forward, resting her head on his shoulder. Connor's arms slid around her, but she pulled back suddenly. "Wait," she said, then turned to look at Brad. He was sitting in a chair across the room, holding a sleeping pup, watching Taylor and Connor silently.

"You do it," she said, and a dull red crept into the boy's cheeks.

"Me? I—I can't. Why would God listen to me?"

"Because you're his child now and he loves you." She held a hand out to him, and he rose, setting the lightly snoring pup on a rug. He straightened and came to take Taylor's hand. The three of them huddled together, bowing their heads.

"God, I don't know what to say," Brad began. "All I know is this little guy needs your help," he said, his voice choked with emotion, "just like I did. Well, you helped me, God, and I figured I was beyond any help from you or anyone else. So please, help the wolf. Don't let the little guy die. Um, amen, I guess."

They opened their eyes, and Taylor smiled at Brad through her tears. "Thank you."

Connor opened his sleep-drugged eyes and reached his arms above his head, stretching. He yawned deeply, peered down at the pups snuggled against him—both of which were snoring away—then glanced around.

Brad was slouched in his chair, two sleeping pups cradled in his arms. Taylor was curled up on the floor, the last pup cuddled close. Connor's heart constricted. Had the pup survived?

He stood up, careful not to disturb the two pups on his cot. He would check on Taylor's little guy. If he was dead, Connor intended to dispose of him before Taylor woke.

But at the sound of his footsteps, quiet as he was, both Taylor and Brad started and woke up. Brad looked at Taylor, his face filled with apprehension—and a loud protesting wail came from the circle of her arms.

She looked down in wonder; then a joyous smile broke out over her face. "I think somebody's hungry!" she exclaimed, and Connor felt like turning somersaults.

He went to Brad and pounded him on the back. "Way to go, buddy!" he said. "And you thought God wouldn't listen to you!"

"Well," Brad said, a smile crossing his tired face, "I'm glad I was wrong."

Taylor came to stand beside Brad, too, and she reached out to rest a gentle hand on his shoulder. "I want you to come back to the ranch house with us," she said.

Brad looked up at her in silence.

"Brad, you're a part of this. You've been a part for a long time. I want you to come and help us care for the pups. And I'd like to talk with you about the future."

"The future?"

Taylor smiled. "I can always use a good ranch hand," she said. "And you probably know Galloway Glen as well as any of us now." She grew serious. "Brad, I want you to think about staying on at the ranch. I can use you. And I'd like to have you there. After all, you're family now."

He stared at her, and Connor saw the play of emotions across his young face: amazement, disbelief, confusion, and finally, hope.

"I'd like that," he said at last, a smile breaking out over his weary face. "I'd like that a lot."

CHAPTER

# Twenty-Nine

When the three of them returned to the ranch the next morning, Taylor's parents took one look at the pups and melted. Then they surged into action. By the time Connor was on the phone to a friend of his, a biologist who worked with captive wolves, the pups were ensconced in a large willow basket lined with soft, fluffy blankets.

Ryan, Lisa, and the twins showed up before long, and they, too, fell victim to the pups' charms. The twins sat on the floor, peering over the side of the basket, watching for the slightest movement or sign of distress.

Figuring the pups were in good hands, Taylor told her mother she needed to go out for a while.

"Are you all right, dear?" her mother asked, her eyes searching her daughter's face.

Taylor nodded. "I just need to talk to someone."

"Duncan?" her mother asked, and Taylor nodded. She should have known her mother would figure out where she was going.

"I want to tell him…about Connor and me. Before he hears it from someone else."

"I think you'll find he already knows, dear. Anyone who cares about you knew how you felt about Connor when he left.

But I do think it would be good to talk with Duncan." She patted Taylor's arm comfortingly. "Duncan has been a good friend."

"Yes, he has," Taylor agreed.

She drove to Duncan's home, a ranch very similar to her own. When she pulled up in front of the house, she saw Duncan on the porch, sitting on the railing, watching her. She walked up and sat beside him.

"I wondered when you'd be coming," he said quietly, staring into the distance.

"I just got back. From Reunion. Where the wolves are."

He slanted her a look. "Your mother told me about the valley, where it was. I went to see it one day." His eyes glowed with the memory. "It's truly a place of beauty, Taylor. I can see why you love it so much." There was no censure, no anger in his voice. Only a quiet resignation.

She wrapped her arms around herself, struggling to find the right words. But there didn't seem to be any words to express what was going on in her heart right now.

"Connor is a good man," Duncan said at last. "He'll treat you well." He looked at her then, a wry smile tipping his generous lips. "He's so besotted he'll probably spoil you rotten, truth be known." His dark eyes caressed her face. "But then, I don't know any woman who deserves to be spoiled more."

The tenderness in his expression pierced her, and she bit her lip. "Duncan...I'm sorry. I—"

He lifted a hand and pressed gentle fingers to her lips, halting the words. "Lass, I know you love him. And I know you care for me. I won't lie. I wish this had ended differently." His hand moved to cup her face, and his eyes were filled with the struggle taking place within him. "But I want you to be happy, darlin'. If it's Connor who will make you so, then I canna try to hold you." His thumb rubbed tenderly along her cheek. "No matter how much I may want to."

Taylor felt her throat constrict with regret at hurting him, and she reached up to cover his hand with her own. "I will always treasure you, Duncan."

He smiled, a teasing light jumping into his eyes. "Aye, lass,

246

as is only right. You've a friend of pure gold before you, and don't you ever forget it."

"Sure, an' you know I won't," she said, smiling through her tears.

His gaze held hers for a moment, then he took both her hands in his. "Know this, lass, and never doubt it: You've a friend forever in Duncan MacEwen. If ever you need me, you have but to call. I will be there. Any time, any place. I've done all I can to help you, to protect you, darlin'. I've always tried to do what's best for you," he said, smiling wryly, "even when I knew you wouldn't agree with me. I won't stop that just because things have changed between us."

She nodded wordlessly, blinking the tears back as he leaned forward to press his lips to her forehead.

"Now get you gone, lass. Your man is probably wonderin' where you've been." He arched his eyebrows. "And it wouldna be right to keep him waitin'."

She turned to leave, then spun around and threw her arms around his neck, hugging him fiercely. "My mother told me today that you've been a good friend to me," Taylor whispered as his strong arms closed around her. "But she's wrong. You haven't been a good friend—you've been my best friend. You helped me survive. You gave me hope." She leaned back, looking up into his dear face. "I love you, Duncan, as I have never loved another friend, man or woman. And I always will."

She squeezed him once more, then stepped back.

He let her go, a sad smile on his handsome face.

*Father, you blessed me abundantly when you gave me Duncan MacEwen for a friend,* she prayed as she walked back to her truck. She pulled the door open and stepped up to slide behind the wheel. *Now I ask you to bless him. Please, Lord, bring him a woman who will love him the way he deserves to be loved.*

The answer, swift and clear, rang in her mind and brought a delighted smile to her lips: *No eye has seen, no ear has heard, no mind has conceived what God has prepared for those who love him.*

When the doorbell rang two nights later, Taylor jumped up to answer it in excitement. Connor's friends were here at last.

She pulled the door open and was suddenly caught up in a gargantuan hug. "Well, you must be Taylor! I swear, Connor didn't even begin to do you justice, little lady."

She laughed breathlessly as the bear of a man finally set her back on her feet. "And you are?" she asked, utterly charmed.

The man pulled a deep bow, graceful for all his girth. "Harry the Harridan, at your service."

The man standing behind him planted one foot on Harry's ample behind and pushed him through the door. Taylor giggled as Harry stumbled inside, tossing a look of mock outrage over his shoulder.

"The caveman here is Alec Stewart, resident biologist and wolf daddy," Connor explained, coming up behind Taylor and slipping his arms around her. Alec had agreed to raise the pups for the next four months. Then he would bring them back to Reunion and reintroduce them to the pack. "And whatever else you do, don't believe a word the man tells you about me."

Alec laughed. "Actually, the one you shouldn't trust is ol' Connor here." His jibe was softened by the obvious affection and respect in the look he gave his friend.

Taylor joined in the fun, showing the men to their rooms, then teasing and bantering all the way into the kitchen, where she introduced the two men to her family. Before long the rooms echoed with uproarious laughter as Harry and Alec regaled them with accounts of Connor's escapades in Washington. Taylor found herself mesmerized as she watched Connor trade stories with his two friends. He'd always been so quiet and reserved, but now he seemed to come alive. He mentioned the names of politicians as though they were just a bunch of guys who lived down the block! And her eyes widened with surprise when she discovered he'd actually been to the White House.

"Wouldn't have dreamed of sending anyone but ol' Con,

here," Harry said, beaming. "After all, I taught the boy all I knew—"

"Which took all of five minutes," Connor interjected playfully.

"Yeah, well, that five minutes got you through one humongous verbal battle with those folks at the White House," Harry retorted.

*What a job,* Taylor thought as she listened. *It's clear Connor loves it.*

Sudden apprehension filled her. She and Connor hadn't really discussed the future, hadn't talked about whether or not he'd be staying around, or when she'd see him again…IF she'd see him again.

The stories that had been so entertaining a moment before now weighed her down, and Taylor soon rose and excused herself, pleading fatigue. She half-hoped Connor would come away from the group with her, but he merely wished her a good night and turned back to correct Harry as he launched into another tale.

Swallowing her disappointment, she trudged to her room. Sasha lifted her head when Taylor came in, stretched in her spot on Taylor's bed, then dropped her head back down with a soft *whuff.*

"Thanks a lot," Taylor muttered. "It's good to see you, too." She grabbed her towel and prepared to stomp into her bathroom, when a light knock sounded at her door. She spun around and hurried to open it. Connor must have followed her after all.

But it was Brad standing there, his expression troubled. "Can I talk to you?"

"Sure." She stepped aside.

He came in and dropped into the large, overstuffed chair beside the window. "I've been racking my brain, trying to remember something, anything, about the hunter who shot Nokomis." Taylor moved to sit on the edge of her bed as he talked. "Tonight, I remembered something."

She could tell from his voice that he was hesitant to tell her about it.

"And?" she prompted.

He licked his lips and stared at the floor.

"Brad, what is it?"

He sighed. "I think I know who the hunter was."

Her eyes widened. "You're kidding!"

He shook his head, but he didn't look happy.

Taylor felt a sudden apprehension. "Is it someone I know?"

"I...I think so. What I remembered was black hair. Long black hair. And broad shoulders."

She felt the color draining out of her face. "Oh, Brad..."

"He was tall," he went on miserably, "and really strong." He shifted his feet. "I'm sorry, Taylor, but I think it was—"

"Duncan," she whispered, filled with disbelief, and he nodded. "That can't be true! You must have made a mistake."

"Maybe." The word was laced with doubt. "I mean, I can't believe Duncan would do something like that. What reason would he have to hurt the wolves?"

Taylor shook her head. None. No reason at all...then her eyes widened in sudden understanding. His words from this afternoon floated back to her: *"I've done all I can to help you, to protect you...I've always tried to do what's best for you, even when I knew you wouldn't agree with me."*

"Oh no," she moaned softly.

"What?" Brad asked.

She bit her lip. "I...you may be right."

Brad slumped lower in his chair. "I was afraid of that. What should we do?" He looked as upset as she felt.

She put her hand on his arm. "Don't say anything. Not yet. Give me a chance to think about this."

He nodded slowly, then rose to leave.

"G'night, Taylor," he said. "Sleep well."

As the door shut softly behind him, she sank back on the bed, certain any chance of that had been completely obliterated.

In the clear light of morning, as she stood brushing her hair, Taylor realized something terrible. Duncan knew about

Reunion, knew the wolves were there, knew where it was. She tossed down her brush and headed for the kitchen. She'd heard Connor's voice coming from that direction a few minutes ago. She needed to talk to him. He'd know what to do.

"Still mad at me for making you take this assignment?"

Connor looked up from his bowl of cereal at his ex-boss, arching one eyebrow. "No."

Harry hooted. "Yeah! Right! You got some amazing photos, every last one of which will probably win you all kinds of awards, and you found the woman of your dreams, who just happens to live in the wilderness, have wolves on her property, and looks like a beauty queen." He looked pointedly around the spacious living room. "Then there's the cruddy shack she lives in—"

"Is there a point to this, Harry?"

"As a matter of fact, there is. I expect an invitation to the wedding. And I expect invitations to visit. I bet they've got great fishing here!"

Connor laughed and leaned back in his chair. "You got it, buddy."

"I still can't believe you won't be coming back to WAC. I am gonna have to calm Irene down, though. The woman's gonna feel terrible that you're dumping her, you know."

Connor slanted his friend a look. "Well, that's just the way it works. She should have known it wasn't meant to last. Besides, I never promised forever."

"Right!" Harry snorted. "I'm not all that worried. You know how resilient women are. I just can't believe you're jumping ship."

Connor nodded thoughtfully. "I know. I was afraid it would be hard to leave. But you know, there's nothing to hold me there."

"Well, you're a rascal, old boy."

"Ain't it the truth," Connor said, laughing. "Ain't it just the truth."

Taylor stood, her back against the wall, in stunned disbelief.

She'd only caught the last part of Connor's discussion with his boss, but it had been more than enough. Connor was leaving, dumping her. He didn't love her. *"She should have known it wasn't meant to last...I never promised forever...there's nothing to hold me...."* She leaned her head back against the wall, refusing to cry.

Resilient, was she? Well, she'd show Connor Alexander just how resilient she really was. She turned and stormed down the hallway, out of the house, almost running over Brad on the back porch.

"Whoa!" he said. "What's the rush?"

"Do me a favor, okay?"

At the fierce tone of her voice, his eyes widened in alarm. "Sure, Taylor."

"Tell Connor Alexander I hope he's very happy in whatever he chooses to do, and that I understand entirely. If there's nothing to hold him here, then he *should* go. The sooner the better! Got that?"

"Well, yeah...but—"

"Good." She pushed past him.

"Taylor, what's going on? Where are you going?"

"To stop a killer." She pulled open the door to her truck.

Brad stopped in his tracks, then spun and ran into the house.


"She said *what?*"

Connor stared at Brad, and the boy shook his head. "I know. It didn't make any sense to me, either."

"Uh-oh," Harry muttered. "Sounds like she overheard us and got the wrong impression."

"I don't know what happened," Brad remarked. "But what worries me most is the bit about stopping a killer."

"What?" Connor surged to his feet, grasping the boy by

252

both arms and all but lifting him from the floor. "Tell me everything you know. And do it fast!"


"See what happens when you trust someone, Father?" She'd been raging for the last hour. "Are you happy now?"

*Trust in the Lord.*

"I *did* trust, and look what happened!"

*Lean not on your own understanding.*

"What's to understand. I'd say it was all pretty clear. Connor Alexander is a bum. And I never want to see him again. Case closed."

She jammed the gears angrily, bouncing on the seat as she sailed over the bumpy ground. Then her eyes narrowed. Reunion was just ahead. And there was a Blazer parked at the base of the rise.

*O God, please! Not the other wolves! Not Sikis!*

Taylor pulled up and slammed on the brakes, sending a shower of gravel and dust into the air. She pushed open the door and scrambled out, realizing as she did so that it wasn't Duncan's Blazer sitting there.

It was Luke's.

She frowned in confusion as she ran. Was Luke the hunter?

She reached the top of the rise and looked down, scanning the valley below her. Relief surged through her when she saw no sign of the wolves, living or dead. Then a gunshot rang out, and she looked up in alarm. It had come from the other side of the rock formation, outside the valley.

She spun, raced back to her truck, and backed out, spinning the wheels furiously. She stomped on the gas, and the vehicle shot forward. As she rounded the rock formation, she strained her eyes, searching. A glint of sunlight caught her attention, and her heart felt as though it had stopped.

Luke was standing there, at the top of a steep, rocky hill, his gun to his shoulder, drawing a bead. About 400 yards away, racing for the woods, was Sikis.

"No!" Taylor screamed, a sob tearing at her throat. "No!"

She laid on the horn at the same time that she stomped on the accelerator. Luke turned, startled, and when he saw her truck, he dropped his gun to his side. She looked back at Sikis and saw him disappear into the woods.

"O God!" she sobbed. "Thank you! Thank you!"

Taylor pulled up near Luke, threw the truck into park, cut the ignition, and slammed out.

"Are you crazy?!" she screamed as she stormed up the steep incline, struggling not to fall as her feet slid in the loose dust and gravel.

Luke flinched at her fury, but stood his ground.

"Go home, *Yazhi.*"

She stopped and stared at him, stunned. "Go—" She broke off, her hands clenched into fists at her sides. "I'll go home, all right. And you'll go with me. And then we're going to call Mom and Dad and figure this out!"

"There's nothing to figure out. The wolves have to go. They've turned people against you. They have to pay for that."

She shook her head. "Luke, this is crazy—"

"No!" His face twisted with rage. "I'll tell you what's crazy! Letting these killers come on your land! Letting them turn people against you! They're the enemy, Taylor. You're just too young to understand."

"They're animals, Luke—"

"They're killers. I've seen them kill." The dead tone in his voice and the strange gleam in his eyes made her shiver suddenly. He didn't look like the man she'd known most of her life. He was a stranger.

He went on, as though the words were pulled from him by some unseen force. "It came out of the woods, just like that one." His eyes went to where Sikis had vanished into the trees. "I was a boy, hunting with my grandfather. We'd killed a deer and were dressing the carcass, when the monster came out of the woods. It attacked Grandfather. He didn't have a chance. Its eyes were wild and there was foam at its mouth and the sounds it made," he paused to shake his head, "they were the sounds of something evil."

Taylor took a step toward him. Wild eyes…foam at the mouth…"Luke, the wolf must have been rabid. Healthy wolves don't attack people."

His eyes came back to her, and for a moment he stared at her as though he didn't know her. A chill raced up her spine.

Then he smiled. "It's okay, *Yazhi*. You go home, and I'll take care of these monsters. They won't hurt us anymore."

"Oh, Luke." Sadness filled her, but not just because of Luke. What made her saddest of all was that she'd been so wrong. About Duncan. About Brad.

About everything.

*God, forgive me. Forgive me for blaming Duncan. Forgive me for blaming you. Forgive me for not seeing.*

"Luke, let's go home," she said softly, reaching out to put her hand on his arm.

"No! You can't stop me!" He swung the gun like a club, and the butt caught her square on the temple. Light exploded in her head, and she was vaguely aware that she was flying.

Then there was nothing.


Luke stood at the top of the hill, looking down at Taylor. The blow had spun her around and sent her flying off the edge. She'd tumbled to the bottom of the incline, then lay still.

His heart was pounding in his chest, and his temples were throbbing. He knew he was here for a reason, but he wasn't sure what. Looking around, he decided he'd better go find his vehicle.

He turned toward the woods, letting his gun slip from his fingers as he did so. Confused, he looked around…saw the vehicle parked at the bottom of the hill. Had he driven a truck this time? He shrugged. He must have.

He made his way down to it and climbed in the driver's seat, turned the key, and headed west, toward the mountains.

Someone was groaning. Taylor could hear the sound, but she couldn't see anyone. Or anything, for that matter. But the sound was growing louder.

"Ohhh…" Awareness flooded her, and with it came pain. Incredible pain. Her head throbbed like it was going to explode, and her arm was on fire. Then there was her leg—she didn't even want to think about her leg.

"God, I think I blew it." She glanced around, realized she was behind the rocky hill Luke had been standing on, and sighed. "Make that, I *know* I blew it."

She grasped her injured arm with her good hand and pulled it onto her chest, gritting her teeth. Oh, yeah. It was broken all right. As for her leg, she wasn't sure what was wrong with it, but she wasn't going to be standing up any time soon.

Taylor stared at the sky. Normally she'd be praying like crazy, asking God to help her, to save her. But she wasn't doing that. Wasn't going to.

Because she knew everything was going to work out.

There was no fear, no worry. She felt nothing but a strong certainty that God was at work on her behalf. As he had been all of her life. She smiled, tears of wonder stinging her eyes. God had finally opened her eyes.

All this time she'd been telling God she couldn't trust Josh, or Duncan, or Brad, or Connor, or anyone. Not even God himself. All this time she'd figured the problem was with them. With everyone else. But it wasn't.

The problem was with her. Within her. She hadn't been willing to let go, to trust things she couldn't see, couldn't understand. Everything had to be proven. Had to make sense. But that wasn't faith. That was leaning on herself.

"Father, I'm sorry." Tears rolled down her face, making a soggy patch in the dry ground beside her throbbing head. "I thought I knew what to do. Thought I was right about Duncan. Thought I could handle Luke. But I was wrong." She looked back up at the sky, regret heavy on her heart. "And I have a feeling I was wrong about Connor, too, wasn't I?"

*I have loved you with an everlasting love.*

"I know, Lord. You've never let me down. When Josh died, you were there. When I thought Connor had betrayed me, you were there. I've probably jumped to conclusions again. You gave me my family and Duncan. You brought Connor into my life. And the wolf. And then Brad." She sniffed, overwhelmed at the enormity of God's care for her. "Even with Luke, Lord, you were there. You kept me alive." She gave a slightly hysterical laugh. "Wounded, but alive. Forgive me, Lord. Forgive me for not trusting you. Again."

*Ask, and it will be given you.*

The assurance floated through her, and she smiled. She had asked, and God had forgiven her.

*Seek, and you will find.*

Her smile broadened. Connor. Her family. When they realized she was missing, they would come looking for her. And, with God's help, they would find her. She knew it. She didn't need to be worried. She was in good hands.


"Do you see her?"

Connor didn't answer Brad's frantic question. He was too busy running up the incline to the edge of Reunion. He reached the top and peered into the valley. His breath whooshed out in disappointment.

"She's not there."

"Maybe she's in the tent," Brad offered, but Connor shook his head.

"I don't think so..."

Suddenly something caught his attention—a sound, floating on the wind. A mournful, sad, haunting sound.

He looked up sharply, straining his ears. "Do you hear that?"

Brad was nodding. "Howling. A wolf is howling."

They stared at each other for a moment, listening, straining their ears. "It's coming from the opposite side of the valley," Connor said, and he raced down the hill, not even pausing to see if Brad followed. He pounded around the rocky structure, but when he reached the other side, there was no sign of Taylor. Just the woods, and the dry ground, and a steep, rocky hill.

"Over there!" Brad exclaimed, pointing at the hill. "I think it's coming from over there."

Connor ran, his heart pounding in his chest. If anything had happened to her, if he'd lost her...

No! He wouldn't even allow the thought to form.

The howls grew louder as he and Brad drew closer to the hill. There was no doubting it now. The wolf was behind the hill. Connor grabbed Brad's arm, pulling him to a halt.

"Hold it," he said. "I want you to stay here."

"No."

"Brad, I don't have time to argue—"

"Then don't," he said brusquely, and ran around the base of the hill.

Connor followed quickly, then stopped and stared.

Sikis, Taylor's wolf, lay on the ground, his head tilted to the sky, howls flowing from his throat. As the last note died on the breeze, the wolf directed his amber eyes at Connor. For a heart-beat he lay unmoving, then jumped up and trotted to a safe distance, watching intently.

That was when Connor saw Taylor, lying motionless on the ground. The wolf had been leaning up against her, covering her.

"Father..." He sprang forward and was beside her in an instant. "O Jesus, please..." Gently he ran his hands over her, checking for injuries. Her swollen forearm told its own story, as did the tear in her jeans and the bruise he could see forming on her shin. Her forehead was badly bruised as well, and Connor felt a towering rage wash over him. He closed his eyes, clenching his teeth. If he got his hands on the person who had done this to her...

"Con?"

His eyes flew open, and he looked into her face. She was conscious, and the look she gave him was one of pure calm and contentment.

"Hi there." She tried to smile.

"Hi," he croaked.

"I'm ready to go home now," she told him, and he uttered a short laugh.

"Okay. I think that can be arranged."

Her eyes traveled past him to Brad. "It wasn't Duncan," she said, and Brad nodded.

"You can tell us all about it after we get you home," he remarked, looking at her with concerned eyes.

She laughed lightly. "It's okay, Brad. I'm not delirious." Her gaze came back to rest on Connor's face. "Well, no more so than any woman who's madly in love, anyway."

Connor stared at her, torn between his desire to laugh and his urge to slip his arms around her and crush her to his chest. "You're a nut."

She smiled. "Well, of course. I'd have to be to fall in love with you."

"Taylor, it's going to hurt like crazy when we move you," Connor told her. "I'll do my best to be careful."

"It's okay." Her eyes were shining with a light he'd never seen in them before. "I trust you."

CHAPTER

# *Thirty*

"Taylor Moira, you're an amazing and courageous woman."

Taylor looked at her brother and laughed. "So I'm amazing and courageous, am I?"

He grinned. "Either that or you're—"

"Plumb daft. I know. Seems to me we've been through this before. So what have I done now?"

Ryan leaned back in his chair, plopping his booted feet on Taylor's kitchen table. "Well, you agreed to marry Connor, which takes an incredible amount of courage right th—"

The rest of his sentence was cut off when he received a sharp smack to the back of his head. Taylor laughed as Ryan spun around to find Connor standing behind him.

"For crying out loud," Ryan complained. "You're already acting like a member of the family."

"I've always been a bit of an overachiever," Connor replied smugly as he moved to wrap his arms around Taylor, cast on her arm and all. "That's why I'm marrying the most beautiful, most intelligent, most wonderful—"

"Puh-leeze!" Ryan exclaimed, crossing his eyes in disgust.

"—woman in the world," Connor finished, and Taylor smiled up at him demurely.

"See?" she told Ryan. "I told you he was brilliant."

"You two are pitiful," Ryan exclaimed.

260

"Yup," Connor agreed. "So, you guys ready to go?"

"All set," Ryan announced, dropping his feet on the floor with a thud. "Mom and Dad and Lisa and the boys are outside." He grinned, wagging his eyebrows. "Let's go howl with the wild ones."

The sun was just setting as Connor drove Taylor's new Blazer up to a line of trees and put it into park.

"Well." He glanced at her. "The moment of truth."

They got out, then went to stand beside her family.

"Wow!" Mark stared in wonder at the line of cars coming behind them. "There's a zillion cars there!"

"Maybe even a trillion zillion!" Mike's face shone. "And they're all coming to see your wolves, Aunt Taylor."

"God's wolves," she corrected him gently. "They belong to God, not me."

Mark cast a quick glance at the cars again. "Yeah, well I hope God told his wolves to show up tonight."

"Me, too," Taylor said, laughing. "Me, too."

"There aren't exactly a zillion cars." Connor shook his head in amazement, a grin on his face. "But there are sure a lot more than I expected."

"Looks like about fifteen or twenty all together," Taylor's father guessed.

"Well, I hope everyone fits in the clearing," Ryan said as he walked toward a group of ten or so people who were gathered in a circle, chattering excitedly. "This way, folks." They turned to follow him to the newly created path that led into the woods.

"I sure hope Sikis and the gang decide to cooperate tonight," Taylor said, watching as more cars pulled up.

"Well, they howled last night, so the chances are good that they're still in the area. But even if they aren't, Brad's got a great program set up to show everyone," Connor said.

"Thanks in large part to the slides made from your pictures," Taylor's mom said with a proud smile.

Taylor slipped her arm through his, looking up at him with eyes that also shone with pride. "They are wonderful photos, Con."

He smiled. "I had some wonderful subjects. By the way, Harry sends his regrets, but he couldn't make it on such short notice."

"That's too bad, especially since this public howl was his idea," Taylor's father said.

"Aye, but it was our hard work that brought it to life," commented a deep voice from behind them.

They all turned to greet Duncan.

"I wasn't sure you were going to get here on time," Taylor scolded lightly.

He met her glance with a smile. "I wouldn't miss it. Not after all the effort we put into this."

The details for the howl actually had been worked out fairly quickly. Connor and Brad had set up a "howling area" about a quarter mile from Reunion, in a clearing in the woods, and the Camus clan had prepared flyers to post. Duncan had taken charge of contacting local resorts to let them know what they were planning. Then there was nothing left to do but wait.

Finally, one warm evening in June, they heard the wolves howling. The next day the posters were put up and anyone who'd agreed to advertise was notified.

"Public Wolf Howl!" the signs proclaimed, directing anyone who was interested to meet at Galloway Glen.

"Well, I'd say our work has paid off," Connor remarked, reaching out to shake hands with Duncan.

"And so it should. Nice Blazer, Taylor," Duncan said, his eyes filled with compassion. Though she'd reported the incident with Luke to the authorities, they had yet to find any trace of him or her truck. The truck was no great loss, but Luke's unexpected violence and disappearance had saddened Taylor and her family.

Connor's strong arm encircled her shoulders, and she leaned against him gratefully. "Well, looks as though we're going to be the stragglers," he said. Taylor followed his gaze to where the last few visitors were hurrying down the path.

"Let's go see if your friends will honor us with their presence," Duncan said.

They reached the clearing and joined the group crowded onto the log benches. Over fifty people listened with avid interest as Brad explained the history of wolves and their interaction with mankind. In the growing darkness, the slides of Sikis and his pack, projected onto a large screen in front of the group, almost seemed to come to life. Then Brad brought out a beautiful, light gray pelt. With sadness in his eyes and voice, he told Nokomis's story.

"There are those who consider wolves one of mankind's greatest enemies." Brad handed the pelt to a somber-faced woman. "I tend to think ignorance is far more dangerous. Nokomis was a creature of great beauty and grace, and her legacy will live on in her pups."

"What happened to them?" the woman asked, brushing tears from her eyes.

Brad smiled broadly. "They're being raised by a biologist."

"Tell me they're not going to a zoo!" a man groaned from the back, and Brad shook his head. "Not at all. They'll be brought back here and reintroduced to the pack next month. And with any luck, in a few years they'll be having pups of their own." Brad glanced at Connor. "Now it's time for what you've all been waiting for."

Connor came forward to explain how to imitate the wolves' howls. "Keep in mind that they change pitch several times in one howl, and they don't howl on the same note. If you want to sound like a wolf, forget everything you learned in choir." Chuckles met this instruction. "Discord is the name of the game. I'll start out. If the wolves respond, you're welcome to join in, a few at a time. Remember, there are quite a few of us here, so be sure to give everyone a chance."

A hush fell over the clearing as Connor turned to face Reunion, cupped his hands to his mouth, exhaled twice, then leaned back and howled. Whispers swept through the crowd, and a few young girls giggled in nervous excitement. Taylor smiled, watching Connor as he gave a second howl, his voice lifting in a haunting imitation of Sikis and his pack.

*Please, Father,* she prayed. *Let them hear the wolves' song...the song you gave them.*

Shivers raced up and down her spine when a lone wolf responded, lifting his voice in a rich and sonorous cry, filled with unutterable longing. Quick tears sprang to Taylor's eyes as a second wolf voice joined the first, and the wondrous music of nature filled the air around them.

Connor turned, his gaze seeking and finding her even in the darkness. She moved forward to stand beside him, grinning as she watched Brad help a young boy with his enthusiastic howl. Others joined in—some cautious, some joyous—and Taylor was moved by the eagerness she saw in their faces.

The sounds rose and soared through the night, rising and falling, echoing over and over, incredibly wild. Incredibly beautiful.

"I think the whole pack is there," she whispered.

"They're playing our song." Connor pressed a gentle kiss to her lips.

"A song of reunion." Happiness filled her heart. "To celebrate their return to Wyoming."

"And your return to me," he added, reaching out to tuck her against his side.

Taylor snuggled close, exhaling a long sigh of contentment and looking at her parents, who now stood beside her. When her gaze met her mother's, a warm glow of pure joy flowed through her.

"'I sought the Lord, and he answered me,'" she whispered.

"'He delivered me from all my fears,'" her mother went on in a low voice, her eyes shining.

"'The angel of the Lord encamps around those who fear him, and he delivers them,'" her father added softly.

"'Taste and see that the Lord is good'"—they turned in surprise to stare at Connor, and his smile broadened as they finished together in quiet chorus—"'blessed is the man who takes refuge in him. Fear the Lord, you his saints, for those who fear him lack nothing.'"

"Amen," Taylor breathed. Then she turned her face to the sky and let the songs of the night and the wonder of Reunion wash over her.

*Amen.*

Dear Reader,

Once upon a time there was a little girl who loved God and her family. Her long-suffering parents loved her dearly, even when she brought home every stray four-footed, furry creature in town. With kindness and humor, her parents nurtured her tender heart and wild imagination. When the little girl approached the mysterious realm of adulthood, she asked herself, "What's the best job I could have?"

"Writing or editing fiction," her self answered. "Especially if it deals with animals!" And, lo and behold, it is so!

Nice little tale, huh? Well, it's 100 percent true. I love God, my family, nature, and reading—and my wonderful parents have cultivated these loves throughout my life. In fact, they are almost as delighted as I am with my job as senior editor at a publishing house. While it's a blast to read some of the best novels in Christian publishing long before they hit the bookstores, what I love most about my job is the authors themselves. These friends enrich my days, teaching me about God and myself with honesty, kindness, and humor. (We do a *lot* of laughing together.) And lately they've been telling me the same thing: "Get out there and write!"

Well, I finally listened to them—and what fun it's been to share my passion for nature, and to create characters and worlds where we learn together about our relationships with God, each other, and the world. Researching and writing *Reunion* has been an amazing adventure. As you read the story of Taylor, Connor, Duncan, and the wolves, may you find your experience equally exciting and enjoyable.

In Christ,

Karen M. Ball

# PALISADES...PURE ROMANCE

## ⟶ PALISADES ⟵

*Reunion,* Karen Ball
*Refuge,* Lisa Tawn Bergren
*Torchlight,* Lisa Tawn Bergren
*Treasure,* Lisa Tawn Bergren
*Chosen,* Lisa Tawn Bergren
*Firestorm,* Lisa Tawn Bergren (October, 1996)
*Cherish,* Constance Colson
*Angel Valley,* Peggy Darty
*Seascape,* Peggy Darty
*Sundance,* Peggy Darty (August, 1996)
*Love Song,* Sharon Gillenwater
*Antiques,* Sharon Gillenwater
*Secrets,* Robin Jones Gunn
*Whispers,* Robin Jones Gunn
*Echoes,* Robin Jones Gunn
*Coming Home,* Barbara Jean Hicks
*Glory,* Marilyn Kok
*Sierra,* Shari MacDonald
*Forget-Me-Not,* Shari MacDonald
*Diamonds,* Shari MacDonald (November, 1996)
*Westward,* Amanda MacLean
*Stonehaven,* Amanda MacLean
*Everlasting,* Amanda MacLean
*Betrayed,* Lorena McCourtney
*Escape,* Lorena McCourtney (September, 1996)
*Voyage,* Elaine Schulte (August, 1996)

*A Christmas Joy,* Darty, Gillenwater, MacLean
*Mistletoe,* Ball, Hicks, McCourtney (October, 1996)

# THE PALISADES LINE

*Ask for them at your local bookstore. If the title you seek is not in stock,*
*the store may order you a copy using the ISBN listed.*

### *Reunion,* Karen Ball
ISBN 0-88070-951-0

There are wolves on Taylor Sorensen's ranch. Wildlife biologist Connor Alexander is sure of it. So he takes a job as a ranch hand to prove it. Soon he and Taylor are caught in a fierce controversy—and in a determined battle against the growing attraction between them...an attraction that neither can ignore.

### *Chosen,* Lisa Tawn Bergren
ISBN 0-88070-768-2

When biblical archeologist Alexsana Rourke is handed the unprecedented honor of excavating Solomon's Stables in Jerusalem, she has no idea that she'll need to rely heavily upon the new man in her life—CNN correspondent Ridge McIntyre—and God, to save her.

### *Refuge,* Lisa Tawn Bergren
ISBN 0-88070-875-1

*Part One:* A Montana rancher and a San Francisco marketing exec—only one incredible summer and God could bring such diverse lives together. *Part Two:* Lost and alone, Emily Walker needs and wants a new home, a sense of family. Can one man lead her to the greatest Father she could ever want and a life full of love?

### *Firestorm,* Lisa Tawn Bergren (October, 1996)
ISBN 0-88070-953-7

In the sequel to Bergren's best-selling *Refuge, Firestorm* tells the romantic tale of two unlikely soulmates: a woman who fears fire, and the man who loves it. Reyne Oldre wasn't always afraid, but a tragic accident one summer changed her forever. Can Reyne get beyond her fear and give her heart to smoke jumper Logan McCabe?

### *Torchlight,* Lisa Tawn Bergren
ISBN 0-88070-806-9

When beautiful heiress Julia Rierdon returns to Maine to remodel her family's estate, she finds herself torn between the man she plans to marry and unexpected feelings for a mysterious wanderer who threatens to steal her heart.

### *Treasure,* Lisa Tawn Bergren
ISBN 0-88070-725-9
She arrived on the Caribbean island of Robert's Foe armed with a lifelong dream—to find her ancestor's sunken ship—and yet the only man who can help her stands stubbornly in her way. Can Christina and Mitch find their way to the ship *and* to each other?

### *Cherish,* Constance Colson
ISBN 0-88070-802-6
Recovering from the heartbreak of a failed engagement, Rose Anson seeks refuge at a resort on Singing Pines Island, where she plans to spend a peaceful summer studying and painting the spectacular scenery of international Lake of the Woods. But when a flamboyant Canadian and a big-hearted American compete for her love, the young artist must face her past—and her future. What follows is a search for the source and meaning of true love: a journey that begins in the heart and concludes in the soul.

### *Angel Valley,* Peggy Darty
ISBN 0-88070-778-X
When teacher Laurel Hollingsworth accepts a summer tutoring position for a wealthy socialite family, she faces an enormous challenge in her young student, Anna Lee Wentworth. However, the real challenge is ahead of her: hanging on to her heart when older brother Matthew Wentworth comes to visit. Soon Laurel and Matthew find that they share a faith in God...and powerful feelings for one another. Can Laurel and Matthew find time to explore their relationship while she helps the emotionally troubled Anna Lee and fights to defend her love for the beautiful *Angel Valley*?

### *Seascape,* Peggy Darty
ISBN 0-88070-927-8
On a pristine sugar sand beach in Florida, Jessica has a lot to reflect upon. The untimely death of her husband, Blake...and the sudden entrance of a new man, distracting her from her grief. In the midst of opening a B&B, can Jessica overcome her anger and forgive the one responsible for Blake's death? Loving the mysterious new man in her life will depend upon it.

### *Sundance,* Peggy Darty (August, 1996)
ISBN 0-88070-952-9
Follow Ginger Grayson to the wilds of British Columbia, Canada, where she meets Craig Cameron, a widowed rancher with two small sons who desperately need a mother. Is free-spirited Ginger ready to settle down in the 1990's last wild frontier? And can Craig risk his heart again, all the while wondering if Ginger can handle his rugged lifestyle?

*Love Song,* **Sharon Gillenwater**
ISBN 0-88070-747-X
When famous country singer Andrea Carson returns to her hometown to recuperate from a life-threatening illness, she seeks nothing more than a respite from the demands of stardom that have sapped her creativity and ability to perform. It's Andi's old high school friend, Wade Jamison, who helps her to realize that she needs inner healing as well. As Andi's strength grows, so do her feelings for the rancher who has captured her heart. But can their relationship withstand the demands of her career? Or will their romance be as fleeting as a beautiful *Love Song*?

*Antiques,* **Sharon Gillenwater**
ISBN 0-88070-801-8
Deeply wounded by the infidelity of his wife, widower Grant Adams swore off all women—until meeting charming antiques dealer Dawn Carson. Although he is drawn to her, Grant struggles to trust again. Dawn finds herself overwhelmingly attracted to the darkly brooding cowboy, but won't marry a nonbeliever. As Grant learns more about her faith, he is touched by its impact on her life and slowly begins to trust.

*Echoes,* **Robin Jones Gunn**
ISBN 0-88070-773-9
In this dramatic romance filled with humor, Lauren Phillips enters the wild, uncharted territory of the Internet on her home computer and "connects" with a man known only as "KC." Recovering from a broken engagement and studying for her teaching credential, her correspondence with KC becomes the thing she enjoys most. Will their e-mail romance become a true love story when they meet face to face?

*Secrets,* **Robin Jones Gunn**
ISBN 0-88070-721-6
Seeking a new life as an English teacher in a peaceful Oregon town, Jessica tries desperately to hide the details of her identity from the community...until she falls in love. Will the past keep Jessica and Kyle apart forever?

*Whispers,* **Robin Jones Gunn**
ISBN 0-88070-755-0
Teri Moreno went to Maui eager to rekindle a romance. But when circumstances turn out to be quite different than she expects, she finds herself spending a great deal of time with a handsome, old high school crush who now works at a local resort. But the situation becomes more complicated when Teri meets Gordon, a clumsy, endearing Australian with a wild past, and both men begin to pursue her. Will Teri respond to God's gentle urgings toward true love? The answer lies in her response to the gentle *Whispers* in her heart.

### Coming Home, Barbara Hicks
ISBN 0-88070-945-6
Keith Castle is running from a family revelation that destroyed his world, and deeply hurt his heart. Katie Brannigan is the childhood friend who was wounded by his sudden disappearance. Together, Keith and Katie could find healing and learn that in his own time, God manages all things for good. But can Katie bring herself to give love one more chance?

### Glory, Marilyn Kok
ISBN 0-88070-754-2
To Mariel Forrest, the teaching position in Taiwan provided more than a simple escape from grief; it also offered an opportunity to deal with her feelings toward the God she once loved, but ultimately blamed for the death of her family. Once there, Mariel dares to ask the timeless question: "If God is good, why do we suffer?" What follows is an inspiring story of love, healing, and renewed confidence in God's goodness.

### Diamonds, Shari MacDonald (November, 1996)
ISBN 0-88070-982-0
When spirited sports caster Casey Foster inherits a minor league team, she soon discovers that baseball isn't all fun and games. Soon, Casey is juggling crazy promotional events, major league expectations, and egos of players like Tucker Boyd: a pitcher who wants nothing more than to return to the major leagues...until Casey captures his heart and makes him see diamonds in a whole new way.

### Forget-Me-Not, Shari MacDonald
ISBN 0-88070-769-0
Traveling to England's famed Newhaven estate to pursue an internship as a landscape architect, Hayley Buckman looked forward to making her long-held career dreams come true. But upon arrival, Hayley is quickly drawn to the estate and its mysterious inhabitants, despite a sinister warning urging her to leave. Will an endearing stranger help her solve the mystery and find love as well?

### Sierra, Shari MacDonald
ISBN 0-88070-726-7
When spirited photographer Celia Randall travels to eastern California for a short-term assignment, she quickly is drawn to—and locks horns with—editor Marcus Stratton. Will lingering heartaches destroy Celia's chance at true love? Or can she find hope and healing high in the *Sierra*?

### Westward, Amanda MacLean
ISBN 0-88070-751-8
Running from a desperate fate in the South toward an unknown future in the West, plantation-born artist Juliana St. Clair finds herself torn between two men, one an undercover agent with a heart of gold, the other a man with evil intentions and a smooth facade. Witness Juliana's dangerous travels toward faith and love as she follows God's lead in this powerful historical novel.

### Stonehaven, Amanda MacLean
ISBN 0-88070-757-7
Picking up in the years following *Westward, Stonehaven* follows Callie St. Clair back to the South where she has returned to reclaim her ancestral home. As she works to win back the plantation, the beautiful and dauntless Callie turns it into a station on the Underground Railroad. Covering her actions by playing the role of a Southern belle, Callie risks losing Hawk, the only man she has ever loved. Readers will find themselves quickly drawn into this fast-paced novel of treachery, intrigue, spiritual discovery, and unexpected love.

### Everlasting, Amanda MacLean
ISBN 0-88070-929-4
Picking up where the captivating *Stonehaven* left off, *Everlasting* brings readers face to face once more with charming, courageous—and very Irish—Sheridan O'Brian. Will she find her missing twin? And will Marcus Jade, a reporter bent on finding out what really happened to Shamus, destroy his chances with her by being less than honest?

### Betrayed, Lorena McCourtney
ISBN 0-88070-756-9
As part of a wealthy midwestern family, young Rosalyn Fallon was sheltered from the struggles brought on by the Depression. But when her father's company collapses and her boyfriend and best friend elope, Rosalyn unexpectedly finds herself facing both hardship and heartbreak. Will her new life out West and a man as rugged and rough as the land itself help her recover?

### Escape, Lorena McCourtney (September, 1996)
ISBN 1-57673-012-3
Is money really everything? The winsome Beth Curtis must come to terms with that question as she fights to hold on to guardianship of her nephew, even facing her deceased sister-in-law's brother. Sent to collect the boy, handsome Guy Wilkerson has no idea that he will fall for Beth, and come to see his own family's ways of living in a new light. Can the two overcome such diversity to be together, beginning their own family?

### *Voyage,* Elaine Schulte (August, 1996)
ISBN 1-57673-011-5

Traveling via ship to the Holy Land, Ann Marie is on a pilgrimage, discovering things about faith and love all the way. But will a charming man who guides her—among the romantic streets of Greece and elsewhere—distract her from the One who truly loves her?

### *A Christmas Joy,* MacLean, Darty, Gillenwater
ISBN 0-88070-780-1 (same length as other Palisades books)

Snow falls, hearts change, and love prevails! In this compilation, three experienced Palisades authors spin three separate novelettes centering around the Christmas season and message.

*By Amanda MacLean:* A Christmas pageant coordinator in a remote mountain village of Northern California is reunited with an old friend and discovers the greatest gift of all.

*By Peggy Darty:* A college ski club reunion brings together model Heather Grant and an old flame. Will they gain a new understanding?

*By Sharon Gillenwater:* A chance meeting in an airport that neither of them could forget...and a Christmas reunion.

### *Mistletoe:* Ball, Hicks, McCourtney (October, 1996)
ISBN 1-57673-013-1

A new Christmas anthology of three novellas...all in one keepsake book!

Also look for our new line:

# PALISADES PREMIER
### More Story. More Romance.

### *Chase the Dream,* Constance Colson
ISBN 0-88070-928-6, $11.99

Alison Austin's childhood dream of being a world-champion barrel racer leads to problems at home and in the arena. Rising rodeo star Forrest Jackson, wounded from the death of his father and abandonment of his mother, is Alison's ideal—and her cousin Jenny's boyfriend. Ultimately, Alison must decide how much she is willing to give up...and to take.

Raised on the circuit, Jenny's love for Forrest is mixed with her love for barrel racing, while bull rider Tom Rawlings rodeos with much different motives.

As the time runs down and the competition heightens, the destinies of these four entwine, leading to a breathless climax. It's rodeo: the rough-and-tumble sport propelled by dreams; where love, life, and death are separated by mere seconds; and where meeting the Master Rider is inevitable.

**Promise Me the Dawn, Amanda MacLean (September, 1996)**
ISBN 0-88070-955-3, $11.99

Set in turn-of-the-century San Francisco and Monterey, *Promise Me the Dawn* weaves the tender love story of spirited English beauty Molly Quinn and Zachary MacAlister, an immigrant who came to America to flee his family's titles, wealth, and influence. During the dark days that follow the 1906 earthquake, Molly and Zachary plan a future rendezvous in the Pacific cliffs.

After they separate, Molly makes a name for herself and becomes the glamorous, new toast of the town. When Zach proposes, Molly decides that she hasn't lived enough yet, and lets him go. But when she later realizes that she may have lost him for good, Molly must reexamine the desires of her heart and turn back to her God before rediscovering the love she nearly lost in *Promise Me the Dawn*.

AND ESPECIALLY FOR YOUNG ADULTS:
Announcing the exciting new
**Pacific Cascades University Series!**

Come and meet nine college students and witness their trials and tribulations as they discover more about relationships, college life, and their world.

*Freshman Blues,* Wendy Lee Nentwig, ISBN 0-88070-947-2 (July 1996)
*Homeward Heart,* Lissa Halls Johnson, ISBN 0-88070-948-0 (July 1996)
*True Identity,* Bernie Sheahan, ISBN 0-88070-949-9 (September 1996)
*Spring Break,* Wendy Lee Nentwig, ISBN 0-88070-950-2 (September 1996)